LOOK AGAIN

LOOK AGAIN

A Logan McKenna Novel

VALERIE DAVISSON

*This book is dedicated to all the animals, wild and tame,
who enrich our lives.*

PROLOGUE

The smell of hot leather and horse sweat, mingled with her own sour body odor, made Gloria slightly nauseous.

She didn't mean to stay so late at the Rope & Ride last night or do that many tequila shots, but who could blame her? This whole weekend had been a bust. First, her rotten horse spooked during horsemanship and landed her right on her butt in front of everyone. Then she was almost late to the interviews and was so flustered she couldn't think of anything cool to say. She just sat there staring at the judges. Besides, she wore last year's outfit. She couldn't afford a new one like the other girls. She hadn't gotten in one good ride. And now it was over.

No more events, no more chances to catch up. And given how the other girls treated her, she sure as hell wasn't going to win Miss Congeniality.

Nope, she wouldn't be going home with even one belt buckle, even though she was so much better than all those other girls. But those girls had better horses and better clothes and better everything! If she had half of what they had, she'd win every single event . . . *every* event, *every* time!

Worst of all was little Miss 'Golden Girl', Cindy Havens. She got her nickname in high school back in Sierra Vista because she was always so goddamned happy. Everyone liked Cindy. She won without even trying. She wasn't rich like the other girls—Gloria had to give her that—she worked after school at *Spur Western Wear*, but still, everything seemed to come easily to Cindy. She caught all the breaks.

Like this weekend. She aced every event. So unless she screwed up royally in this last ride, Cindy was sure to be crowned Rodeo Queen tonight.

Gloria watched from the back side of the grounds now as Cindy took her gorgeous buckskin stallion, Beau—the horse that should have been hers, had she been able to afford him— around the arena for her final run.

They were beauty in motion, horse and rider as one, enjoying themselves immensely. Cindy leaned forward and let Beau out. The crowd held its collective breath. He was going so fast around the arena, that the slightest misstep would mean disaster. But, as usual, Cindy pulled it off, pulling up in front of the judges to the cheers and roar of the crowd. Cindy would go home with the Queen's saddle, and the crown for her new hat.

Gloria, on the other hand, would just be going home— broke, tired, and without a single ribbon to show for all her trouble, let alone the saddle. She slipped out the side exit. No need for her to stand there smiling while they gave the crown to someone else.

It was so unfair!

She'd called in sick Friday and Saturday to be here. She'd slipped a few extra bucks out of her mom's wallet for gas. She'd done everything she could—it's not like she hadn't tried, but nothing ever worked out for her. Nothing. Ever.

On top of everything else, tomorrow morning she had to start packing. This was her last rodeo. Last month, her dad, who had been out of work for over a year, informed the family that they were moving. He'd gotten a job somewhere in Oregon. They were leaving in June, as soon as school was out.

As she silently stewed, a flash of color caught her attention. A skinny kid—maybe seven or eight years old and all decked out in a western snap shirt, jeans, and boots, totally engrossed in the pleasure and challenges of eating a huge cone of bright pink cotton candy—walked past her on his way to the front of the arena, probably to rejoin his parents. Backlit by the afternoon sun, he looked like part of a Norman Rockwell painting her mother had on the kitchen wall.

For some reason, this irritated the hell out of her. Making sure no one was watching, she nudged a dusty black rock from along the fence with the toe of her boot until she had it in the perfect position. Then, drawing her foot back, she carefully aimed, kicked, and sent it flying.

Bullseye! Hit him right between the shoulder blades. Now why couldn't she do that in her events? If they gave out buckles for kicking rocks at kids, she'd take first place.

Startled, the boy dropped his cotton candy. He looked around but couldn't see his assailant. Looking down at his treat lying in the dirt, the boy scrunched up his face and went running for his mother.

Gloria allowed herself a small smile.

Yep. Better get used to it, kid. Life's not fair.

Feeling somewhat better, she made her way back to her trailer to pack up her horse and gear and get on the road. After last night's bar bill, she was out of money; she'd have to settle for a can of chili for dinner. Her horse didn't know it yet, but he wasn't getting *any* dinner. Teach him to lose every frickin' event.

If she left by seven, she would be home by eight-thirty. Her mom would make her give her horse a good rub down and unpack everything tonight, so she would be on time for school tomorrow.

Located practically on the border of Mexico, Sierra Vista was ninety miles south of Tucson. Another good reason to leave tonight. If she hung around and left in the morning, Cindy would want to drive down together, looking out for each other on the road in case either one had car trouble. Like she would want to drive her old truck and beat-up horse trailer next to Cindy's shiny new rig. Like they were friends.

Right.

If only she could have taught Cindy a lesson before she left.

3 WEEKS LATER

MOVING DAY

Most of the boxes were packed, but Gloria asked her mom to leave the television set until last so she could check the weather report. July thunderstorms could and often did cause flash floods that washed out roads around Tucson, which they had to pass through on their way to Oregon. Her dad had already scheduled the electric company to turn off the power today, but they said it would stay on until five tonight.

She grabbed a Pop-Tart bag out of the box her mom had left on the counter for her and ripped open the corner with her teeth. They were better warmed up, but the toaster was already packed. She sat cross-legged on the floor to enjoy her breakfast, without taking her eyes off the television screen. Local news was next. She hoped she hadn't missed it.

A female reporter dressed in a green pantsuit, buffeted by what Gloria knew were hot, dry winds full of gritty sand, stood in front of the blackened shell of a horse trailer. She blinked her eyes and spoke into the mic. Miles of mostly empty, scrubby desert stretched out behind her, edged by a string of low, hazy mountains.

Gloria reached over and turned up the volume on the TV.

"*. . . standing here on the side of Coyote Way about eighteen miles west of Highway 92. Early this morning, acting on an anonymous tip, highway patrol located a previously reported stolen vehicle and property belonging to Cindy Havens of Sierra Vista, Arizona. We were able to speak with Miss Havens about an hour ago. She is not available at this time to speak with us on camera, but this is what this reporter has learned so far.*

"*Monday morning, five days ago, Miss Havens reported the theft of both her horse trailer and her horse. According to her statement, she was to give an equine education workshop to young riders as part of her Tucson Rodeo Queen duties that day.*

"*When she went to bed Sunday night, she said her horse was in his stall, the trailer outside, and her truck already packed with what she needed. When she woke in the morning, her truck was still there but both horse and trailer were gone.*"

The reporter turned to her left and brought a short man in uniform into the frame. The young man's hands rested on his equipment belt, and he looked uncomfortable.

"*I have with me Officer Rogers, who was the first on the scene. Officer Rogers, can you tell me what you discovered when you arrived?*"

The officer cleared his throat and leaned into the mic.

"*Well, the trailer was gone—totaled, somebody torched it.*"

"*And Miss Haven's horse?*"

"*The horse . . .*"

Officer Rogers looked down at his feet and cleared his throat then continued.

"*We found the horse staked out about twenty yards from the trailer.*"

That was all the officer was inclined to say. The reporter prompted him.

"Was the fire . . . did it reach the horse?"

"No, no, the fire did not reach the horse."

The officer stared stoically into the camera, standing at parade rest, unwilling to say more.

"And what condition was the horse in? Where is the horse now?"

The officer clearly did not want to answer this question, but he did.

"The horse was left without food. There was a water bucket nearby, but it was empty—probably kicked over—when I arrived. The metal parts of the trailer that were left had cooled off, so I knew the horse had been out there at least a couple of days."

The young officer looked like he might be sick.

"Any other news about his condition? You're sure the fire hadn't reached him?"

.". . No, but his back tendons had been cut . . . I'm surprised coyotes didn't get him."

The reporter looked properly shocked. She leaned in, moving the mic even closer to the officer.

"Is the horse expected to survive?"

Officer Rogers regained his composure and spoke in a more formal, emotionless tone.

"The owner was contacted and sent the vet out right away, but it was too late. They put the animal down about an hour ago."

Grinning ecstatically, Gloria switched off the TV, unplugged it, and carried it out to the U-Haul where her mother was tucking blankets around a dresser mirror.

"What'd the weatherman say?" her mom asked.

"Clear skies all the way to Oregon!"

1

Logan pulled on her running shoes and laced them snugly. They cost more than all the rest of her clothes combined, but were springy, waterproof, and in Logan's mind, worth every penny. She swore they made her run faster.

She pulled on her gloves and patted her pockets. Poop bags . . . leash . . .

Dixon, Logan's two-year-old labraheeler, panted impatiently at the door, raring to go. The labrador/blue heeler rescue had been intended as a gift for Ben last year after he lost his best buddy, Purgatory, the Greater Swiss Mountain dog he'd raised from a puppy. But Dixon had other ideas. Before they even brought him home from the animal shelter, he had attached himself to Logan and that was that.

Ben took it in good-natured stride, but last Christmas he finally got his very own dog, an eight-week-old English Cream Golden Retriever they named Max, as he was the biggest puppy in his litter. If his polar bear paws were any indication, the vet said he would probably top a hundred pounds when he was full grown.

Max had potty trained pretty quickly, but that was about all he'd learned to do. He chewed on everything and still had his sharp piranha-like puppy teeth. They didn't know how to break him of gnawing on their hands like chew toys. Leash walks were a trial and taking him on her run with Dixon was out of the question. Within seconds, he had himself and anyone trying to walk him hopelessly tangled in his leash.

And true to his breed, Max loved everyone and assumed everyone loved him and would appreciate his exuberant greetings. Not everyone did. Some people didn't want forty pounds of furry puppy love jumping and nipping at them, trying to reach their face to give them a proper doggie kiss.

Right now, Max had both paws up on the top of the child gate Ben had optimistically stretched across the doorway, barking and wriggling, begging to go with them.

Logan leaned over the gate to kiss Ben goodbye and gave Max a scratch behind the ears and under his chin, "As soon as you learn to behave, you can come with." Then to Ben she said, "Hopefully the rain will hold off an hour. Do you want me to bring breakfast burritos back from Pirates? Sausage?"

"Sure, I'll have coffee ready. Oh . . . and I wouldn't say no to a cinnamon roll," he added over his shoulder, with a waggling of blonde eyebrows over denim blue eyes.

Ben turned back to the kitchen where he was working on tonight's dinner. A large hunk of raw beef sat on a cutting board on the counter, along with a few cloves of garlic, assorted onions, potatoes, and carrots. "That'll give me time to get the pot roast in the cooker. It needs at least eight hours," he said.

"Mmmmmm!" Logan's mouth started to water.

Ben knew the way to a woman's—or at least this woman's—heart was through her stomach. Ben's great cooking was half the reason she married him. Logan could boil water and make top ramen, but that was about it. Ben put her in charge of salads. The easy ones with only three ingredients.

Logan promised to be back within the hour, with breakfast in tow. They always got enough to share with Dixon, who had a cast-iron stomach. Monster puppy Max, on the other hand, had a delicate constitution and could only eat a special (a.k.a. expensive) dry kibble with a scoop of pumpkin on top. Poor Max. But they'd learned the hard way not to deviate from his diet or they'd all be up all night with him. With a bucket and a mop.

Today, though, everyone was in good health.

Logan tightened the scrunchie that kept her thick, wavy auburn hair out of her face, then leaning down, she clipped on Dixon's leash before heading out the door.

The air was crisp and cold. Warming up, they jogged down Barber Street and zigzagged across a few others until they reached the small sprinkling of shops strung along Highway 101. The five-block stretch pretty much constituted the entire downtown of Depoe Bay. But in spite of its size, between charter boat fishing and whale watching tours, Depoe Bay attracted its share of tourists. It also claimed to have the world's smallest harbor, which no one bothered to dispute.

Dixon didn't really need a leash, as he stayed on Logan's left and heeled perfectly, but Logan was a law-abiding citizen, and Dixon was a good sport about it.

The shops were closed now, but even in the winter they had a fair amount of tourist traffic. In the summer, it was wall-to-wall tourists with caramel apples, lattes, and cameras taking selfies at the sea wall which ran along the other side of the highway, opposite the shops.

Once they were across Highway 101, Logan took in the spectacular view. Winter weather was blustery, but that suited the locals, which Logan and Ben could now call themselves after buying a home here a few years ago. It was the best decision she ever made. Well, that and marrying Ben.

She smiled and picked up the pace. Stretching her long legs, she turned right, heading north. Finding a good rhythm, she let her mind go blank. Running, for Logan, was moving meditation. She'd never had the patience to sit on a Zen pillow and chant for an hour, but give her a stretch of open road and she was a happy woman. Feeling the cold air pushing against her face, breathing it deeply into her lungs, heart pumping, her body working smoothly in unison—there just wasn't anything else that gave her this same feeling.

Being a somewhat rural area, there were no sidewalks after you got out of town. Running along the 101 wasn't the safest thing to do, but Logan had reflective strips on her jacket and had learned where to zig or zag to avoid being right on the road. Other than that, she just had to trust her reflexes and hope some guy in a pickup truck didn't come around the corner with only three hours of sleep the night before.

A couple of miles later, she turned around at Fogarty Beach. Sometimes she stopped to let Dixon play there, but this morning she wanted to get to Pirates Coffee before the cinnamon rolls sold out. Good decision. When Kathy, her favorite barista, saw her coming, she waved and popped the last two in a to-go bag for her.

Ten minutes later they were home. Leaving her sandy shoes outside, Logan unhooked Dixon and let herself into the house carrying a warm paper sack from which delicious aromas were rising.

"Door Dash comin' through! Get your fresh, hot breakfast right . . ."

Before she could finish her sentence, her husband stomped across the front hallway right in front of them with a big trash bag, chunks of foam and blue fabric leaking out of it, in one hand and a broom in the other. Without speaking, he disappeared into the kitchen and straight out to the garage, letting the door slam behind him.

Logan and Dixon exchanged looks.

Max's muffled barking came from behind the bedroom door, so Logan peeked in to see what was what. Ben had Max safely secured in his crate, but there was no longer a lovely, brand-new, expensive, denim dog bed on the floor next to it.

Ahh . . .

"Max, you're in big trouble, buddy . . . ," she whispered, pulling the door shut quietly behind her.

Hoping to soothe the savage beast (Ben, not Max), Logan laid out the food, cinnamon roll front and center, put Dixon's portion in his dog bowl by the sink, poured herself a large mug of coffee, and sat down to wait.

After much banging in the garage of the trash can lid and who knows what else, Ben stomped back in and plopped down in his chair. Not even bothering with a fork, he grabbed the cinnamon roll and polished it off in three huge bites.

Wow. Impressive.

Sitting back, licking his lips, Ben took a long draw of the hot coffee Logan carefully pushed in front of him and said, "I don't know what I'm going to do with that dog!"

He started in on his burrito. Between mouthfuls, he said, "I'm in the middle of a couple of projects. I can't take him with me because he barks his head off or rips up the seats in the truck. And I can't leave him here. I don't want to keep him cooped up in the crate, but if I leave him loose in the house—well, you saw what he did to his dog bed. Purgatory was *never* like this . . . ," he grumbled.

But Purgatory wasn't a puppy, Logan thought, but was wise enough not to say this out loud.

She did, however, have an idea. She'd ask the crew tomorrow.

2

The Cormorant Coffee Crew consisted of Logan and her two friends, intrepid local reporter, Samantha Badger, and her sister-in-law, Jean Pullman. Most Wednesdays found them at Pirates. Logan peeled off her jacket and headed over to the picnic table where Sam was already saving their seats.

Without taking her eyes off of her laptop screen, Sam held up her finger in the universal 'just-a-minute' signal and pushed her signature hot pink cat-eye glasses back up on her nose. She tapped in a few more lines, then quickly scanned what she had written before hitting send.

Mother to a rambunctious one-year-old, Miss Magnolia, as well as a full-time reporter for the *NewsTimes,* Sam was one of the busiest women Logan knew. But she was also the most fun. It was always a party when Sam was around. How she packed that much energy into her barely five-foot frame was anyone's guess.

"Sorry about that," Sam said. "Just had to get that sent off. Now I can focus on what's *really* important—food!"

Logan laid her jacket on the bench and the two of them got in line at the counter.

They'd just started in on their cheesy breakfast burritos when the front door let in another customer, along with a gust of wind and rain.

Jean Pullman had arrived. Heads turned. They always did.

A dramatic skunk stripe accented the tall woman's dark hair, which she wore swept up and off her face, tucked into a neat French twist. Jean even looked French, or like most Americans expect French women to look. Minimal makeup, expensive but simple wardrobe, graceful, and completely composed.

In addition to being a well-loved family physician in Lincoln City, ten miles north of Depoe Bay, Jean was also Sam's sister-in-law and the Lincoln County Medical Examiner. The county couldn't afford a full-time position, so Jean only wore her ME hat on Wednesdays. Her office was in Newport, ten miles south of Depoe Bay. She joined them at Pirates on her way.

Logan met Sam and Jean several years ago when a young man, the owner of the house that Logan and Ben were buying in Depoe Bay, was wrongly accused of murder and had no way of proving his innocence until Logan stepped in to find the killer. The women's combined skills had come in handy more than once since, including solving another murder and a missing persons case.

But mainly they were friends. And this morning, the mystery Logan brought to the Cormorant Coffee Crew had nothing to do with murder or a missing person, but with Ben's puppy challenges.

Once Jean had her tea, she joined them at the table, where Logan was telling Sam about Max's latest round of destruction.

"You should have seen Ben," she said, finishing up the story, "Stomping through the kitchen with what was left of Max's brand new dog bed sticking out of the trash bag. I've never seen him so pissed!"

"Dogs need to learn who's boss," Jean said, taking a bite of her croissant without dropping a crumb.

Logan doubted any animal—canine or human—would dare disobey Jean. Even her wardrobe was obedient. Her jewel-toned flats never had a speck of sand or mud on them. Today's shoes were a brilliant, peacock blue . . . and dry.

"Well, duh!" Logan said, letting out an exasperated huff. "But how? Ben isn't trying to teach him to *do* anything, just *not* do some things. How do you train a negative?"

"Rolled-up newspaper," Jean said with a shrug. "One whack on the nose . . ."

Ignoring Jean, who she hoped was kidding—Logan had no intention of ever smacking any dog, even if that worked—she turned to Sam. "Didn't you do a story on some miracle dog trainer a couple of years ago? It was a woman . . . she had an unusual name . . . is she still around?"

"Which one? I've done a couple dog stories," said Sam. "You mean that agility phenom, Autumn Whitney, the kid who took all the prizes with her miniature Schnauzer last year?" Sam said.

"No," Logan said, "She was national, lived back east some-where. This one was local."

Sam tucked a strand of her shiny, jet-black bob behind her ear and tapped something into her phone, which was always, like her laptop, charged and within reach. She held it up for Logan to see.

"Oletta," she said. "Oletta Hartley. *Adventurous K9* out in Eddyville."

"Yeah! That's the one," Logan said. "They had that little school bus that came and picked up the dogs and took them out to her ranch, right?"

"I remember that story," Jean said. "They had seatbelts for the dogs and everything. Very well organized."

Sam popped the last of her burrito into her mouth, licking her greasy fingers before wiping them off on her jeans. "I don't know if she takes puppies," Sam said, swallowing. "I think her doggie day camp is kind of a fitness and socialization thing for grown dogs. She's got trails and a pond where they can swim. It's right off the highway, but it goes back a ways behind the house; they're out in the country. We got some great pictures of all the dogs playing together. She even has horses."

"Do you have her contact information?" Logan asked.

Sam said she thought she still had the woman's personal email and cell phone number in her files. She'd text it to her when she got home.

Jean threw her trash away, then leaned down to give Sam a hug, "Don't forget we get Miss Magnolia this weekend. We're going to check out the new octopus at the aquarium."

"What happened to the old one?" Logan asked.

"Died," Jean said, lifting her messenger bag onto her shoulder. "They only live a few years. This one was brought in by a crab fisherman last month. Female. She had some injuries but is doing great now."

Logan mentally added that to the list of fun things to do next time Amy brought Ian down. Her five-year-old grandson loved all animals, wild or tame.

"Oh, and Baylee's back!" Jean added. "She was spotted off Otter Crest."

"That's awesome!" Logan said.

Baylee was a popular female resident gray whale in Depoe Bay. Whale watching season didn't really get started until Baylee showed up. The whales had been late this year on their annual migration up from Baja on their way to Alaska.

"Any customers waiting for you today?" Sam asked Jean hopefully. Sam was always looking for a scoop and all deaths in Lincoln County of undetermined cause went to Jean first.

"Sorry, no one awaits my attention that I know of," Jean said. "But if any floaters came in overnight, I'll let you know." Looking back at her sister-in-law, she added, "But you're still welcome to come down. You can write a breaking news story of me working on my budget or perhaps sit in on some scintillating Zoom meetings later this afternoon."

Sam rolled her eyes.

"I'll pass, thanks, but you can't blame a girl for tryin'!" she said, gathering her things.

As the three friends went their separate ways at the door, Logan reminded Sam to send her the dog trainer's contact information and headed home to see what Max had destroyed in her absence.

They really needed to get that dog into some kind of obedience class and sooner rather than later.

3

Even though it was already April, other than a few days of unseasonably warm weather at the end of February, winter clung stubbornly to the central Oregon coast. As much as Logan loved cool temps, soft rain, and sipping a hot toddy by the fire, even she was getting tired of gray skies and muddy shoes.

So Sunday morning on the way home from her run, when the sun pushed aside the gauzy clouds to fill the sky, Logan closed her eyes and reveled in soaking up every bit of the sun's warmth on her face.

Even the neighbors said this winter had been the longest, rainiest one they had ever experienced, or at least could remember. A gnarly ice storm in January knocked the power out for almost a week in many parts of Lincoln County, including Depoe Bay. After that storm, Logan invested in a fleece-lined wool beanie, a thicker pair of gloves, and some L.L. Bean water-resistant pants.

Logan and Dixon rounded the corner and started up the gravel drive to the house. The front windows were lit an inviting, warm yellow and smoke curled out of the chimney. She loved their new home. The fact that Ben was waiting inside was a huge plus. How had she gotten so lucky?

When they got inside, Ben had good news. Oletta Hartley, the dog trainer Sam recommended, had returned their call. She couldn't promise anything, but said she'd be happy to take a look at their puppy and make some recommendations for behavior modifications. Were they available today?

An hour later, they were on their way. The forty-five minute drive to Eddyville went by quickly. They saw two red-tailed hawks, sitting stoically, one on a fence post, one at the top of a tree, presumably scanning the area for prey. Or maybe they were meditating. Who knew?

Luckily, both Max and Dixon loved to go 'bye-bye-in-the-car!' The minute they opened the back of the SUV, both dogs jumped right in. Currently, they were each pressed against their respective back windows, noses stuck as far out of the crack as they could get them, madly sniffing, happily drinking in myriad scents and fresh air rushing by. Ben only lowered the windows a few inches. He was worried about them jumping out, which was a possibility, Logan had to admit.

A wood and wire gate stretched across a gravel road that led into the property. Welcome sign on the left, with a metal cutout of a grazing horse above it. A sign on the right instructed them to 'STOP. Do Not Open Gate! HONK!'

They did and a tall woman in jeans, work boots, sweatshirt, and open jacket, who they assumed must be Oletta, emerged from around a berm up the hill and waved them toward a gravel parking area on their right. A thick, honey-blonde braid lay over one shoulder. Logan approved of the practical wardrobe.

An assortment of dogs, including a German shepherd, a small doodle of some kind, and a curious Doberman joined Oletta to greet the new arrivals. Introductions made—canine butt sniffing and human hand shaking—Oletta led them all over to a long stretch of grass on the other side of the arena and picked up a bright orange rubber ball. Ignoring the humans, she addressed Dixon and Max with a mischievous grin.

"You've been cooped up in that ole' car for a while, right guys?" she asked. "Let's see if you can get this before Hawk does!"

Tossing it a few times in the air to get all the dogs excited, Oletta wound up and threw the bright orange ball a *very* long way down the field. A natural athlete herself, Logan was still impressed by the power in that throw.

Must have played softball.

Dixon and Hawk streaked after the orange dot, the other dogs joyfully running behind, trying to catch up. Hawk, the German shepherd, caught it on the first bounce, raced back, and dropped it at Oletta's feet. She repeated this nine or ten times until tongues lolled out of the sides of doggie mouths and much panting and drooling ensued. Dixon snatched it midair once, but Hawk was far and away the best at this game. The other dogs didn't seem to care as long as they got to participate.

Picking up a hose, Oletta filled some oversized, stainless steel water bowls, letting the dogs get a drink and relieve themselves. Then she led everyone over to a couple of split log benches where they could sit and talk. Max had immediately wanted to be as close to Oletta as possible and jumped up beside her. The other dogs were lying close by. Hawk lay at her feet, Dixon at Logan's. Logan scratched Dixon behind his ears.

"Now, tell me about Max," Oletta said. "He's your dog, right, Ben?"

While Ben talked, Logan observed Oletta, curious how she would handle it when Max started chewing on her with his needle-sharp puppy teeth or jumping up to lick her face. But within minutes, Max was settled down with his chin resting on her leg, perfectly relaxed, eyes at half-mast.

Wow.

Logan tuned back into the conversation. Oletta was giving them some tips. "Whatever you do, both of you have to do it," she said. "Start simple, be consistent. Decide on your commands and stick with them. Use 'off' when he jumps on you or someone else, not 'down', because 'down' means you want him to lay down. Very different command."

Logan still couldn't believe Max was being so well-behaved. She couldn't help herself and interrupted, "How'd you get him to be so calm?"

"Tired him out first," Oletta laughed. "A tired dog is a good dog. Puppies have a lot of energy."

Oletta ruffled Max's fur, rubbing him behind the ears, "I'd love to have him," she said, standing up and handing Ben the leash. "He's a great dog."

Ben asked about the doggie daycare camp she ran, so she showed them a couple of the trails and the pond where the dogs swam. It looked like doggie heaven, so Logan and Ben agreed to have both dogs come out once a week for socialization and exercise.

"The school bus will pick them up at 9:00 a.m. Wednesday mornings at the movie theater parking lot in Newport," she said, "and bring them back at 5:00 p.m., happy and tired. Don't worry if they sleep for the next twenty-four hours after their first day, especially the puppy," she said, walking them back to their car. "I've got about fifteen regulars—all breeds. Most are local but they come from all over. They run and swim and play and nap, then do it all over again. Max and Dixon will be exhausted when they get home, but in a good way. I guarantee Max won't eat his dog bed on a Wednesday."

She promised to do a little training with Max on those days, too, then walked them back to the car. Dixon padded beside Logan, then jumped in the back without prompting or a leash.

"Someone obviously did a good job with your labraheeler," Oletta observed, "where did he get his training?"

"I have no idea. We just got lucky with Dixon," Logan explained. "He came that way. He's a rescue. I'm not sure what he's been trained to do besides maybe chase seagulls at the beach. He's good at that!"

Oletta laughed and told the dogs she'd see them on Wednesday.

4

Sixty-five-year-old Carl Muller sat at his patio table under the outdoor heater, as he had done every morning for the last few months, watching the sun slowly lighten the sky from blackened charcoal to dove gray. Oregon was often gray. Not his favorite color.

Taking his time, he savored his cappuccino. A small plate in front of him contained one buttery croissant and a spoonful of marionberry jam. The jam was a gift from the stone mason who'd done their fireplace. The label said *Gingifer's Preserves.* Carl had taken a jar of it back for Astrid on his last trip to New Jersey and she loved it.

He dabbed his mouth with the linen napkin and debated a second cup of coffee. Deciding against it, he crossed his legs and leaned back in his chair, half closing his eyes.

It was so quiet here. Nothing like New Jersey or New York, almost three thousand miles away, where he had lived most of his life. Or even farther east, across the Atlantic, where he'd run after everything fell apart. Those were scary times. But good ones, too. He wondered what his life would have been like if he had been born into a different family, had a regular job—but he couldn't imagine it.

It's not like he had a lot of say. He'd grown up in the business. He and his first wife, Maria Teresa, a Bartolomeo, were promised to each other as kids, to solidify ties between the families. They married out of high school. Maria had popped out two Agostinis by the time he got his business degree from NYU.

Those were the glory days. Everyone in all five families was rolling in money. And everyone knew who you were. You had respect. Corner tables were reserved and front-row seats to any Broadway show Maria wanted to see suddenly became available. Custom suits. Stretch limos. They never paid for anything. People took care of them, and they returned the favor. And you always had friends. It truly was one big *Family*.

Then along came the trials in '85 and '86, essentially destroying their world. Like rats in a hole, everyone turned on each other or scattered to save their own skin. One of his best friends, and one of the Family's top enforcers, Salvatore, a guy with over a hundred kills to his name and countless 'messages' that landed his victims in the hospital instead of the morgue, testified for the Feds. Sal did a measly fifteen years and was now back out, cashing in on his crimes. He was all over social media, selling signed baseball bats, his previous weapon of choice for breaking arms, legs, and kneecaps.

Carl had been lucky, though. He'd gotten out before the sweep. Louis got him a private jet to Switzerland until things cooled down. Switzerland didn't have extradition to the U.S. until the mid-nineties and by then the FBI was busy with a few other domestic problems, like the World Trade Center bombing and Oklahoma City. And then came 9/11. In 2001, the Mafia was the least of the FBI's concerns.

Carl pushed his plate away, wishing he could shove the memories away as easily. His words to Astrid came back to haunt him.

When I turn fifty-five . . . when I turn sixty . . . we'll go soon, Astrid. Soon.

To put her off for a while, he bought this property out here in Oregon, a couple hours from Portland. Lots of trees and open fields. He promised to build her a fine home.

Just be patient, Astrid. We have plenty of time. Why don't you start sketching out some floor plans? Horses? Sure, we can get some horses. All the horses you want.

And then, without warning, time ran out. Astrid was diagnosed with pancreatic cancer. Because she hadn't complained, it was fairly advanced before they discovered it. Damn doctors gave her less than six months, but Carl would not accept that. He put a rush on everything. Told Louis he was leaving.

If he could just get Astrid out here, to fresh air and green trees in Oregon, he knew she would get well. Houses take time to build, but Carl knew how to speed up the timeline. Even in Oregon, commissioner's kids needed braces or a vacation to Disney World, so with a few well-placed 'gifts' to the right people, Carl had all the permits by Astrid's second round of chemo; utilities were being brought in from the road, and the builder had started framing the main house.

And if bribes didn't do it, a little intimidation provided by Fred Davies, a local cop he had in his pocket, did. Although Oregon born-and-bred, the Toledo patrol officer's late mother was from Jersey. When he put the word out he needed some West Coast muscle, one of his cousins in Scranton put them in touch. Davies was as dirty as they came and happy to take a side job now and then.

Astrid finished her last treatment two weeks before the move and couldn't wait to see their new home in Oregon.

At the last minute, Carl had Astrid's kitchen garden area marked off with stakes and string to welcome her to her new home. He knew she would like that.

Then three days before they were to leave, Astrid died.

Carl still couldn't believe it. He stared into space, seeing only her soft, blue eyes smiling at him with trust and love.

Her blonde hair and smooth, ivory skin. She hardly ever wore makeup. Didn't need to.

He should have retired when she wanted him to. What had those few extra years bought him? Money? More money? What good was money without Astrid? Besides, what was there to spend money on in this god-forsaken backwater? There wasn't a decent deli in miles. They had to get everything flown in.

His cappuccino turning sour in his stomach, Carl got up and went into the house to talk to John about the croissants.

5

Logan kept it short, but she and Dixon got in a good, solid run in plenty of time for all of them—canines and humans—to wolf down Ben's delicious bacon and eggs breakfast and go potty before piling into the car. Oletta said the little school bus picked the dogs up promptly at 9:00 a.m. Since the Newport theater was only fifteen minutes away, they arrived early and were waiting when the little, yellow school bus turned into the parking lot.

There was no mistaking it. It looked like an official school bus, but had *Adventurous K9* printed in large, black letters on both sides. It had been fitted inside with seatbelts for each canine passenger, two to a seat. Four dogs were already strapped in, happily panting or looking out the windows. Logan snapped a picture with her phone to send to Amy. The bus rolled to a stop a few feet away.

The door whooshed open and the driver, a trim woman with a ready smile and short, steel-gray hair got out of the bus to greet them. "Hi, I'm Paulette," she said, taking the dogs' leashes, "And this must be Dixon and Max!"

Logan worried how they would react to such a new experience, but both dogs followed Paulette up the steps without hesitation. She had them loaded up and strapped in securely within minutes, then climbed back into the driver's seat.

"What time should we be here to pick them up?" Logan asked.

"Get here by five," Paulette said, "I might be a few minutes either side, depending on traffic, but I try for as close to five as I can."

With that, she pulled the door shut and they watched the little school bus drive away.

All of a sudden it was very quiet.

Logan looked at Ben.

Ben waved his arms in the air and shouted, "A day without the kids!"

Logan laughed. Having dogs was kind of like having kids. Parenting of any mammal was a full-time job.

Once home they made good use of their free time. Ben worked in the garden and got his paleo lasagna made (he was trying out a low-carb diet, so the noodles were replaced with long zucchini slices). It was foil-wrapped and tucked into the fridge so all he had to do was put it in the oven later.

Logan put some laundry in and ran the vacuum, then went into a corner of the living room where she set up her music, looking forward to a few hours of uninterrupted creative time. Her chair faced a large picture window on the east side of the house that showcased the forest. Brown and gray streaked cedars rose tall and straight, their lower branches nodding over the back deck. A few feet into the forest, a moss-covered snag provided shelter for any number of critters and was a great hunting perch for the barred owl that nested farther in and visited occasionally.

She drank in the view then lifted her violin out of its case. After some minor tuning, she tucked Bella under her chin to try out some variations of a new composition she'd been working on. Lovingly crafted for Logan's Appalachian great-grandmother by a young, Italian immigrant, Bella was an exquisite instrument.

LOOK AGAIN

She'd promised her former music student, Brandon, a contribution to a recording he was putting together when she and Ben flew down to Jasper, CA, her old hometown. They were going down in June to visit family, including Ben's nephews, Calvin, Cooper, and their little sister, Casey. Logan's daughter, Amy, her Scottish botanist husband, Liam, and her very active five-year-old grandson, Ian, lived just down the street. Ian and Casey, born just weeks apart, were practically growing up together as siblings. They both entered kindergarten last fall.

People assumed Ben was Ian's natural grandfather because they were both blue-eyed towheads. He never corrected them. He had walked Ian's mom, Amy down the aisle, so his role in the family was now official if not genetic.

After a late lunch at the Horn, Logan and Ben decided to play tourist, wandering around the shops in Depoe Bay. Logan almost stopped and got some caramel corn from Ainslee's but remembered Ben's diet. She'd have to grab a couple of bags next time she went down to see Sam's baby, Miss Magnolia. Sam was never on a diet, and Logan could scarf hers down in the car on the way home.

Around three-thirty, Logan's cell phone rang. She retrieved it from her jacket pocket where she'd left it this morning after snapping a picture of the little yellow bus to send to Amy.

"Hello?"

"Logan? Hi, it's Oletta, at Adventurous K9."

6

Logan immediately worried one of the dogs had been injured or run off or . . .

"I am so sorry," Oletta said, "but the bus won't start, and Mom can't do her regular drop-off route this afternoon."

"Oh, that's okay," Logan said, relieved. At least the dogs weren't hurt. She put her phone on speaker so Ben could hear.

"Keegan is working on it, but it needs a part we can't get until tomorrow. Normally, my husband, Lane, would bring your dogs back in his truck, but he's got a full load already. The owner of the other three dogs we picked up this morning is an elderly man who doesn't drive—he sends his dogs out here every week to get some exercise."

Logan didn't know who Keegan was, but she was glad someone was working on the little school bus—it seemed to be an essential component of Oletta's business.

"No worries, Oletta, we can come pick them up," she said.

She filled Ben in on the way back to the house.

"I'll call Clay," he said. "Let him know I can't make that emergency communications thing tonight."

After they lost power and cell service during the big ice storm this winter, their handyman and friend, Clay, a ham radio operator, had talked Ben into studying to get his Radio Technician License and tonight was the first meeting.

"No, you go ahead," Logan said. "I can drive out to get the dogs."

"Are you sure you don't want me to go with you?" Ben said.

"No, thanks for offering, but I'm good. Besides, I'll bet we'll be home and tucked into bed before you are."

Ben should have taken that bet.

The drive out to Eddyville took less time than before, or seemed to, probably because she knew the way. She queued up some Allison Krauss. Logan loved Krauss's old bluegrass albums, but one of her more recent recordings, a duet with Robert Plant, *Can't Let Go,* was a new favorite. As she flew down the highway, Logan turned up the volume and joined in, belting out the end of the chorus. She almost missed the turnoff but braked just in time and rolled up to the gate. Oletta came out to let her in.

"I hope you don't mind," Oletta said, "but it was getting late, so the dogs are up at the house. Lane's feeding them all dinner. He'll bring them down after he lets them out to do their business."

Logan said that was fine with her, she was in no rush. She did wonder how Max's digestive system would handle whatever dog food they used, but decided not to ask. If it didn't agree with him, they'd find out soon enough.

"I was just about to get the horses," Oletta said, "It's been a crazy day. Rattlesnake in the sweet feed. They're not usually out this early."

Rattlesnake?

Logan looked quickly around her feet, but Oletta didn't seem to be worried, so she tried to relax.

"I needed a little equine therapy. Working with my horses is my happy place. Would you like to meet my guys while you're waiting?" Oletta asked.

"Absolutely," Logan said. Like many pre-teen girls, Logan had gone through a horse-crazy stage. She fell in love with the powerful animals after watching Saturday afternoon movies like *Black Stallion* and *National Velvet*.

When they got to the gate, Oletta whistled once, then waited. Logan waited and watched expectantly. She felt like a kid at Christmas.

First to come around the corner, a large bay ambled toward them. Obedient to Oletta's call, but not in any big hurry. A little white around the muzzle. Logan later learned this was Draco, a gentle twenty-three-year-old horse they bought for her mother, who still liked to ride. A younger, charcoal-gray, medium-sized horse with a shiny, long, jet-black mane and tail made a beeline for Oletta, nudging her with his nose. Gorgeous animal.

Last, but not least, a long-legged colt trotted right up to Logan and started nosing around her jacket. Curious about the newcomer, the other horses meandered over to check Logan out, too, almost knocking her down.

"This is Reign, my two-year old roan, and the one trying to get into your pockets is Hondo, the baby," Oletta said.

Although Logan was thoroughly delighted at being surrounded by the beautiful beasts, it was a little nerve-racking. They were like big, friendly dogs. *Really big* dogs.

When the meet and greet was over, they walked the horses back to the arena. Putting Hondo and Draco into their stalls, Oletta lifted a rope halter off a hook by his stall, slipped it on Reign, and led him into the arena.

"Lane's probably playing catch with the dogs in the back," she said. "You're welcome to watch me work for a while. I try to get a few hours in with him every day."

She explained that Reign was the horse she was currently getting ready for Nationals—whatever those were. Hondo was next up, as he got older. Logan readily agreed and sat on an overturned crate, her back by the east wall so she could observe without being in the way.

The arena itself was enclosed, but arched, open-air windows had been cut all around the top half of the walls, letting fresh air in but keeping horse and rider protected from rain and snow. Covered in a soft, almost powdery dirt, the ground inside the arena was smooth and free of potholes or anything else a horse might trip on. Most of the space was empty, except for some equipment around the edge, a large tractor tire in one corner, and a raised wooden structure on the left. At the south end on their right were the three horse stalls, water, feed barrels, and tack room.

"This is so cool. It's huge!" Logan said. "Was it here already when you bought the property, or did you have it built?"

"No, we built this place ourselves back in 2015," Oletta said. "Everybody pitched in."

She explained it was where she got all of her horses ready to compete in national trail riding events.

"How many events are there?" Logan asked.

"I do about fourteen or fifteen every year," Oletta said. "Next one's in Veneta. Reign's just starting out."

"Is it kind of like a rodeo competition?" Logan asked. "Do you rope calves or do barrels?" Those were the two events she could remember from the rodeo she saw when her friends Thomas and Lisa Delgado took her to a rodeo in Southern California.

"Some rodeos have trail competition events," Oletta said, "but not the other way around. Different setup. Some people in this area did rodeo when they were young and lived in Colorado or Arizona, or even California, where there's a lot more of that, but they do all trail competitions now."

In an aside, she added, "Barrel riding is for cowgirls with younger bones."

For the next few minutes, Logan watched as Oletta put Reign through his paces. The beautiful horse was a joy to watch, and Oletta's patience was impressive.

More time must have passed than she realized because when Lane brought the dogs down, their shadows were long on the ground. Oletta walked Reign back to his stall and secured the gate. "I'll feed them in a minute," she said as she walked her out.

Logan lifted a very tired but happy Max into the back of her car and Dixon hopped up on the left. Max stretched out puppy-style, chin on paws, and promptly went to sleep. Dixon took up his position by the window.

"Speaking of trail riding," Oletta said. "I've got my next event this weekend, April 5 – 7, out at J Fisher's, but on Wednesday we've got tracking training for Hawk and Kraken at our Schutzhund club. Why don't you and Ben join us? And you can bring Dixon and Max. They'd have a great time. We usually grab a bite to eat after and Outback's patio area is dog-friendly."

Logan said she'd check with Ben, but it sounded like fun. She was sure Ben would be up for it. Maybe they'd pick up some training tips. Lane said he'd text her the directions and went to open the gate for her. She waved as she pulled onto the highway.

Ben's radio class started at 7:00. Logan checked her mirrors, then pressed her lead foot on the accelerator—just a little. Depoe Bay was less than an hour away. If she got lucky, she'd beat her husband to the lasagna.

7

John Clemens Carter was in the zone. Opening both doors of the custom-built, 18.7 cubic feet capacity, Sub-Zero refrigerator, he poked around in the crisper drawer and then went back to his iPad on the black quartz counter.

Arugula . . . olives . . . prosciutto.

Closing his eyes for a minute, he visualized what else he might need, then added veal and melon to the list. And those croissants Carl wanted. It was just he and the boss banging around in the big house now that Astrid was gone, but they were expecting an important guest this weekend and that meant beefing up the grocery list. He'd decided on his signature saltimbocca and of course a good wine. Wine was his specialty. Maybe a nice Cabernet Franc.

He carried his iPad over to the breakfast bay and scooted in behind the table on the u-shaped, built-in bench seat. The fit was a little tight, but he could still slide in. 'Built-like-a-fireplug' his dad always bragged, 'like all us Carters,' before clapping him on the back and gathering him into a bear hug at every holiday gathering. He missed his Pa.

Sunlight streamed into the kitchen through floor-to-ceiling mullioned windows. He loved this view—looking out at all the green. Astrid would have been so happy here. The view used to include the stringed demarcation for her future vegetable garden, but Carl had him take it down after she died. He would never admit it, but it had been painful to look at every day.

Half an hour later, finished with his menus and shopping list, which he knew would have to be adjusted depending on what was available at the market, John gave his ponytail a practiced tug to tighten it. He kept his long, white hair neatly trimmed, but it still reached almost to his belt. A few years ago he thought of cutting it, but Astrid told him she loved the color and thought it made him look distinguished, so it stayed. It was thick enough and his hairline had only receded a little, so it didn't look like one of those old guys with five strands of scraggly hair left. He was old, but not as old as Carl. He and Astrid were—had been—about the same age, at least a decade younger than Carl.

He thought back to when he first met Carl and Astrid, back when he owned Johnny's, his upscale steakhouse in Brooklyn.

It had been a Thursday night with a good, steady crowd.

He'd known who Carl was, of course, everyone did, so when he saw who was at table nine, he made sure to bring over a complimentary bottle of wine and take care of their order himself.

This became a regular habit, so when Johnny's went belly up in the depression they called a recession, along with half the other restaurants in the city, he said yes to Carl's offer to become his personal chef and sommelier. In hindsight, he shouldn't have.

If it had only been working for Carl, he'd have turned him down. He'd have stayed as far away from that dark, rotten world as possible, but he found a way to rationalize his decision. In his mind, he worked for Astrid, not Carl.

The moment he'd seen saw the tall, fresh-faced blonde at table nine, he was hooked. Why she married a cockroach like Carl he'd never understood. He later learned that Carl had met her when he was in Switzerland. She sure wasn't from around here.

Maybe Carl was different there, away from Jersey. Astrid may not even have known he was a Agostini or what he had done in America. That begged the question, once they returned to America and she did find out, why did she stay with him for all those years? He'd never asked, of course, and she never brought it up.

Even though he lived in the house and saw and heard most everything that went on within the crime families, all he ever talked about with Astrid was the menu or giving his opinion when asked about what car she should buy. Carl insisted she get a new one every year. Astrid didn't have a clue about cars, nor did she care. He remembered her tripping into the kitchen one afternoon with an armful of showroom brochures, dumping them on the counter, and then throwing her hands up in mock surrender.

"You must help me, John!" she laughed. "Carl says I must pick one by tonight!"

He'd learned to keep a delicate balance between the feelings in his heart and the expression on his face, and to control his body language, which always threatened to betray him. He would never dishonor Astrid. That was his main reason for never telling her how he felt. The other was the assurance of what Carl would do to him if he ever found out. First, he'd have his balls chopped off, then have them dissolved in a vat of acid, or fed to the hogs, before throwing what was left of him off a pier. There were so many choices.

Of course, now that Astrid was gone, it didn't matter. He'd never told her, and now he never could. He wasn't sure how he felt about that.

He was almost finished with his grocery list when the phone rang. After the cell towers had gone down during January's ice storm, Carl had instructed him to get a landline with extensions throughout the house. The very next day he had people out installing them. He didn't want to miss a call. Even though Carl was ostensibly retired, he kept in touch with Jersey. And New Jersey had been calling a lot lately.

As if on cue, the phone rang. *Speak of the devil.* Carl picked up in the living room on the first ring. Without trying to, John could hear Carl's side of the conversation. The boss's voice was deep and still had more than a hint of Jersey.

"Louis," he said.

That would be Louis Agostini, the old don who kept an iron grip on the remaining Family business back east. The old guys still respected and rewarded loyalty. Louis was the one who had helped Carl escape to Switzerland years ago when things got hot. Carlo Agostini became Carl Muller. When things cooled down, he laid the groundwork for his return. Carl had worked for Louis ever since. Louis was also the one who allowed Carl to 'retire' and move away. Permission to leave the Family was hardly ever granted. John had never seen it done before.

John tuned back into the conversation.

"No, I understand," Carl said, "Business is business. Of course you want to see it for yourself. I'll show you when you get here. We can go over the numbers then."

John listened a while longer but learned nothing new. These two were experts on not giving much away on the phone. It was just habit for them not to mention specifics. At the end of the call, Carl said, "And Louis—thank you."

That may have been the first time John ever heard Carl thank anyone for anything. It made John wonder what he was thanking him for.

8

Carl was back on track. He smiled to himself at the joke. Using his thumb and index finger on the trackpad of his laptop, he zoomed in, examining the plans. It really was going to be gorgeous. Everything was coming together.

This wasn't the original plan, of course. He bought this property, plus the lot next door, to give Astrid a start on her dream—lots of open land. It was just the start, he'd promised. He would buy her more over time. No rush.

Then she got sick. He sped up the timeline and bought a few more properties. All through third parties of course—different names. No sense tipping his hand to the sellers and jacking up the prices. He had a map of checkerboard properties in his office as they closed. Every time he got another one, he'd color it in green and spread the map out on the table—then have Astrid show him where she wanted the house and where they might keep her goats and maybe some horses.

He realized now he'd gone a little crazy that year. As if buying more land would keep her cancer at bay. Spending a big chunk of his capital. He had left enough for them to live on comfortably out here in the sticks, but not much else.

Then one morning, not long after he lost Astrid, Carl woke up and looked around. Sitting here staring at the trees, riding horses, and feeding goats was Astrid's dream, not his.

It was way too damn quiet here.

What he needed was a project. One that would replenish his bank accounts. He didn't want to go back east. Except for Louis, who was pushing ninety, everything was being run by the younger guys now. And some of them weren't Agostinis or even one of the original five families. No, he needed to make a new life for himself here—but how?

For a few months, he sifted through ideas. He knew how to make money in Jersey. The city was jammed with people and businesses and greedy mayors and government officials. Millions of dollars traded hands every day, all waiting for the Family to skim their share in one way or another. Kept them all fat and happy.

Out here, everything was spread out. If there was money, people must keep it stuffed in their mattresses, because he didn't see any of it floating around. Human nature being what it was, though, there must be an undercurrent of slime around here somewhere. But even if he could find it, he didn't have the well-established connections, distribution routes—and frankly, the muscle—to get his cut, like he used to.

But there had to be something. Maybe gambling.

He wasn't Indian, so a casino was out. Besides there were already a couple closer to Portland. There were lots of vineyards around here. John knew wine, but when he asked him about making their own wine, John said it usually took several years before a first vintage was ready. Carl didn't have that kind of time. John could also help him design and set up an upscale restaurant, but he quickly ditched that idea. People wouldn't drive for hours just for a good meal. There had to be something else to draw them here. Something they couldn't resist.

Then it hit him.

A casino wasn't the only way to gamble.

He did some research. Fifty-five acres. That's all it took for a decent horse track. By pure accident, he already had most of that. And Oregon allowed on-track betting. There was nothing like it out here already. He quickly saw the possibilities. Fine dining, fine wine, the touch of glamor, the cold hard cash piling up in the bank. The $1,200/night rooms in the lodge. A few, very exclusive suites. Maybe even a helicopter pad for Louis.

After all, Louis would be bankrolling this. He just agreed to the loan. For the lion's share of the profits, but since he was putting in most of the buildout money that was only fair. That he would do the deal at all was a result of his gratitude for how Carl had handled himself—the loyalty he'd demonstrated—by not turning traitor back in the eighties. For always doing what he was told. Without any hesitation, Carlo got on that jet and left the country. America, the greatest country in the world. Left Maria and the kids without a second glance. Then stayed in Switzerland until they told him it was safe to come back.

He was waiting to hear about one or two more properties. The realtor said with the very generous cash offers he'd just made, they were all but done deals. She would call him later, tonight. He'd decided it was safe to deal directly with the realtor for these last two deals now that he had the rest. He didn't have time to go through his usual third party. With any luck, since he was paying in cash, the realtor said they could close in two or three days. As soon as he had proof in hand, Louis promised to send the money to get the project started.

Astrid wanted horses, well, she was going to get them! He was naming the racetrack after her. *Astrid Meadows and Cedar Lodge.*

Lacing his fingers together behind his head, Carl leaned back in his chair. It was good to be back in the game!

9

Wednesday morning dawned fair and dry, although a storm was predicted to come in later that day. Logan hoped it would hold off until tonight. She was looking forward to seeing what Schutzhund was all about and seeing Oletta work with her dogs.

They decided Max would have more fun running around with the other dogs at Adventurous K9 and swimming in the pond, so they left him with Oletta's mom for the day and just took Dixon. Down to four humans and three canines, they decided to take the Hartley's large SUV. Oletta drove, Lane rode shotgun, Logan and Ben took the roomy back seat, and the dogs happily jumped in the back.

On the way to Springfield, Lane turned halfway around in his seat, explaining what they'd be seeing today when they got to the Schutzhund club.

"Schutzhund means 'protection dog' in German, but really, it's a triathlon sport that has three phases of training: tracking, obedience, and protection."

Logan thought the protection part sounded scary and brought to mind lunging, snarling German Shepherds going after prisoners in the movies.

She looked up at Kraken and Hawk in the rearview mirror. They didn't look vicious. Both dogs looked relaxed and happy. Kraken had joined Dixon at the window watching traffic go by, while Hawk was lying down. Still, to Logan, dobermans always looked a little dangerous, even when they were just lying there. What Lane said next reassured her somewhat.

"We only do the tracking part," he said. "We've trained all of our dogs to track. Oletta's done some search and rescue work with Hawk."

"Are there competitions? Is this where the police train their dogs?"

"There are competitions. You can take this sport as far as you want to go, as long as your dog is up for it. You can have an expert train your dog, but everyone in this club is an owner and handler. We all train our own dogs."

He went on to explain that today there were no competition events, just people in various areas on the club grounds, working with their dogs. When they arrived, the parking lot was already filling up. Oletta found a spot in the shade, and they unloaded, making sure they all had water and snacks.

As they trekked across the field, Logan was glad she'd worn her hiking shoes and long pants. It was dry but uneven, and on one side there was a stretch of long grass which may or may not contain a patch of blackberry brambles. It was hard to tell from here.

The first person they came to was a woman holding an excited young dog on a leash.

"Hi, Mandy," Oletta said. "How's Thunder doing?"

"Oh, hi, Oletta!" Mandy said. "He's doing okay. Got about half this time. Van's setting it up again, now."

Not wanting to interfere with whatever training was going on, Logan kept Dixon at her side and watched as the man walked back to get the dog.

"They're doing straight line tracking," Mandy explained. "That's my husband, Van. Basically, you walk a straight line, placing treats—hot dog slices for this one—on every footstep, first, then walk back in those same steps to get your dog. You want them to lead, but if they're young and just starting out, you keep them close. You make sure they stay between your feet and on track, keeping their nose to the ground to follow your scent in a straight line. Gradually you leave fewer treats-maybe every third step, until all they're doing is following the scent—nose to the ground—then they get a big reward at the end!"

Logan watched as Thunder gobbled up hot dog slices one after the other. He missed a few, but not bad. Van and Mandy repeated the exercise a few more times and Thunder only left two on his last run.

After they said their goodbyes, they walked across the field to a shaded area under a large tree, edged by the usual mix of salal and smaller bushes. Ben pulled out a water bottle and gave all three thirsty dogs drinks out of a collapsible bowl from his pack.

"Okay, Hawk," Oletta said. "You're up! Let's show 'em what you can do."

Logan and Dixon stayed with Ben and Kraken so she could watch Hawk in action.

Lane grinned, pulled off his jacket, and took off at a trot, quickly disappearing into the brush. They waited about three minutes, then Oletta held Lane's jacket under Hawk's nose so he could get a good whiff, and said, "Find!"

Hawk shot away like a bullet; Oletta following close behind.

Logan felt her arm almost jerk out of its socket as Dixon, nose to the ground, took off after Oletta.

Thankful for her morning runs, Logan was able to keep up, but just barely, as Dixon pulled her along, zigzagging down a hill, across a stream, and up to a jumble of broken concrete blocks piled next to a small outbuilding.

When she got there, Hawk was standing perfectly still, looking intently at the pile of rubble. Dixon barked once and then sat very still, staring at the same place.

"Nice job, guys!" Oletta said as Lane pushed one of the slabs away and crawled out, effusively praising both dogs. They gave them a five-minute play session of fetch with an old tennis ball Lane pulled out of his pocket, then walked together back to the field.

"Wow," Logan said. "That was fun! I've never seen Dixon take off like that."

"He's a natural, all right. And you didn't do too bad yourself. How do you feel about doing some search and rescue training with me and Hawk?" Oletta said.

Dixon wagged his stubby tail as if he understood the invite.

"Sure," Logan said. "Sounds like fun!"

They agreed to get together when Oletta returned from Nationals next week.

"Let me know what day and time and we'll be here," Logan said.

"Well, if you can get away for a couple of days we can do a trail ride, too. You can stay in the trailer," Oletta said. "It's my son's, but no one is using it right now."

Logan looked forward to the training for Dixon, but also to spending time with a new friend. She really needed to get out more, anyway. There was a fine line between being content staying at home with her music and Ben and being a recluse.

10

The rest of the afternoon went by quickly. Around five-thirty, Oletta and Lane took a break for an early dinner. Logan and Ben quickly joined them.

The weather held, so the four friends were able to enjoy their meal al fresco on Outback's patio. Everyone ordered steaks, the specialty of the house. Oletta and Lane got the prime rib. Ben's paleo diet allowed his New York strip, but he had to have steamed vegetables and a salad with it and no bread. Logan shamelessly put away an eighteen-ounce bone-in ribeye, medium rare, with a fully-loaded baked potato, and an ice cream brownie-cookie thing for dessert. There was salad involved, but she only stabbed a few forkfuls of lettuce.

She sneaked a few pieces of the steak to the dogs, as did everyone else, so when they piled back into the car, everyone was happily stuffed. Logan snuggled up next to Ben in the back seat and rested her head on his shoulders. She loved his warm, solid presence. Nothing like spending a day outside, tromping around open fields, then ending it with a superb meal and a good man to make a girl happy.

It was dark before they pulled through the gate onto the gravel drive. A few fat raindrops began plopping on the hood of the car, announcing the impending arrival of Weatherman Kyle Scott of Channel Five News' promised storm. Looking out through the windshield at the quickly approaching dark clouds, Logan wished she had brought her warmer—and waterproof— winter coat. They had to get Max first, but she wanted to get on the road before the worst of the storm hit.

Oletta parked next to Logan and Ben's car. They loaded Dixon in the back and Lane and Ben went up to the house to retrieve Max.

"I'll be right up," Oletta said, clamping her hat on her head before a gust of wind could blow it off. "I just want to check on the horses."

Hawk trotted beside her, and Logan followed behind him. Kraken went with Lane.

Oletta explained she wanted to make sure Hondo hadn't gotten out of his stall and into the tack room again. He'd had a fun adventure last week, she said, nosing and nibbling his way into everything, pulling blankets off shelves, one of the bridles off the wall, and knocking over a couple of her competition trophies. She had Keegan put in a more secure latch, so Hondo was probably fine, but she'd feel better knowing he hadn't gone exploring.

"Come on," she said, "You can help me tuck them in."

A clap of thunder boomed not too far away. Logan was happy to follow her into the short walkway between the arena and the stalls, which was warm and dry. As soon as she entered, Logan inhaled the wonderful, horsey smells of saddles, barn wood, and hay. She looked into the tack room as they passed. It was horseless, so apparently the new and improved latch Keegan had installed had held.

But something was wrong. No nickering sounds and no beautiful horse faces leaned out over their stall doors to greet them and beg for a chin scratch.

LOOK AGAIN

Before Logan could process this information, Oletta sprinted ahead and ran out the back door. Like a magic trick, she disappeared, leaving nothing but a black rectangle cut into the arena wall just past Draco's stall, which was empty. All of the horse stalls were empty.

Feeling for the flashlight in her pocket, Logan dashed after her. The minute she stepped out of the protection of the barn, angry gusts of wind whipped her hair into her face. She squinted into the dark but could only see a few feet in front of her, where the light spilled out from the open doorway.

Grateful for the compact, tactical flashlight Ben insisted she carry in every jacket pocket, Logan shone its strong beam around the immediate area, searching for the horses. Almost immediately, Draco's large form emerged from the shadows, plodding toward her. He didn't have on a halter, so there was nothing to grab onto but his mane, but he didn't give her any trouble when she patted his side and sort of leaned on him to coax him into his stall.

Once he was in, she realized he was soaking wet. Making an executive decision she hoped was right she grabbed a blanket and threw it over his back to keep him warm for now, then secured his stall door and rushed back outside to help Oletta find the other two.

Her flashlight beam found Oletta leading Reign up from the field through an open gate. A huge wave of relief flooded through her, but then she saw the look on Oletta's face.

"Is he okay?" Logan asked. "Where's Hondo?"

Oletta didn't answer right away. Once she had Reign inside, she ran her hands over his body and down each of his legs, lifted up each hoof, and checked his eyes and ears. Satisfied, she left him for a minute and did the same for Draco, then took a big breath and came back out.

"These guys are okay. They know enough to stay close to home, but Hondo's a baby. He's still out there," she said.

After snatching a headlamp off a hook on the wall, Oletta whipped out her cell phone and called Lane. Briefly explaining the situation, she asked him to grab Hawk's vest and GPS collar from its charger in the laundry room.

By the time Lane and Ben got to the arena, Oletta had Reign saddled and ready, Hondo's halter and a lead rope wound around the saddle horn. Next she slipped on Hawk's vest and attached his GPS collar. She tucked his lead into one of her pockets, so he was free to run ahead.

Ben would stay put with Lane in case Hondo were to find his way back on his own.

"Even if he walks in on his own and isn't seriously injured, he's been out in this weather, the temps are falling, and he could easily develop hypothermia," Oletta explained. "Thanks, Ben. Lane will show you what to do and how to set up the heating fans."

"Do you want me to call your vet?" Logan asked, wanting to do something.

"The vet's over an hour away," Oletta said, getting one of Hondo's horse blankets out of his stall. "If Hondo does have hypothermia, the vet wouldn't be able to get here in time. A small horse like that will need help now, not later. You need to warm their core. And we're set up for it."

"There must be something I can do to help," Logan said.

"Yes, there is," she said. "Thank you—both of you—I really appreciate your staying to help. Logan, what you can do is check along the highway. See if you can spot him along the shoulder. Go west, like you're going home. That's where our property comes up to the road—that's where he could get through."

No one voiced the obvious, that in this storm and on such a dark night, a driver might not be able to stop in time even if they saw an animal walking across the road. Hondo could have been hit by a car and be seriously injured or lying dead on the road. That was not the way Logan wanted to find him.

"Couldn't he wander off to the right?" Logan asked.

"I don't think so. There are several trails. Some lead up into the hills, another one would take him to the lower part of the property where the pond is. That side's fenced. He can't get out that way. So he's inside or out by the highway. There's a steep drop-off to a ravine up Coyote Run Ridge. That's where I'm headed first."

"Do you need a long lead for Hawk?" Logan asked, looking around for one.

"No, he won't need it. I'm going to send him out ahead," Oletta said, holding one of Hondo's blankets under the doberman's nose, letting him get a good whiff. "Hopefully Hondo won't be too far away."

But as she mounted up, Oletta's face looked grim.

11

Assignment received, Logan squeezed Ben's arm as she hurried out to their car, wishing everyone good luck. At the last minute, she went back in and grabbed a rag she saw hanging on a nail outside Hondo's stall she had seen Oletta use on him before.

Logan let Dixon up into the passenger seat and cracked the window a few inches so he could smell the air as she drove. Then she let him get a good whiff of the rag. Finding a real horse in a fierce storm at night was much more difficult than finding a person hiding in some rubble in a fun doggie game of hide and seek. That was Hawk's job, but Dixon's nose was better than her eyes—particularly at night, so there was always a chance. She didn't want to miss Hondo because he was out of the range of her limited vision.

Putting her headlights on bright—oncoming traffic be damned—she began crawling along the shoulder, hoping she wouldn't get rear-ended in the process. Luckily, due to the late hour and the storm, there weren't many other cars on the road. Oletta told her when she got to the red barn, to turn around. That's as far as their property ran in that direction. No one said how many passes to make before giving up, but with Hondo's life on the line, giving up wasn't an option.

Dixon seemed to get the idea they were looking for something, because he sat glued to the open window, sticking his nose as far as it would go, sniffing intently, completely focused.

Once she rounded the bare road cut, Logan pressed on the brakes and began rolling slowly along the gravel shoulder, peering into thick stands of trees as they passed, looking for a glimpse of four long legs and a swishing tail, a silhouette, or a long face with a pair of alert ears twitching back and forth.

Hopefully, Oletta and Hawk would find him, and they would all be safe and warm inside their stalls before she got back, but as the storm intensified and another burst of hail hit the car, she felt herself growing more and more anxious.

By her fifth pass, the rain was coming down so hard it was almost impossible to see beyond her headlights on the road. Nothing but gravel, a row of mailboxes, and ghostly edges of clumps of brush. No Hondo.

It had been almost forty-five minutes. Maybe Oletta and Reign had found him and were too busy to call and let her know. If Hondo was injured that made sense. She almost decided to give Ben a call to find out when Dixon burst out barking, jumping up, planting his front feet on the arm rest of the passenger door, anxiously pushing his nose as far as it would go out the top of the open window.

Logan pulled over, unsure what to do. Dixon kept barking, nosing around the window, trying to get out. It was probably just a raccoon. She couldn't see a thing in the dark. *Still . . .*

Putting the car in reverse, she angled it back and forth a few times until her headlights shone into the brush.

Well I'll be damned . . .

"Dixon! You found him!" She reached up and gave Dixon an enthusiastic scratch on the back of his neck and put the car in park.

LOOK AGAIN

Not twenty yards away, she saw the back of Hondo's head and neck sticking up from a ditch on the side of the road, struggling to climb up a slippery embankment. He must have tried to cross a stream or fell into a ditch or something and gotten stuck. Poor little guy! His dark coat and mane blended perfectly into the night; she would never have seen him on her own.

She couldn't get through to Oletta, so she called Ben who put Lane on. She gave him her GPS coordinates and said she and Dixon would wait with Hondo until help arrived. She didn't see any blood, but he seemed to be favoring his right front leg. She would try to get down there and calm him, so he didn't thrash around anymore.

Not wanting to take Dixon out in the rain, she told him, "Good find!" several times, then locked him in the car, making sure she had her keys in a pocket. With the headlights and her flashlight, she found a way down into the ditch. Knee-deep in freezing water she sloshed her way over to the frightened colt.

Coming up on him from his right side, Logan wrapped her arms around his neck, reassuring him with her body, talking to him in a soothing voice, while keeping herself clear of his frantic front hooves.

"Whoa there, Hondo. That's a good boy. Your mama's on her way," she said.

Hondo tried again to lurch up the muddy bank. There was a lot of power in his hindquarters, even if he was a baby. Logan didn't want him to strain anything trying to get out. She kept talking and rubbing his neck, "You calm down, now . . . you don't want to mess up that pretty pedicure you got the other day . . . Mama's on her way . . ."

After a minute or two, Hondo stopped lurching, but he was still shaking pretty bad. Logan had no way to help him out and the ditch was quickly filling up with muddy water. They stood there like that in the hard rain for what seemed like forever.

Then Logan heard the sweetest sound she'd ever heard, Hawk's bark! *The cavalry's arrived!*

Oletta deftly slipped Hondo's halter over his head and with Logan in the back pushing and Oletta pulling, they got him up and out, but he was definitely in pain and avoided putting any weight on his right front leg.

Logan watched Oletta agonize for a few minutes, then reach into her pocket for her phone, but it must have fallen out on the trail, so she borrowed Logan's to call Lane and have him bring their horse trailer. He would then call the vet to meet them at the arena.

"I'd rather have the vet see to this leg first, but we need to start treating Hondo's hypothermia right away," Oletta explained.

Logan waited until Lane arrived and they got Hondo into the trailer as carefully as possible, then she ran back to her car and drove to the arena. When she and Dixon got there, Oletta had Hondo in the warm stall Ben and Lane had prepared. She started to work on him while Lane was unsaddling Reign.

Oletta explained what she was doing as she worked. The fans were blowing warm air that Hondo would breathe into his lungs, bringing his body temp up faster. She had several blankets lying on him and plenty of water for him to drink.

Right now, she was pressing a warm compress against the colt's neck. This was the next best thing to a warm IV the vet would provide. It warmed the blood pumping through his veins, warming his core, not just the exterior of his body, which was what they needed to do to stave off hypothermia.

Normally, she would keep him here and stay with him through the night, taking his temperature frequently until he was out of the woods, but they would have to see what the vet advised when he got there. If Hondo's leg was broken, which seemed very likely, they'd have to transport him to the animal hospital in Corvallis. Either way, it was going to be a long night.

Logan and Ben offered to stay and help, but there wasn't much they could do, so they collected Max from Paulette and got in the car. Oletta offered to loan Logan some dry clothes, but she said she'd turn the heater up in the car and they didn't have far to go.

On the way home, Logan told Ben the story of Dixon's barking his head off and making her stop to look and then seeing Hondo. Technically, Dixon hadn't tracked Hondo, but still, he'd earned some extra treats when they got back.

Ben told her Lane had not been able to reach Oletta, either, so he couldn't tell her where Logan and Hondo were, but somehow, in the middle of a storm and on a muddy trail, Hawk had followed Hondo's track and gotten Oletta there anyway. What an amazing animal! How could he track Hondo through all that rain? You'd think that would have washed away any trace of scent. She'd have to ask Oletta about that.

Reaching between the seats, she laid her hand on Dixon's warm side, which was rising and falling rhythmically as he slept.

"I'll bet you'd like to learn to do that, wouldn't you, Mr. Nose?" she said.

12

Oletta checked and double-checked her living quarters horse trailer again, ticking off the items on her checklist one more time. Fuel tank, oil, tires, backup generator, batteries, water bucket, hay bags, saddle, bridle, ropes, halters, blankets, leg wraps, extra everything . . . She'd already packed her food and clothes, including her chinks and wild rags. Oh, and her new hat. Normally, she'd have on the Nationals silver belt buckle she won with Diamond, but that was tucked away in the ribbon case. She hadn't had the heart to wear it since he died. Automatically, she reached up and touched the frame of the photo of the striking palomino paint.

She didn't like leaving Hondo so soon after his ordeal. It was still touch and go, but with round-the-clock medical care and access to a doctor, the animal hospital was the safest place for him right now. The vet had operated successfully on his fracture, now it was just a waiting game to see how he healed.

Hondo had no idea how lucky he was, but she knew how close they had come to losing him. The thought infuriated her! This was no accident. Someone had opened the gates and let her horses out into the icy teeth of a storm—and she was pretty sure she knew who that someone was.

She'd deal with them later, but for now, she forced herself to focus. She had to be in Veneta, ready to compete, bright and early tomorrow. That meant getting there tonight to set up and get the schedule and a map of that day's course with its obstacles that all riders and their horses would need to navigate. You never knew what order the obstacles would be in—part of the challenge was seeing how you and your horse handled the unexpected.

That only gave her a few hours to run through her checklist again and get on the road.

J. FISHER TRAINING
VENETA, OR
SATURDAY AFTERNOON
APRIL 6

Gloria Merrick was nobody's fool. With barely concealed pent-up rage, she yanked off Sienna's saddle and tossed it on the ground.

It was obvious this whole thing had been rigged! And Oletta wasn't even supposed to be here! But oh, no, she'd showed up—unbelievable! And even though they hadn't announced today's scores, Oletta no doubt had the highest. She almost always did.

Giving her horse a cursory rub down, Gloria roughly exchanged halter for bridle and stabled her in the barn. She threw hay in the feed trough, but didn't bother checking the water level or making sure it was fresh.

The old sorrel mare didn't complain. She'd learned this treatment was normal from humans—at least this one.

When Gloria got back to her trailer, she grabbed a Budweiser from the cooler in her truck and threw herself down into her camp chair. Leaning forward, elbows on her knees, she pressed the cool can against her forehead.

A trim, efficient-looking woman in jeans, boots, and cowboy hat came around the corner.

"Hey, Gloria!" she said, "got a minute?"

Gloria looked up at her unexpected visitor. It was Julie, owner of J Fisher Training and the sponsor of today's clinic.

There was only one camp chair. Gloria didn't get up and didn't offer her a beer. She popped the top on her own, took a long drink, and waited. Unphased, Julie cheerfully perched one butt cheek on the open tailgate and got to the point.

"Noticed Sienna had some trouble out there today, especially on the bridge," she said.

Gloria said nothing.

"Sienna's a good horse. I think she can do it," Julie said. "She just needs a little more work."

Again, no response.

Undaunted, Julie plowed ahead. "Look, I'm doing an extra clinic this month," she said. "We're going to include a lot of water work. I think Sienna would really benefit from some extra practice. I'm happy to hold you a spot. Your horse has good potential."

"Not unless you can waive the fee," Gloria snorted. "Six hundred dollars is a little rich for my blood. I'm not like the rest of these bitches who can afford to go to clinics every other week."

She glared up at her guest. The woman needed to know that she knew what was what. She also knew she should keep her mouth shut, but she was tired. Tired of losing. Tired of watching Oletta win. Oletta shouldn't have even been here today, but she was.

"I know Sienna's a crap horse, but even if I could afford better, whatever horse I have, we're not going to get any points in *your* events, *are we?*"

Julie stood up briskly and brushed off her jeans. She gave Gloria a hard look.

"Suit yourself," she said and made her way toward other, friendlier campfires.

Gloria sat and stewed a while, working her way through a couple more beers. It was always like this. She never fit in. Just like back in Arizona when she was a kid doing rodeo. When her dad moved the family out to Oregon, she'd taken up competitive trail riding, thinking it might be different—maybe easier. But no. It was the same.

Gloria sat staring into space until dusk softened the day. The aroma of BBQ reached her along with friendly laughter and her stomach involuntarily growled. Dinner was included in the event fee.

Might as well take advantage of it.

She squirmed in her chair for a minute, debating. She didn't have to talk to any of them. She would grab some food and bring it back to her trailer to eat.

Without making eye contact, she quietly walked past the circle of women sitting in camp chairs, laughing and talking, while balancing paper plates on their laps. Denise was telling a funny story, which meant Donna must be there, too, along with Oletta. The Three Musketeers.

Even though Philomath was practically right next door to Eddyville, where Oletta lived, she had never once even asked Gloria over for a cup of coffee.

Back at her campsite, Gloria wolfed down her food and fumed. She might have a chance of making friends if they all weren't friends with Oletta first. They probably just liked her because she had great horses. First it was Diamond, and now, taking center stage with her two-year-old blue roan quarter horse, Reign. He was just gorgeous, and Oletta always braided his shiny black mane and tail perfectly. Reign was young, but already everyone could tell he was going to be good. Oletta had always been lucky.

Gloria stabbed a hot dog and loaded it up with beans. As she chewed, she stared into the night. Maybe it was time Oletta got *un*lucky.

13

The ground crunched slightly under Oletta's boots as she stepped out of her trailer. There wasn't a true frost on the ground, but it was still damn cold for April. She clamped her hat down, pulling her coat tighter. Retrieving one flake of alfalfa and two of hay, she tucked them under her arms and hustled up to the barn. Her own breakfast would be a granola bar and a bottle of orange juice from her mini-fridge after she fed and watered Reign. Lane said Hondo was doing fine, but she was anxious to get home.

Taking a path behind the trailers so she didn't wake anyone, she passed one of the new women they talked with last night. Hannah something. Good rider. Had a nice little three-year old paint. She'd picked up some good tips from her. They'd exchanged phone numbers yesterday and she looked forward to seeing her in Eugene at the indoor trail riding event this summer.

Cocooned in a horse blanket, her friend, Donna, sat on the steps outside her trailer, her hands wrapped around a steaming mug of hot coffee. Toasting Oletta with her mug, she nodded good morning. Donna was pushing seventy, but still could outride them all, ranking high every year in Nationals.

Most of the others were still in their trailers, but lights were coming on one by one. By the time she got back, Oletta knew the sun would be up and the campsites filled with the smell of sizzling bacon and strong coffee.

She flipped on the light as she stepped inside the barn. As light flooded the building, she saw a scrawny woman with long, black hair scrabbling over and out the open window of Reign's stall.

Gloria!

Dropping the flakes of hay and alfalfa, Oletta rushed forward, then forced herself to slow down so she wouldn't frighten Reign. When she got there, she just stared. She couldn't move.

No!

She couldn't tear her eyes away from what she was seeing. It was Reign, but he didn't look like the majestic champion he was. His beautiful braids had been hacked off in uneven chunks, leaving only an inch or two of his glossy, black mane sticking up in odd spikes from his neck. What was left of his mane was a stubby, ragged mess. It would take months if not years for it to grow back.

Murmuring what she hoped were calming words—as much for herself as for her horse—Oletta did a quick visual check of his back end. It was as she feared, she'd gotten to his tail, too, leaving no more than a stubby brush. He wouldn't even be able to keep the flies off this summer.

Anger filled her whole body, lodging deep in Oletta's gut. She needed to confront the coward who'd done this, but first, she needed to see to Reign. She leaned in, stroking his neck, running her hands over his body. Reign nudged her, wondering why she didn't bring in his breakfast. At least he didn't seem to be physically injured in any way.

LOOK AGAIN

Hardening her anger into resolve, Oletta went back for the hay and alfalfa she'd dropped, filled Reign's corner feed bin, and refreshed the two buckets of water in his stall with a hose on the opposite wall. Then, giving Reign a final once over, she patted him on the side, secured his stall door, and took off at a run to confront the horrible woman who had done this.

Pushing past anyone in her way, Oletta stalked straight to Gloria's trailer and began pounding on the metal door.

"Gloria! Get your butt out here!"

The trailer remained dark and silent.

Any campers still in their trailers emerged to see what was going on, gathering in a sort of half circle behind Oletta.

"Come out here, you bitch! I *saw* you!" Oletta demanded, banging on the door again with her fist.

The door to the trailer opened and a sleepy-looking Gloria, barefoot, pushing her hair out of her face, looked out, squinting into the morning light.

"Quit banging, Oletta," she said. "And stop yelling. What are you talking about, anyway? Saw me where?"

Quivering with fury, Oletta kept her arms by her sides but balled her fists.

Speaking through clenched teeth, she said, "At the *barn*, Gloria. Don't play dumb with me! I *saw* you climbing out of Reign's stall just a few minutes ago and you know it!" Her voice raised and she added, "I saw what you did!"

"You're crazy, Oletta," Gloria said, fully awake now. "I've been here all night, here in my trailer. If you saw anyone, it wasn't me. You're probably just imagining things."

Oletta held up a hunk of what used to be Reign's tail that she'd picked up from the floor of his stall and shook it in Gloria's face. "This . . . *this* is not a figment of my imagination, Gloria! You did this to my Reign—and I know you're the one who let all three of my horses out last week. Hondo's just a baby! He could have *died*! They all could have! What is *wrong* with you? Why do you have to be so *hateful*?!"

For a second, real fear flashed across Gloria's face. Oletta could see it in her eyes.

"If I wanted to hurt your horses, Oletta, I would have." With a smirk, she added, "And maybe someone should! Serve you right for cheating all the time. As for this morning, I was right here and you can't prove otherwise, so go take a piss, Oletta. You look like you could use one."

Oletta shook with rage, "You touch my horses again, Gloria, I'll kill you!"

Dismissing Oletta with a shrug, Gloria turned to go back inside.

But Oletta wasn't done with her. Letting out a strangled warrior yell, she grabbed Gloria by her hair and dragged her outside.

The women gathered behind her let out whoops and cheers!
"Catfight!"
"Go get her, Oletta!"

14

SUNDAY EVENING

John finished up the last of the dinner dishes and hung the towel neatly on the oven door. Untying his apron he tossed it in the washer on his way out to the back patio. He repurposed the leftovers from last night's dinner, so there hadn't been much to clean up.

Carl had already disappeared into his office while waiting for an important call. All excited about the new project, John knew he wouldn't see his boss again until breakfast.

Grabbing his warm jacket off a hook by the door, John fished a pack of American Spirit cigarettes out of his pocket and shook one out. Only three so far today. Better. He'd planned on quitting for Astrid, but now, what was the point?

Stepping outside, John slipped on his coat and let the door close behind him. He looked across the bare backyard—which had yet to be landscaped—at the thick stand of trees. Using a Zippo lighter from the same pocket, he cupped his hands and lit his cigarette. Dropping the lighter back in, he took a deep drag and relaxed, allowing himself to enjoy that first rush of nicotine as it buzzed through his system.

His eyes rested on the trees. He now recognized a few. Cedars, some various pine trees, and Douglas Firs. They were all very different from the ones that lined the streets in their Harrington Park neighborhood back in Jersey. City trees were tamer. Maples and oaks with broad crowns and thick branches that invited tree swings and lost their leaves every fall.

The trees here were tall, straight, and prickly. Oregon trees—particularly at the coast where he went for drives on his day off, did not invite climbing or swings. He kind of liked the fact that nature in the Pacific Northwest didn't cater to humans.

He took another drag of his cigarette and blew the smoke out slowly, not focusing on anything in particular. He had a lot to think about.

Last night's dinner had gone well. The minute Louis Agostini's chartered jet touched down at PDX, a town car whisked the old mob boss down the I-5, depositing him at their front door just before six. After taking his hat, long wool coat, scarf, and leather gloves—very East Coast, Louis still wore a hat, although he'd switched from a fedora to a wool cap at some point—John went into the kitchen to finish dinner preparations. Carl took Louis into the office to talk business, which presumably had something to do with the blueprints spread out on the long table in his office. They'd been delivered in long tubes last week and Carl had not shown them to John or volunteered what they were for. Big secret.

Which just made him more curious.

Half an hour later they emerged from the office. John served Louis and Carl cocktails and canapes in the living room by the oversized stone fireplace.

During dinner, Carl and Louis reminisced about the old days, the idiots running the country, and how the younger generation "don't know nuttin' from nuttin' about honor or loyalty." With a little wine, or maybe just to bond with Louis—remind him he was still one of the regular guys—Carl fell right back into the street talk of his younger days. His accent got thicker by the glass.

When it was time to go, John brought Louis his coat. The old crime boss thanked him for the excellent meal and apologized for not being able to stay longer. He had a doctor's appointment in the morning back in Jersey. Only Louis could get his doctor to come in on a Sunday. And he hadn't said, but John knew it was probably a house call.

Louis next expressed his sympathy to Carl for the loss of Astrid.

"She was a good woman," he said, adjusting his hat.

After accepting Louis' condolences, Carl walked him out to the purring town car, where the driver stood waiting, holding the back door open. Steam from the exhaust pipe swirled up, colored red by the taillights. Louis pulled his coat tighter and lowered himself into the car with surprising ease. The driver shut the door with a solid click.

Once he was settled, Louis lowered the window and looked out at Carl. "Friday," he said. "No guarantees after that."

The tone wasn't threatening, just matter-of-fact. Whatever it was Carl was getting from Louis, the offer wasn't open-ended or unconditional.

"Absolutely," Carl said. "Probably before. I should hear tomorrow. I'll call you as soon as it's done."

Louis nodded once, then settled back in his seat as the window raised smoothly and sealed him inside. John went back into the house, but Carl watched until all he could see were the taillights heading north on the highway.

After Louis left, John offered Carl some Amari. His boss usually enjoyed an after-dinner drink, or sometimes an affogato by the fire. Tonight he just asked for an espresso.

While waiting for his double shot with three sugars, Carl sat in one of the two matching wingback chairs in front of the fire. When John returned he motioned for him to put the cup and saucer down next to his phone, which buzzed just as he did. Carl grabbed it before it danced off the table.

"Audra!" Carl said. "Good timing, my guest just left . . . No, that's okay. I was in a meeting earlier, anyway."

Sitting up straight and leaning forward, he skipped the rest of the niceties.

"So what'd they say?"

Whatever Audra said 'they'd' said, it must have been good, because Carl did an uncharacteristic fist pump punctuated with a silent 'Yes!'

With no good excuse to stay, John went back to the kitchen, but he could still hear Carl's side of the conversation.

"So cash got us a three-day close. But it's a done deal, right?" Carl said. "They can't wiggle out of it?"

He seemed satisfied with her answer, then asked, "What about the other one?"

Couple of beats of silence.

"Okay, call me as soon as you know," he said.

John was at the kitchen sink when Carl unexpectedly came back into the kitchen. The look on his face was grim.

"Changed my mind," he said. "Make it a bourbon. Neat. I'll be in my room."

Until about four o'clock in the morning, John lay awake, a feeling of unease growing in his chest. Something was up and it didn't feel good. He had so many questions.

Whatever the answers were, they were in Carl's office.

15

The next morning, Carl had his usual breakfast on the patio, followed by a cigarette. As John cleared the table, a whiff of tobacco triggered an intense craving. He'd given up cigarettes when Astrid got sick, making sure she had clean air to breathe, but started up again after she died. Now he was trying to quit for himself, but it was very hard to quit smoking when you lived with someone who did.

The rest of the day passed at a tortuous crawl. Now that he had decided to snoop, John couldn't wait for his boss to leave so he could get into his office and see what was going on.

Carl spent most of the day doing something in there, then after dinner, took his espresso in the living room. John waited for an opportunity, but none presented itself. Once Carl parked himself in front of the TV, he wouldn't budge 'til midnight, and worse, he was a light sleeper.

As the opening music for *Predators* started up, John resigned himself to try again tomorrow. Eventually, Carl would have to leave the house.

Frustrated and increasingly anxious, John turned in early, but didn't get much sleep. All he could think about was how to get into that office. Carl had been acting strangely for the last few weeks, going from morose and numb to suddenly full of energy, focused on whatever this project was.

Maybe now that Astrid was gone and not around to soften him, the old Carl was re-emerging. The real Carl.

He remembered watching the two men at dinner. With Carl's long bones and fair hair, and Louis' short, squat body and sunken eyes, the two men had few physical features in common, but a life of violence and crime left its mark on both faces. When you looked again, under the skin, the two men were brothers at heart.

John stared at the ceiling and took stock of his life. He asked himself a question he'd been asking himself more and more often lately. Why was he still here?

TUESDAY

John steeled himself for another long day, but just before lunch, Carl got a call and said he was going out for a while. John waited until he could no longer hear Carl's car before trying the office door. It was a testament to how much Carl trusted him that it wasn't locked. Or maybe it wasn't trust, just that Carl considered John a piece of furniture—useful, but not a threat.

Approximately twelve by fourteen, the office wasn't that large. After all, Carl was supposed to be retired.

The only window in the room took up the top half of the wall directly across from him, above a credenza, and looked out over what would have been Astrid's vegetable garden but was now bare dirt ending in trees. Carl's desk was on the right, facing into the room. A long, rectangular table covered in blueprints ran almost the full length of the left wall, opposite the desk. Above the table, a large black and white map had been tacked onto a cork bulletin board with push pins. Sections had been colored in green.

LOOK AGAIN

John flipped on a light switch and went to examine the map on the wall. Except for a few labels, it had little detail. It showed Highway 20 running east to west—or vice versa—and had dots for a few nearby towns, like Philomath and Toledo. The bottom right corner told him he was looking at a map of Lincoln County. In the middle was Eddyville. The sections looked like plot outlines, including what must be this property, although it was only labeled with a number, not an address. All but one of the plots adjacent to or surrounding this one were colored in a green highlighter pen.

What are you up to, Carl?

He knew Carl had bought the two lots directly adjacent to this one so he could build this house and have lots of land for Astrid. Those lots were colored in green, but so were a lot of others. Did Carl own those, too? And if so, when had he bought them and why?

Knowing Carl could return any minute, John got out his phone and went to work. Without moving anything, he let his eyes pour over the blueprints on the table in front of him. Occasionally he would lift up a corner and capture an image of what lay beneath.

At first, none of it made sense.

One drawing was labeled *Cafe Zurich*. Was Carl planning on opening a restaurant? If so, why hadn't he consulted him? Carl didn't know anything about the restaurant business.

Another drawing was an exterior elevation for a three-story mansion, much larger than this house, the one Astrid had designed. Why would Carl need a bigger house? They were knocking around in this one as it was. Several of the bedrooms hadn't even been furnished yet.

The next sheet represented what looked like floor plans for each level of the house. A long hallway opening into individual rooms, each with its own balcony or patio.

Each room had a name:

Saint Moritz . . .

Basel . . .

Lucerne . . .

It took him a few minutes, but even then he wasn't sure of what he was seeing until he saw the last drawing, an artist's rendering of the finished product, a zoomed-out, birds-eye view of all the buildings and exterior features combined, including a large oval in the middle. Three-inch high, embellished, gold script across the top removed all doubt.

Astrid Meadows and Cedar Lodge.

John stood there, stunned. Then, after closing up the office, leaving it as he had found it, he returned to his room, his mind flooded with questions.

Had Carl lost his mind?! How could he do this?

Naming a racetrack after Astrid and giving the rooms in the lodge Swiss town labels only gave the project a thin veneer of class. Like everything these guys did, no matter how pretty on the exterior, Astrid Meadows and Cedar Lodge would be rotten inside. Built with one goal in mind. Making money.

With casinos, the house always won. Horse racing was no different, but it had an additional layer of filth: doping. The Family owned other racetracks. He'd heard the talk. Beautiful horses dropped dead on Louis' tracks. But as long as they made money, no one cared.

This would have made Astrid sick, to see her dreams turned into this nightmare. At least she wasn't alive to see it. John sat down heavily on the edge of his bed.

So that's what Louis' involvement was. He should have known. John ran back down to the office to take one more quick peek at that map.

It was all right there.

So that's what all the fervent phone calls were about. Carl must have sunk all of his own money into buying up the land

and now needed Louis' money to build out the racetrack and lodge.

Just then he heard Carl's car pull into the garage. Making sure he hadn't disturbed anything, John turned out the light, and quietly closed the door behind him, willing his heart to stop pounding.

The question that entered his mind as he hurried into the kitchen and started preparing dinner, was just how badly Carl wanted that last property and to what lengths he was willing to go to get it.

16

Carl reached for his phone in the dark. Tapping on the screen, large, bright numbers informed him it was one o'clock. He fell back on the pillow. He'd gone to bed at eleven. The realtor wasn't going to call tonight. Tomorrow at the earliest.

He still had time. So why was he lying here awake, staring at the ceiling? He couldn't keep his mind from going over the plans. Over and over . . . plans that would never become a money-making reality unless he got that last piece of property by Friday. There was time, but he was cutting it way too close.

He threw off the covers and got out of bed. Reaching for his robe, he stuffed his feet into his slippers and put his phone in his pocket. Quietly, he padded downstairs to his office. He sat at his desk for a while, but there really was nothing more he could do until he heard from the realtor, so around three a.m. he took half an Ambien and went back to bed.

A few hours later, when the phone did ring, he jerked awake, forcing his eyes open wide, blinking furiously. The sky had lightened. It was six a.m. He tapped on the screen to take the call.

"Hello?" Carl said in a groggy voice.

It wasn't the realtor.

Damn.

A thin, thready voice. "Carl, it's Louis."

Carl pinched himself hard, trying desperately to clear his head of the Ambien fogging his brain.

"Yeah," he said. "I'm right here."

"Carl, I want you to listen. I don't have much time. Paulo will be back any minute."

Carl had to strain to hear him.

"I'm in the hospital . . ."

"The hospital!?"

"Yeah," Louis said, "Not to worry. I just wanted you to know. I had a slight problem. A small heart attack . . ."

"A heart attack?" *Could heart attacks be small?*

"Yeah," Louis said, "Go figure, a life of booze and linguini? Didn't see that one coming."

He coughed, laughing at his own joke.

"The reason I called is this," Louis continued. "I know I said Friday, but you need to get me that proof as soon as you can—Thursday at the latest—they're gonna operate Friday."

He took a shallow, ragged breath.

"You know I'll honor our deal. You are the only one left who knows what loyalty means and that we take care of our own," he wheezed.

He paused again to catch his breath.

"If I make it, deal's on," he said. "I look forward to coming out for the grand opening. But if I don't, Paulo's gonna be a problem," he said. "Paulo won't give a shit about our agreement."

Carl's heart sank. Paulo was Louis' son and had a very different vision for the Family's business. It definitely wouldn't include loaning Carl any money. The younger generation was more into drugs than racetracks, which took longer to pay off. They could make more in a month running drugs than a racetrack could pull in all year.

"I'm leaving instructions," Louis said, "but I can't guarantee he will honor my wishes. You understand?"

"I do, Louis," Carl said, fully awake now. "You'll have what you need by Thursday at the latest. I swear."

And he would. He had to. There was no other choice. Kissinger's famous quote—at least he thought it was Kissinger who said it—popped into his head.

'The absence of alternatives clears the mind marvelously.'

And so it did.

Without making a conscious decision to do so, Carl went to the closet—fully awake now. Taking a metal box down from the top shelf, he laid it on the bed and checked the contents. Good. Next, he made sure the wire transfer had gone through. Until the loan from Louis came in, this was almost the last of his money. He hoped it was enough to get the job done.

Finally, he left a note on the refrigerator for John not to wake him. Then he went back to bed and slept like a baby until noon.

By tomorrow night the Hartley property would be his.

17

After her morning run with Dixon, Logan texted Oletta to make sure they were still on for her to come out for a couple of days of search and rescue training. Oletta said she was looking forward to it and to come anytime. If she got there before lunch, they'd fit in a trail ride first to get Dixon used to being around horses.

Ben was taking Max down to Newport this afternoon to practice leash walking around other people and dogs, and later Clay was coming over for dinner and to help Ben practice for his radio technician test. Logan loved that Ben could fend for himself and didn't make her feel guilty for doing things on her own.

Her late husband, Jack, had wanted her to be with him twenty-four-seven, his own little cheer squad and helpmeet. She hadn't realized how manipulative and selfish he was until a year or two after he died.

Clay was also Ben's movie buddy. Whenever she had a music gig or was out of town, Ben and Clay watched guy movies like John Wick III where fifteen people die in the first five seconds. Logan didn't get it. It was like her otherwise gentle husband had some throwback caveman gene that surfaced on movie night.

They had come to an agreement, though. Ben wouldn't make her watch the *Mad Max* trilogy if she didn't make him watch *Babette's Feast* or any other painfully slow, foreign film with subtitles. They even pinky swore, which everyone knows is binding in the state of Oregon.

Logan looked in her closet. Since she was only staying one night out in Eddyville, she pulled out some sweats, a hoodie, and a long-sleeve black t-shirt and stuffed them into a backpack along with her toothbrush, hairbrush, and underwear. She'd toss her running shoes in the car but wore her boots. Oletta's recommendation. Said that way her feet wouldn't slip through the stirrups. Made sense.

She was on the road by nine with a large coffee, cream, no sugar in the cupholder. Dixon was in the back, his nose sticking out of the window, sniffing for all he was worth. When she picked up speed on the highway, he switched to looking out the back. They pulled up to Adventurous K9 at about ten-fifteen.

Keegan let her in. She parked and let Dixon out.

"Hi, Logan," Keegan said. "Oletta's on her way down. She's got the horses saddled up in the barn. You can meet her in there."

The young man bent to give Dixon a scratch behind the ears, then said he needed to get back to work. Walking to the little carport area where the vehicles were kept, he hopped on a green and yellow John Deere mini tractor, started it up, and bumped out toward the field where she and Oletta had found Draco and Reign the night of the storm. It was also where Hondo had wandered off toward the highway, getting stuck in that muddy ditch—almost getting himself killed. It looked very different today. Today the sky was clear and sunny, not dangerous at all.

LOOK AGAIN

Logan looked back at the road leading up to the house and saw Oletta walking toward her, waving, Hawk trotting by her side. Logan waved back and waited.

Lane stepped onto the porch and yelled, "Oletta! That realtor's on the phone again—Audra something—you want to talk to her?"

"It's your turn!" Oletta yelled back. "Tell her we're not interested. Maybe she'll believe you."

When Oletta got closer, Logan got a good look at her face. *Wow.*

Purple and black splotches decorated her right eye from brow bone to cheekbone, some fading to yellow. The inside corner of her eye was bright red.

"Ouch!"

Oletta gave her a rueful smile, "You should see the other guy—or in this case, girl."

She promised to share the whole story once they were on the trail. Logan couldn't wait. When they got inside the arena, Logan asked how Hondo was doing.

"He's doing good," Oletta said. "Just waiting to see how the leg heals. It was a bad break, but he'll be home soon."

When they got to Reign's stall, Logan was in for another surprise. Although he didn't seem injured in any way, Reign no longer had a mane, just a stiff one-inch brush along where his beautiful hair used to fall gracefully over his neck, and when he turned, she could see his tail had been docked, too. It was all neatly trimmed, but way shorter than it was last time Logan saw him. Oletta had spoken with great pride about her horse's 'spa days' where she spent hours giving them baths and braiding Reign's mane and tail before events. Why would she cut his mane and tail this short?

Logan didn't want to be nosy, but she had to ask.

"What happened? Did his mane have some kind of health issue with it, like ticks or something, or is that just something you need to do every now and then to keep it healthy?"

"Nope," Oletta said, "Not planned. Somebody hacked it off. I just evened it out so it didn't look so bad."

Logan couldn't wait to hear the whole story and if it tied in with the black eye, but for now, she needed to pay attention. While the dogs sniffed around, Oletta had already started giving Logan a mini-riding lesson, helping her mount Draco, adjusting the stirrups for her, showing her how to hold the reins. Draco didn't really need direction, she said. He would follow Reign. Logan was glad she'd worn her boots. Her feet felt much more secure in the stirrups than they would have with slick, no-heel running shoes.

Oletta swung a leg over Reign's saddle and led the way out the lower gate, crossing the field, the dogs running ahead. Over her shoulder, she explained they were going to Salmon Creek. Just a short ride today. About forty-five minutes. They'd be home in time for lunch.

Lunch? Ben's breakfast had already made its way down to Logan's hollow leg and her stomach was absolutely empty. Why hadn't she thought to bring some snacks?

18

For the next twenty minutes, Logan gave herself over to the beauty around her, and the calming clop and thud of their horses' hooves, occasionally clattering across rocks when there wasn't a bridge. The trail crossed the same stream several times.

The sound of an engine snapped her out of her nature reverie. She looked around for the source of the mechanical noise. Off to the right of the trail, about a couple of football fields away, Keegan was riding the John Deere in slow circles, flattening anything in his path, smoothing out an area she guessed was about as big or bigger than the arena back on the upper level.

"What's he doing?" Logan asked, standing up in her stirrups to see better. Dixon and Hawk sat and panted.

"He's clearing the briars and brush, making a new field and exercise area for the horses," Oletta said. "We're always doing something around here. Ten acres doesn't sound like much, but it's a lot to keep up and I'm always getting ideas for things I want to do, like more trails!"

Logan's butt was getting sore, and since riding single file made conversation difficult, Oletta still hadn't told her how she got that black eye or who cut Reign's mane and tail. She tried to shift her seat in the saddle to get more comfortable.

She'd have to ask Ben to pick up some Epsom salts so she could soak her sore muscles in a nice hot bath when she got home. She doubted the little trailer had anything more than a shower in it and probably not a ton of hot water. She prayed it had some, at least.

Oletta must have taken pity on her because a few minutes later she directed Reign off the trail into a small clearing next to the stream and dismounted. Logan gratefully followed suit, handing the reins to Oletta, who tied them loosely in some brush.

"They won't go anywhere," she said.

Digging her fingers into her lower back, Logan leaned back and stretched until it popped.

Much better.

Again, following Oletta's lead, Logan flicked the top off her water bottle and drank greedily, emptying almost half of it. She hadn't realized how thirsty she was.

Before they sat down on some nearby logs, Oletta reached into her pocket and pulled out a giant PayDay bar, tore open the wrapper with her teeth, and held it out for Logan. "Want some?"

A woman after my own heart.

As the sun warmed their faces, they sat and chewed and watched the horses. Long necks down, placidly resting. Even without his mane, Reign was a beautiful animal.

A fly landed on Reign's flank, and he contracted the muscles a few times quickly to shake it off. He was momentarily successful, but without a tail to follow up with a flick, the fly came right back.

"I'm going to have to slather him with fly ointment this summer," Oletta said.

During the next few minutes, Oletta summarized the series of events at the J Fisher place three days ago, including her brawl with Gloria at the end and someone calling the police.

"Did they arrest her?" Logan asked.

"Nope," Oletta said. "I showed them what she had done to Reign, but since he wasn't physically harmed, even if I could prove it, they could only give her a ticket. The one cop had horses himself and was disgusted by what she'd done. He took me aside and said he'd document the incident so in case she ever did something like that again there'd be a record of previous similar behavior which might influence a judge, but without hard evidence, there wasn't much else they could do."

"But you saw her running away, right?" Logan asked. "Doesn't that count?"

"Not without video," Oletta said. "And the other cop was ready to haul us both in for fighting, so I wasn't going to push it."

"Did anyone else see her running back to her trailer to hide?"

"No," she said. "It was early. And if they did, they would have spoken up. I've been friends with those women for years and they all know Gloria. No one would have covered for her."

"So that's it?" Logan said. "She just gets away with it? What about her letting the horses out in a storm? Isn't that illegal? I mean, you must be able to get her on trespassing or something! Hondo could have died!"

"I have even less proof of that," Oletta said. "No one saw her do it and she didn't leave any evidence behind, but I can't think of anyone else who would have done it. It must have been her."

"Did the police at least take a report?" Logan asked. "Maybe animal control has some kind of penalty or law that applies to her cutting Reign's mane and tail at least."

Oletta laughed somewhat bitterly, "No, in fact, the police told me I was lucky they didn't arrest *me*. I was the one who pulled her out of her trailer. In the one cop's mind, I started it."

"So how did it end?" Logan asked.

"They asked if she wanted to press charges, if you can believe it! I scratched her up and she had a sprained ankle—which she probably got when she scrambled out the window of Reign's stall."

"Well, did she?" Logan said. "Press charges?"

"I could tell she wanted to, but with my friends there, she knew better. They knew what she'd done, and they would have raised hell if she had."

With that, Oletta stood up and went to get the horses. Once they were both remounted, Logan asked, "So there's nothing you can do?"

Oletta's eyes flashed something fierce, "Not legally, but word gets around. I don't think we'll be seeing her for a while. Julie already banned her from future clinics and phoned a friend of hers at OHC—she's scratched from the next Eugene event, too."

As Reign stepped back onto the trail, Oletta added, "I shouldn't have lost my temper, shouldn't have let her get under my skin, but when it comes to my horses . . . I just saw red. It took two women to pull me off of her before the cops came."

Logan would have bought a ticket to see that.

19

After lunch, which was a big spread of make-it-yourself sandwiches with all the fixings, including potato salad and oatmeal cookies, Logan got her backpack from the car. Oletta walked her over to the trailer and showed her where everything was. She was relieved to see her lodgings included hot and cold running water, a small shower, and a toilet that flushed.

"We'll give you time to settle in," Oletta said. "I've got a couple of phone calls to return. The dogs and I will pick you up in an hour."

"Perfect," Logan said.

"You could cook in here, but Mom's making dinner up at the house," Oletta added. Then she turned to Dixon and said, "And we'll have some chicken for you after we play hide and seek."

The rest of the day flew by, as good days do. Oletta put Hawk and Kracken through their paces, laying a trail and having them take turns finding Logan. Then they switched and had Dixon try it. No problem. Straining at the leash, he pulled Logan straight to Oletta. She increased the difficulty a couple of times, but even with a broken scent trail and a longer, more convoluted route, he only hesitated once.

Even though she hadn't trained him, Logan found herself inordinately proud of her dog.

After dinner, Dixon stretched out in front of the wood stove with Hawk and Kraken while Logan helped with the dishes. Dinner had been a hot, cheesy, bubbly Mexican dish with layers of ground beef, corn tortillas, black olives, onions, and some kind of peppers. She'd have to get the recipe for Ben.

Oh, and the margaritas weren't bad either. On the rocks. Fresh lime. Salted rim. Made from scratch, not a mixer. Awesome. Those were Oletta's contribution.

Lane said his goodnights and went to bed early, Kracken trotting faithfully behind. When she first met Lane, Logan hadn't realized he had neuro-Lyme disease. She'd looked it up and it was one of those conditions where people had good and bad days. The day she'd met him he was walking around great. But he had his down times and when one of those hit, Kracken was Lane's service dog, bracing when he needed to lean on his shoulders to push himself up. He also helped Lane get into his mobility scooter, which allowed him to get around the uneven grounds of the property. It was amazing how much dogs could learn to do.

7:00 P.M.

"Guess it's just us chickens, then!" Paulette said with a wicked grin, hanging the dish towel over the edge of the sink. "You ever play golf, Logan?"

Golf as it turned out was not a miniature putting green set up in the den, but a card game.

"Pretty simple," Paulette said. "I'll let Oletta explain the rules. No betting or chips, but whoever loses has to clean out the stalls first thing in the morning."

Paulette set them up on the kitchen table while Oletta made another round of margaritas. Deftly shuffling the double deck,

Paulette dealt each woman fourteen cards face down, which Logan was told to arrange in two rows. The remainder of the deck went in the middle of the table with one card turned over to start the discard pile.

The whole point of the game was to end up with the lowest number of points. If you could get one of the seven cards in your top row to match one in the bottom row, they canceled each other out to zero points. The rest of the rules sounded confusing at first, but being a double Math and Music major, Logan caught on quickly. It was a fast-moving game. There was enough strategy to keep it interesting—you had to pay attention to what the other player had so you didn't discard a card they needed—but it wasn't so difficult she couldn't play even after another round of Oletta's margaritas. *Was this her second, or her third?*

By nine-thirty, Logan had three more points than Oletta and nine more than Paulette, so she was designated tomorrow morning's 6:30 a.m. horse shit shoveler. She good-naturedly accepted her consequence. After receiving instructions on where to find the pitchfork and where to put the manure, Logan pulled out her trusty pocket flashlight and carefully picked her way back to her trailer. Oletta told her she'd meet her at the arena around 7:00 a.m. and they could get the horses fed and watered together. Logan was welcome to join them for a human breakfast before she went home. She planned on taking them up on that offer.

20

Thin clouds dimmed the already meager light of the crescent moon, but Gloria could see well enough. The air on her face was cold and at the moment, all was quiet. Most people were home in bed at this hour. Dressed in dark jeans, jacket, and boots, she all but disappeared against the backdrop of the trees.

She frowned. She had managed to pull her car a few yards off of the highway in some thick brush, but the back end still stuck out. Coming from the west no one could see it, but anyone coming from the east would spot it for sure. If she had more time, she would camouflage it better—cut some branches and lay them across the tires and trunk, breaking up the silhouette, but it would have to do.

Besides, she reassured herself, if anyone spotted it they would think it was a junker that broke down—abandoned on the side of the road—as it should have been and would be as soon as she could afford something better. She'd picked up the Chevy Tahoe for a couple thousand dollars two years ago—her dad always said, 'buy American', but with 240,000-plus miles on the odometer, it had given her nothing but trouble. She hated that car. Maybe she'd get lucky, and someone would steal it.

She reached into her jacket pocket to pull on her gloves and winced. She lifted up her sweatshirt to make sure the ace bandage hadn't come loose. It hadn't, but a giant, technicolor bruise spread from her left armpit to her waist. Only bruised, not broken, the doctor said—but what did he know? It still hurt like hell.

She lifted the backpack from the ground and slipped it on, avoiding her ribcage area. Then, gauging the distance to the other side of the ditch, she jumped. Landing hard, a sharp pain shot up her side. Almost made her pass out. When she recovered, she clenched her jaw and told herself to toughen up. Focus.

Dark clouds lurked on the edge of the horizon, just behind the treetops, against the night sky. Time to get moving.

While picking her way through blackberry brambles and over tree roots, Gloria sorted through her thoughts and gathered her nerve. She should have finished the job last time. She'd given Oletta more chances than she deserved.

But had she taken the hint? *No.*

Some people needed a stronger message. She chuckled to herself. It's not like she didn't know how to deliver one. Twenty years ago she wouldn't have put up with this crap. In fact, she *hadn't.*

It all came flooding back. 1989. Tucson Rodeo. Her rival, Cindy Havens, newly crowned Rodeo Queen, taking all the prizes that should have been hers. Smug bitch. But she'd paid Cindy back.

She hadn't rushed it, either. She bided her time, waiting for the perfect opportunity. Which made it all the more satisfying. She remembered standing there watching her handiwork—thrilling at the satisfying popping, sizzling sounds of her rival's horse trailer, rocketing up in flames! And just a stone's throw away, Cindy's stupid horse, dripping blood, knocking over his bucket, frantically searching for water that wasn't there.

The very thought gave her a renewed burst of energy. This was going to be fun!

If she had parked right in front, she could have hopped the fence and been in and out in five minutes, but she wanted to come in from the fields so she didn't wake anyone up at the house. She also wanted to avoid the security light trained on the entrance gate.

A few minutes later, Gloria broke out of the trees. The arena was just ahead. Silhouetted against the sky, the arched windows cut out along the top of the structure reminded Gloria of a Moroccan courtyard she had seen once in a book in middle school about the Arabian Nights.

But she wasn't here to sightsee. From previous visits, she knew that the right side of the building in front of her was the soft dirt-floored, open-air arena where Oletta trained her horses. She headed toward the left, where three horse stalls and a trophy room anchored that end of the building. Using her leg muscles, which were good and strong from all the heavy lifting she did at work, she easily jogged up the steep, rocky embankment.

Now that she had decided on a course of action, she felt surprisingly calm. Nor was she worried about being caught. What she had to do wouldn't take long.

Gloria slowly pushed the barn door open and stepped inside. She had to admit, Oletta kept her place in good shape. The door slid smoothly on its runners and didn't make a sound. A wooden half wall, upon which horse blankets and saddles rested, separated this area from the arena.

To avoid making noise with her boots, Gloria took her time. The old horse, Draco, was in the first stall. He pretty much ignored her, as did Reign in the middle stall, but the yearling came right over, stretching his neck out to investigate. She couldn't resist rubbing that soft nose and scratching him between his ears. He was so beautiful and gentle! She could never afford horses like this. Her horse ran the other way when she saw her coming.

The last door led to the trophy room. She hadn't had time to explore it when she was here last time. Tonight, she allowed herself the luxury. After all, after tonight, it wouldn't exist.

Leaving the door open, she went inside. Oak bookshelves made into display cabinets lined the small room. They were crammed with blue, red, and white ribbons, belt buckles, plaques, and silver and gold trophies. Gloria ran her fingers along the front of one of the shelves, noting what each award was for.

On the opposite wall hung a framed picture of Diamond, Oletta's gorgeous palomino pinto, the one that died. Many of the trophies in this room were won with that horse. She remembered Oletta taking first in Nationals two years ago. If she'd had a horse like Diamond, she would have beat her.

And now Oletta had Reign and was already bringing Hondo along. Always a step ahead.

Gloria shook her head in disgust. She had no need of a trophy room, or even a trophy shelf. She only had a few 2nd and 3rd place ribbons to show for all her years of competing. She kept them in the back of her underwear drawer. Until she got more, it would just be embarrassing to put them up.

She should have more. And she would have if she didn't have to compete with Oletta all the time. Everyone wanted to keep her down. It wasn't her fault!

Swallowing the bile that rose in her throat, Gloria turned her back on the trophy room and got to work.

21

Gloria looked around for a good place to set up. Spotting a large barrel with a piece of plywood laid across it, opposite Draco's stall, she walked over, slid her backpack off, and dropped it at her feet. From the center section of her pack, she removed two family-sized bags of potato chips. Ripping the first one open with her teeth, she dumped it carefully onto the plywood, mounding the chips into a pile with her hands.

Stepping back, she visually traced the imagined trajectory that ran from the pile of chips on the plywood base up the post and straight up to the open rafters and the roof. This was so perfect. Every inch of this place was wood.

Satisfied, she looked around for a good location for the second bag. There. Opposite Hondo's stall was a stack of crates. One bag would probably do, but she wanted to make sure.

After eating a few of the chips first (salty and oh, so delicious!), she repeated her earlier actions, making a second pile on top of the crates. Finally, she stuffed the now-empty foil bags into her pack.

She learned this trick from her otherwise useless father. Her dad was too cheap to take them on real vacations where people stayed in hotels, but he did manage to take them car camping sometimes.

Once, when it was time for dinner, she wondered how he was going to get the BBQ going. She didn't see the can of lighter fluid he sometimes used at home. Her idiot dad had probably forgotten it. With a heavy sigh, thirteen-year-old Gloria prepared herself to eat cold hot dogs.

When her dad started stuffing potato chips under the briquettes, she thought he'd lost his mind. But he just smiled at her. Then, with a magician's flourish, he touched a lit match to one chip and *Whoosh*! The oil in the chips made them burn, baby, burn!

It was the one useful thing her father ever taught her. And chips had a secondary advantage, which she found very useful tonight. The fiery inferno would consume the evidence. Not even a trace would be left for arson investigators to find. No accelerant, no devices. Nothing leading back to her.

Striking the fireplace match she brought with her, Gloria reached out to ignite the first pile of chips when Draco, the old horse, neighed. Bobbing his head up and down he stretched his neck toward the open barn door just outside his stall and stared into the dark.

Gloria froze.

"Hello?" she said.

Was someone out there? Probably nothing, but still . . . she'd better check. Gloria quickly blew out the match and took a tentative step outside.

22

The man checked his pockets one more time. Good. He had what he needed.

Where the moon broke through the dark clouds that filled the inky sky, it scattered pools of pale light at the foot of the trees, which were now a mass of deep, impenetrable shadows. The air was still.

On his right, almost out of his field of vision, a flash of movement caught his eye. His heart rate spiked, then settled down. Just a coyote. He watched as it silently trotted across a corner of open ground and disappeared into the brush.

He kept walking.

Fifteen minutes later he arrived.

Eerily silhouetted against the sky, a large, wooden structure loomed up ahead. Avoiding the front, he skirted the building and climbed up the berm to the back entrance. He was surprised but pleased to find the tall, sliding barn door already open. A security light on the other side of the building made it difficult to see the dark interior. He gave his eyes a minute to adjust.

Taking extra care now, he cautiously stepped forward. He hadn't come this far to turn back now. He made out the shape of a wheelbarrow to his right, and just inside the barn, the vague outline of tools that had been hung on the wall.

Instinctively, he put his hand on the grip of the gun in his pocket. It wasn't his usual weapon, but he always kept a drop gun around. Untraceable. Smaller, but it was good insurance.

Suddenly, a woman's silhouette materialized in the doorway, right in front of him. His heart almost stopped. He froze.

The woman stood perfectly still, peering into the dark. Listening.

Noiselessly, the man shrunk back into the deeper shadows as far as he could go, his back pressed against the wall.

"Who's there?" the woman said in a harsh whisper.

A mouse skittered by, its scratching louder than fireworks on the Fourth of July.

Cautiously, the woman ventured out a couple of steps. So close, he could have reached out and touched her. He held his breath, afraid to make even the slightest sound.

Then one of the horses broke the tense silence with a neigh, startling both humans. After that, everything happened very quickly. The man involuntarily jerked, and the woman whipped around, seeing him for the first time—and his gun, which he had automatically pulled out of his pocket and aimed. Their eyes locked. The woman ran. But not far.

One shot and she was down. A split second later, a frenzy of barking split the night.

Fuck! Now what?

A metal door screeched, and a woman's voice called out, "Dixon, quiet! Hello? Is anybody there?"

The man looked behind him. Not more than fifty yards away, a woman stood in the doorway of a trailer, holding onto her dog. And she was looking straight at him.

Now was not the time to lose it. Keeping his panic at bay, he crouched down and surreptitiously picked up his brass. Then, carefully pocketing his gun, he waited until the woman and dog went back inside.

And then he ran. Whether she had seen him or not, he had no idea, but he couldn't take any chances. He'd deal with that later.

As for the other woman, the dying one, her blood slowly seeped out from beneath her body, spreading into a crimson halo.

With everyone gone, the night settled back into a quiet calm.

Soon, though, although there was no one but the horses to hear them—came scurrying, scratching creatures, followed by tiny crunching sounds. Never one to miss out on a meal, the rats had discovered their unexpected bonus of a salty, greasy midnight snack.

23

Before the sun had even peeked over the horizon, Dixon nosed Logan awake, wanting to go on their usual morning run.

"We need to do some chores first, Lassie," Logan groaned, rolling out of bed, exchanging her pajama bottoms for jeans. Knowing she had stall-mucking duty, she had slept in her sweatshirt.

Dixon cocked his head.

Splashing some water on her face and quickly pulling her hair back into a loose braid, Logan pulled on her boots and jacket and exited the trailer, heading toward the arena, Dixon at her heels.

The air carried a sharp tinge of pine. She could get used to this. Something about the fresh air, riding, hiking, and playing with the dogs suited her. Even the horse manure smelled good.

Entering the arena, she switched on the light. Stopping at the tack room first to pick up some berry treats for Hondo, she gave each of the horses a couple of goodies and nose rubs, then went to get the wheelbarrow Oletta said was just outside the back barn door.

She ran through Oletta's instructions in her mind. She was to fork the manure into the wheelbarrow and when it was full, roll it over to the compost pile. At the far end of the walkway, she lifted the pitchfork off the wall and leaned it against Draco's stall.

The wheelbarrow was right where Oletta said it would be, just outside to the left of the door, but that's not what froze Logan in her tracks.

Not more than twenty feet away, a woman's body lay sprawled on the ground, face down, her head turned slightly to the right. One arm flung above her head, reaching toward the gate, one bent to a square at the elbow as if being sworn in before taking the witness stand. While her own body absorbed the shock, millions of neurons fired in Logan's brain, recording everything as the sun began to rise incrementally lightening the sky.

Cold monochrome turned to blush, then living color, the woman's lank, black hair in sharp contrast to her white skin. A thick pool of black spread out from the left side of the body like an ink blot. Logan watched, mesmerized, as the sun's thin fingers reached out and touched it, transforming it from dull maroon to deep, glistening crimson.

Telling Dixon to stay, she carefully picked her way over to check for a pulse. Cold, waxy skin verified what she already knew. That and the hole in the woman's back.

Suddenly, the sun's rays passed behind the clear dew drops that had gathered on the woman's hair, igniting them in a split second of dazzling beauty. And then it was gone.

Shaky, Logan stood up. Controlling her breathing she retraced her steps to the barn. Since there was no rush for an ambulance, she called Oletta first, and then dialed 911.

Whoever this woman was, she was beyond her help. Not wanting to disturb the scene any more than she already had, Logan sat on a bale of hay inside the barn and waited.

24

Oletta entered the arena at a run. Logan stayed where she was. When Oletta got to the doorway and looked outside, she reached a hand out to steady herself against Draco's stall.

"Oh, my god!" she whispered. "It's Gloria."

"*The* Gloria?" Logan asked, coming up next to her. "You mean the one who gave you that black eye three days ago and hacked off Reign's mane and tail?"

This was not good.

"Yes," Oletta said, still staring at the corpse lying twenty feet away.

"When was the last time you saw her?" Logan asked, knowing that was one of the first questions the police would ask once they discovered the two women knew each other.

"Not since Fisher's," Oletta said. "They pulled us apart; she got in her trailer. I went with Julie to clean up and take care of Reign. When I got back, she was gone. She left as soon as she could."

The full consequences of how this would look seemed to be dawning on Oletta. The next words out of her mouth were tinged with desperation.

"I haven't seen or heard from her since then. I don't even know where she lives," she said, coming back inside. "I know this looks bad, but what was she doing here? And who did this? That looks like someone shot her . . . there's so much blood. The police are going to think I did this because of what happened out at Fisher's."

"Okay," Logan said, knowing she needed to help Oletta calm down before the police arrived. "I know this doesn't make any sense, but it will. Let's get through today and then we can sit down and figure this out."

"She's right, hon," Lane said, coming up behind Oletta. "This makes no sense, but there has to be a logical explanation. We'll find out who did this."

Everyone agreed the best way to handle this was to give brief statements—without elaboration—to the police. Most cops were honest, but Logan knew that some law enforcement officers were only interested in clearing cases and would focus on the most convenient suspect, not necessarily the guilty one. Rick had told her once that on average, only half of all homicides were ever solved, anyway. Every cop wanted to improve those numbers and were often under great pressure to do so.

For now, all they could do was wait.

A fire engine rolled in first. Two young firefighters—both calendar-worthy in Logan's opinion—descended from the cab. One brought an EMT kit, although they told him the woman was already dead.

Lane took them through. Verifying there was nothing they could do for their victim, they came back—slower this time—and asked if anyone else needed medical assistance. No one did, so they climbed back into their fire truck. Logan overheard the driver radio in and ask someone to send out the ME or Deputy ME if Jean Pullman was not available. After a few more minutes of mostly listening to whoever was on the other end, he disconnected and let Oletta, Lane, and Logan know an ambulance and two sheriff's deputies were on their way.

It might take a while because they were both coming from home. Being a rural county on a budget, Lincoln didn't have round-the-clock law-enforcement coverage. Neither the Oregon State Police (OSP) nor the Sheriff's Department had patrols between three and seven in the morning.

Oletta started to go in and feed the horses, but the fireman shook his head and told her to stay put. The detectives would eventually let her go in to care for her animals, but until then, it was a crime scene. Off limits.

Oletta did not look happy, but when Logan assured her the horses at least had fresh water, she grudgingly obeyed. She, Logan, and Lane went and leaned against her car.

"I miss my dogs," Oletta said. Lane had left Kraken and Hawk in the house with Paulette so they wouldn't be underfoot.

Twenty minutes later, a black, Ford SUV with SHERIFF printed on the side in large, gold, block letters pulled in. With a look of relief on his face, the fireman started up the truck while Lane opened the gate. As the two vehicles passed each other—one coming in, one going out—it was obvious the drivers knew each other. The fireman rested his elbow on the open window and leaned out.

"Hey, Grant," he said, grinning. "What took you so long? What'd you do, stop for donuts?"

Without looking up, the thick-shouldered driver in the Sheriff's vehicle gave him the finger, finishing with a toodle-oo wave. The fireman was still laughing as he turned onto the highway.

The man called Grant parked and he and a passenger got out of their car. Both men wore dress slacks, shirts, and ties, although that's where the similarity ended.

The tall one with pasty skin and a full head of unruly, black hair was Detective Monson—early sixties with a serious, quiet manner—looked like he slept in his clothes. Might have. Detective Grant was the shorter, younger, and buffer of the two. The one who'd flipped off the fireman. His pale blue dress shirt was crisply ironed, and his straight, sandy hair neatly combed.

Logan recognized them immediately. Her brief interactions with them had not been pleasant. Monson even once had her on his list of murder suspects in the death of a local charter boat captain, until—with the help of the Cormorant Coffee Crew—she'd identified the real killer.

Monson raised his eyebrows but made no comment about Logan turning up at yet another one of his crime scenes.

"Ms. McKenna," he said, acknowledging her presence. Then he turned to Oletta and Lane. "And you are Mr. and Mrs. Hartley?"

Oletta drew in a deep breath. "Yes, it's—she's this way, through here," she said, leading the way.

Monson instructed Lane and Logan to stay where they were, then followed Oletta through the walkway leading to the back of the arena. Fine with her. Logan had no desire to see the dead body again.

She also knew what to expect next. The detectives wouldn't let anyone leave until they'd taken all of their statements. They would also keep them separated so they couldn't coordinate lies and get their stories straight should they be guilty or involved in some way. In her case, Logan had no story to get straight. She didn't know anything but the victim's name—and she only knew that because Oletta had told her.

25

A few minutes later, when the state police arrived, they posted an officer at the gate and went in. The young officer was to admit only official vehicles and keep everyone else out. Doggie daycare was canceled for the day, but there were always FedEx deliveries, curious neighbors, and soon the media would arrive.

The trooper, a newbie trying to make a good impression, stood at parade rest, doing his best to look intimidating, and made sure no one came in without a badge or a note from their mom.

Logan knew Wednesday was Jean's day to be at her ME office in Newport, so she wasn't surprised when she was next to arrive, an ambulance right behind her. If Jean was surprised to see Logan there, she didn't show it. Jean was every inch the professional and got right to work. Grant came out to wave her in. From where Logan sat, she could see straight through the arena and hear most of what was said. She tried not to look past the detectives to the body.

After her initial examination, Jean stood and peeled off her gloves.

Monson, who had been patiently waiting, asked, "Time?"

"Can't tell you much, yet. She's cold, but rigor mortis hasn't completely developed. She hasn't been dead long. There could be other factors. Right now I'd estimate between midnight and three a.m., but that could be off by a couple of hours either way."

Disposing of her gloves and booties in a plastic receptacle set up for that purpose by Grant, she nodded to the waiting ambulance staff that it was okay to take the body now.

"Cause of death?" Monson asked, although it was pretty obvious to him.

Jean gave him a look, then said, "Gunshot of course, but she has some other injuries. Looks like she got a few abrasions and contusions sometime in the last few days. Her ribs are wrapped with an Ace bandage. May or may not be related to this. Any idea who she is?"

"No formal ID on her," Monson said. "Car keys in the backpack along with some trash, a water bottle, chip bags, matches. Probably a camper or day hiker. We're looking for a vehicle now. Hopefully, she drove in, and her wallet will be in there."

Jean nodded.

"Birdwell?" said Monson. More of an assumption than a question. Lincoln County didn't have enough unnatural deaths to warrant its own morgue. Cyndi Birdwell was the Medical Examiner in Portland and did all their autopsies.

"Yes, I'll be sending her up to Cyndi, but not right away. I'm going to park her at Hanson's. Give me a chance to check her out more closely, see if there's anything more I can tell you."

They walked back out to the parking lot.

"No one heard anything, I suppose?" she asked, looking up at Oletta and Lane's house and the trailer where Logan had stayed.

"Not that we know of," Monson said.

"Well, not that anyone's admitting," said Grant.

Leaving the crime scene techs to their work—they had already taped off the scene—Monson emerged from the arena and asked Oletta if there was anyone else on the property besides the three of them.

"Just my mother, Paulette. Lane and I are at the house. Mom has her own place," she said, "just behind ours." "That's where she's at now, taking care of the dogs."

Monson looked at Logan.

"Oh, and this is Logan McKenna," Oletta added. "She came here yesterday for some tracking training practice for Dixon there. She was our guest last night. She stayed in my son's trailer, just up there." She pointed up the hill.

Monson nodded.

"Do you have other employees? Anyone else here last night?" Monson asked.

"No," Oletta said, "Keegan helps out now and then, but he doesn't live here. He has a regular job, but does odd jobs as needed around here, then he goes home at night."

"Was he here yesterday?"

"Yes, but only for a short time," she said. "Like I said, he goes home at night."

"And what time did Keegan leave yesterday?" Monson asked, flipping open a small, spiral notebook.

"I don't know, exactly," Oletta said. "Sometime mid-afternoon. Maybe two or three? He had lunch with us, then he had a few things to finish up. I know his daughter had a doctor's appointment at four, so before then."

Monson finished scribbling, then said, "We'll need Keegan's full name and contact information, and how long he's worked for you before we leave. Any other part-time help?"

"No," Oletta said. "We used to have more employees but cut back during COVID and haven't rehired."

Next, Monson had Logan wait in her car and Lane sit in his while he took Oletta over to the shaded carport where the work vehicles were kept and took her statement. Logan thought suit-and-tie Detective Monson looked funny perched on the seat of the mini John Deere tractor.

Grant went up to the house to talk with Paulette, then came back to Logan. He began by asking how she knew the Hartleys and then filled in a timeline.

"What time did you arrive yesterday?"

"Well, I don't remember the exact time I got here, but it was around ten. We got our trail ride in before lunch, which was around twelve. Her mom made sandwiches, and Keegan joined us up at the house. So did Lane."

"What happened next?" Grant asked.

"Umm . . . Oletta walked me to her son's trailer," she pointed to the travel trailer where she had stayed. "and showed me where everything was. Dixon and I laid down for about an hour. I played some games on my phone, then Oletta picked me up and we spent the afternoon doing tracking training. They give all her dogs search and rescue training. Hawk is great at it. I was interested in learning more—getting Dixon here started. That's why she invited us out."

At the mention of his name, Dixon raised his head and looked at Grant. When Grant did not respond with a behind-the-ears scratch or a treat, he went back to resting his chin on his paws and just listened.

"Then what? Did you see the deceased at any time during that day? Did she come to see anyone here for any reason?"

"No, until I saw her . . . this morning," Logan said. "I'd never seen her before."

"Okay," Grant said, "what did you do after the training?"

"We fed the dogs, she took care of the horses, and then we had dinner. Paulette—Oletta's mom—made a Mexican casserole and then we played cards for a while."

Logan skipped the part about the margaritas. Detective Grant didn't need to know about those. It wasn't exactly critical information for the investigation.

"Who was there for dinner? Did Keegan stay?" Grant asked.

"No," Logan said. "Keegan had already gone home. I don't know what time, just sometime after lunch and before dinner. It was just Paulette, me, and Oletta's husband, Lane."

"What time did the card game break up?"

"Nine-thirty or ten. I think it was around ten when I got back to the trailer," Logan said.

"Did you go right to sleep?"

After four margaritas? That answer would be yes.

"Yes, pretty much," Logan said. "It had been a long day."

Grant scratched the back of his neck and then asked, "Did you wake up at any time during the night—hear or see anything?"

"Not really," Logan said. "Dixon barked once—woke me up. I looked out, but didn't see anything. I thought it was probably a racoon or a deer—he barks at those at home all the time. We live in Depoe Bay, on the edge of town. Lots of wildlife—we even saw a bear once."

"What time did your dog start barking?"

"I'm sorry, I didn't look, it was the middle of the night, and I was only half awake," Logan said, "but it was still very dark outside, so not approaching sunrise yet."

"Did you go outside to see what he was barking at?" he asked.

"No," she said, feeling slightly defensive. It could have been a gunshot that woke Dixon, but how was she supposed to know that last night, and what could she have done about it anyway? Even if she had called the police right then, the killer would have been long gone by the time they got there, and they'd be right where they were now.

"I poked my head out the door. I think I stepped out onto the top of the little stairs there and said something like 'Hello? Anybody there?' But no one answered and I didn't hear or see anything. I only did it for Dixon. He's not satisfied until I get up to check out whatever he's barking at. Then he settles back down."

"Okay," Grant said, dropping that topic for now, "I'd like to ask you a few questions about this morning. I want you to walk me through what happened. I know this must be difficult, so if at any time you need to take a break, let me know."

Logan nodded. She didn't want to talk about this, but, of course, she knew she had to. Grant let her tell the story in her own words.

26

"Well, remember I told you I lost at cards the night before? The deal was whoever lost had to clean the horse stalls this morning. Oletta showed me where things were the day before. Said it was simple. Move the horses out. Get the wheelbarrow. Pitchfork the manure into it. When the wheelbarrow gets full, dump it in the compost pile out back, then put fresh hay down."

She didn't know how much detail she needed to go into but figured if he wanted to know more about how to muck out a stall, she'd send him a link to the YouTube video she'd Googled last night before she went to bed. She had wanted to make sure she did it right. A part of her wanted to impress Oletta and Paulette with her horsewoman skills.

"Dixon and I usually go for a run at 6:00 a.m.," she continued. "This morning, he got me up like clockwork. I got dressed and we walked down the hill to the arena."

She pointed to the open door leading to the horses. The memory of her discovery beyond the barn door on the other end, which she had conveniently shoved to the back of her mind, came back in full color and sharp detail. A lifeless body.

The scraggly black hair spread out on her shoulders and onto the ground . . . and all that blood.

"When I went outside to get the wheelbarrow—that's when I saw her."

Not wanting to interrupt the flow of her narrative, Grant kept his questions short.

"Then what?"

"I called Oletta," Logan said. "Told her what I found, then I dialed 911."

Grant looked up from his notes.

"Why didn't you call 911 first?"

"It was pretty obvious the woman was beyond help," she said. "I checked for a pulse," she added somewhat defensively.

Grant clarified a few points then thanked her for the information and told her they would contact her later for a more complete statement or if they had additional questions.

"And if you think of anything else—sometimes after a traumatic event our brains kind of freeze—things may come back to you in bits and pieces. If you think of anything at all—even something you think is insignificant, please give one of us a call."

He handed her his card and said she was free to go—for now.

He walked her back up to the trailer to get her things, with the usual admonition of 'don't leave town' in case they needed to talk with her again.

The detective did not ask her if Oletta knew the murdered woman, so Logan didn't volunteer that information. She just told him that she—Logan—had never seen her before, which was true. The police would discover Oletta and Gloria's history soon enough.

Logan also didn't hear Monson ask Oletta how she got the black eye, but maybe he did when he talked with her alone. She hoped Oletta didn't lie. It was one thing not to volunteer information, quite another to lie to the cops.

What a mess.

LOOK AGAIN

Grant escorted Logan to her car while Monson shadowed Oletta and Lane as they fed and watered the horses. When they were done, they walked the three animals to the fenced-in area at the back of the property. Monson reminded them that no one, horse or human, was to go beyond the tape until officially notified that the scene had been cleared. Then he and Grant went back to talk with the OSP trooper.

With nothing more she could do, Logan waited until Oletta and Lane got back to say her goodbyes. She offered to stay and help, but what her friends needed most right now was some quiet time to sort all this out. She gave Oletta a huge hug, then thanked her for yesterday's trail ride and told her to thank her mom for the delicious meals. Then she loaded Dixon in the car and headed home.

It wasn't until Logan was on the road that the full impact of the last five hours hit her. A woman had been shot—murdered—and Oletta not only knew her—but had good reason to have pulled the trigger.

Within the next few days if not the next few hours, as soon as the police discovered the connection between the two women and learned about the violent fight they had at the J. Fisher event last weekend, and what Oletta suspected Gloria of doing to her horses last week, they'd be looking at Oletta as a prime suspect.

Yesterday, when she told her about the incident at Fisher's, Oletta said someone called the cops to break up her fight with Gloria. That meant a police report. Probably, anyway.

Did Oletta shoot Gloria to defend her horses? Was it an accident? Had she shot a warning shot to scare her off, but shot her for real instead? Had Gloria come back to get even? No one pays a social call in the middle of the night. Was Gloria there to do real harm to the horses, not just let them loose or cut off Reign's mane and tail this time? Had their feud escalated?

Logan squinted out the windshield in concentration, running all this past Dixon, who listened patiently but kept his opinions to himself.

"I can see that if Gloria is as awful as Oletta says she is, she would come back to do more damage, but how would Oletta know she was even there to come down and try to stop her? And wouldn't she just try to scare her off, not shoot her? And how did she hear her? She and Lane's house is twice as far away as the trailer where I was, and I didn't hear anything.

"Well, I didn't, but you might have. Is that why you barked? I'm pretty sure I would have heard a gunshot, but maybe not. Gunshots are loud. And that still doesn't explain why Oletta went out to the arena in the middle of the night.

"She could have called Gloria to meet her there—set her up somehow, but why would Gloria agree to drive all the way out here or do anything her perceived enemy asked her to do?

"No," Logan said, shaking her head and making eye contact with Dixon in the rearview mirror, "I can see why Gloria might have been there, but not how Oletta could have known she was there. There is absolutely no logical reason for Oletta to have come down to the arena in the middle of the night and certainly not with a gun. Does she even have a gun?"

Furrowing her forehead in concentration, Logan tried to think of all possible scenarios. Coming up empty, she let out a frustrated huff. She consulted Dixon again.

"I can't see how she could have done it, Dix, but if Oletta didn't kill Gloria, who did?"

27

John was seated at the kitchen nook, working on next week's menus. *Nathan's Naturals* in Toledo opened in an hour. They got much of their fresh produce on Wednesdays. He wanted to get there before everything was picked over. While he finalized his list, Carl walked in and went to the refrigerator.

"Do you want me to make you something before I go?" John asked. His boss had slept through breakfast, which was unusual.

"No," Carl said, taking out a container of leftover lasagna from last night's dinner and then putting it back. "I'll fix myself something later, I know you need to get on the road."

Getting a coffee cup out, Carl began making himself an espresso.

John raised his eyebrows, but kept his mouth shut. Carl never did anything for himself if John was around to do it for him and he certainly never concerned himself with inconveniencing anyone else's schedule.

John did want to get going, though, so he tucked his laptop under his arm and grabbed his keys. After looking out of the window, he went back for a light jacket. Never hurt to have an extra layer, even if he left it in the car. In Oregon, even on warm days, it usually stayed cool until noon.

Leaving Carl to his coffee making, he promised to be back in time for lunch.

"I'll see if they have some of that Boar's Head Black Forest ham you like," he said.

Even though the Toledo Farmer's Market didn't officially open for a few more weeks, several of the vendors came into town to supply local grocery stores. A foodie at heart, John had connections. Easily identifiable by his snow-white ponytail and naturally gregarious from his restaurant days, John knew everyone's name and life history, from store owners to clerks to farmers, and they knew his. Well, his name, anyway. He didn't divulge his boss's prior occupation, just referred to him as a retired businessman from back east if anybody asked.

He parked and consulted his list as he headed toward the produce section of the store. *Radicchio and porcini mushrooms.* A stout woman with frizzy, red hair saw him come in.

"John!" she said, waving him over with a bunch of Swiss Chard. "How the hell are you?"

Greta and her husband had a farm out near Philomath. She was stocking the organic section. In the cart he saw several types of lettuce, asparagus, and green onions waiting to be unloaded.

After mutual bear hugs, he asked after her family, and they talked food. He told her what he was looking for and she made him up a couple of bags. Spotting some fennel, he asked her to pick out a couple of good bulbs for him.

"What do you have in mind for these little darlins'?" she asked, placing it in his cart.

"I'm thinking roasted," John said. "Olive oil with a sprinkle of Parmigiano . . ."

Before he could go into the full recipe, there was a commotion at the back of the store.

"Oh. My. God!" It was Tessa, one of the clerks. "My mom and dad live in Eddyville!"

Both he and Greta went over to see what was going on.

By then several other employees were gathered around. Tessa turned the volume up on her phone and held it up high so everyone could see and hear the YouTube video that was playing.

John squinted. Without his glasses, which he'd left in the car, he didn't see distance well.

A short, young woman with black hair, a reporter of some kind, was standing in front of a fenced, rural property. A little shaky, the video looked like it was being recorded on the fly. Behind the reporter, a Sheriff's vehicle, an ambulance, a van, and a couple of other cars were crowded into a small area between the front gate—which was closed—and a large, wooden barn-like structure. Yellow crime scene tape left no doubt that something very bad had happened here.

Tessa shushed everyone so they could hear what the reporter was saying. She tapped the bottom of her screen and started the video over.

"Good morning. Today is Wednesday, April 10, and this is Samantha Badger reporting for the *Lincoln County News Times*. I am standing in front of 98612 Highway 20, Eddyville, Oregon, personal residence of Oletta and Lane Hartley and place of business for Adventurous K9, a daycare camp for dogs.

"At 6:17 a.m. Willamette Valley Communications Center in Salem, Oregon received a 911 call from a woman later identified as Logan McKenna, an overnight guest of the property owners, reporting the discovery of an injured and possibly deceased woman on a gravel path on the far side of the structure behind me. Sheriff's deputies were dispatched, along with fire and ambulance. Death was verified at the scene by Lincoln County Medical Examiner, Jean Pullman.

"Identity of the victim and cause and time of death have not yet been officially released," she added. "But stay tuned. Updates to this news bulletin will be posted as soon as new information becomes available. This is Samantha . . ."

The rest of the audio trailed off as the person holding the phone quickly returned it to her. Until the video stopped, they could see a young man in uniform hustling back to the front gate where a firetruck was waiting to get out and a sheriff's vehicle was waiting to get in.

Later in the day that video would be edited, but the news cycle being what it was, the reporter must have decided to post it raw for now.

"Wow," John said.

"Don't you live out that way?" Greta asked.

28

Sam pushed her glasses back up on her nose and checked the number of hits her online news bulletin had received so far, then scanned the comments and responded to a few. Channel Five had better visuals, but she had the scoop and some exclusive content from the OSP officer manning the gate before the sheriff's deputies shut him up. It paid to show up early and make friends.

The very young and very helpful state trooper described the murder victim as a forty-something female with long, black hair. About 130 pounds, 5'6"-ish. Hard to tell exactly with her laying on the ground in a pool of blood, he'd said.

Sam had been careful not to use the trooper's name, but his boss would figure it out. Poor guy probably caught a rash of shit for spilling his guts to a reporter once her story hit. He was already in trouble for leaving his post to hold her phone so she could make that first video for her news bulletin.

All's fair in love and news. He wouldn't make that mistake again.

Because Sam monitored her police scanner twenty-four-seven, she had been the first reporter to arrive on the scene yesterday. Although radio airwaves were public, police had become more cautious in what they broadcast. Rarely, if ever, did they say, 'possible homicide.' That would bring every reporter and camera crew in the area running out to the scene.

Instead, they used less definitive phrases like 'person down' or possibly 'person with gunshot wound.' But Sam knew most law enforcement locals and could usually break their code. This one was definitely worth a trip.

When she arrived on scene and saw a large wooden structure and part of the parking lot cordoned off with crime scene tape with a bunch of law enforcement vehicles, including her sister-in-law's car and the crime scene tech's van, she grinned broadly. Her instincts had paid off.

It wasn't that she was happy someone was dead—probably murdered—but she was happy to beat Channel 5 to the scene and hopefully get the scoop. That was her job.

But it wasn't just that. Ever since Sam was a kid, she possessed a strong sense of justice. So did Jean and Logan. They all liked getting to the truth and making the bad guys pay. That's one of the reasons they were friends.

Speaking of Logan, her long-legged pal just blew in the front door of Pirates Coffee, shaking the rain off her jacket, the faithful Dixon at her side.

The barista called out, "The usual?"

Releasing her thick, wavy hair from its scrunchie, Logan ruffled the moisture out with her fingers and said, "Yes, thanks, Kath, and add a bacon burrito for Ben. I'll pay now but pick it up when I go."

"Okay, just give me five minutes' notice before you leave and I'll have it ready," Kathy said.

Tail wagging slightly, Dixon stopped at the counter and looked up in hopeful anticipation.

"Come here, you cutie!" Kathy said, reaching into a large, glass jar of dog biscuits, tossing him one. He snapped it out of the air with practiced ease.

Logan slid onto the picnic bench across from Sam while Dixon laid at her feet to enjoy his treat.

A few minutes later, Kathy delivered Logan's breakfast: a sausage burrito with the works, a large cinnamon roll, and her Cormorant Coffee Crew mug filled with scalding hot brew. Sam had already finished her food but held out her own CCC mug for a refill.

"How was your run?" Sam asked, pushing her laptop to the side, but not closing it.

"Good," said Logan, wrapping her hands around her mug. "Sorry, I'm late. We did an extra couple miles. I needed to get all that . . . what happened yesterday . . . out of my brain."

"I usually do that with sex," Sam deadpanned.

Logan almost squirted coffee out of her nose.

"Lots and lots of sex," Sam said. "Tim has to call in sick the next day."

Kathy let out a guffaw from behind the counter.

"So," Sam said, "Spill! I want to hear everything. I got bare-bones info out of the OSP guy, but I need more. What did the sheriff's deputies tell you?"

29

"**D**idn't Jean fill you in?" Logan asked.

"*Our* Jean?" Sam said, peering at Logan over her glasses, librarian style. "I got more information out of the cops. You know she won't tell me anything until she has 'official results' and it won't 'affect the investigation'."

Sam rolled her eyes. Logan nodded and took another drink of coffee.

Jean was a stickler for the rules. And rightly so. Logan and Sam were more likely to bend or break a few now and then.

"You were there," Sam said, pulling her laptop over in front of her, fingers poised over the keyboard. "You found the body. What do you think happened?"

Logan took a big bite of her breakfast burrito and thoughtfully chewed, then reached for a paper napkin and wiped off her mouth.

"Off the record," she said, swallowing.

"Of course," Sam said. "Just notes for now, I promise not to use anything I can't verify another way."

That was always their deal. And Logan wanted to talk. Talking to Sam was exactly what she needed. Last night she had been too tired to give Ben anything but a short summary of what happened. This morning all the facts were jumbled in her brain. Laying it all out for Sam would help her straighten out the events in her mind and construct a clearer picture.

Also, Sam wasn't biased. She hadn't met Oletta or spent time with her or Lane. Logan was having a hard time being objective and knew Ben was, too. She liked Oletta and therefore wanted to defend her new friend, even though she knew she might be involved. She certainly had plenty of motive.

When she was done laying it out for Sam, Logan sat back. "That's about it. I called Oletta and then dialed 911."

"What was Oletta's reaction?" Sam asked.

"Seemed normal to me," Logan said. "She looked as shocked as I was."

Telling the story helped her feel less stressed about it but hadn't provided any answers as to who killed Gloria or why. Sam said Oletta was the obvious suspect. The one thing they both agreed on was why Gloria may have been there.

Caught in the act of chopping off Reign's mane and tail by Oletta, then getting into the fight with her at the J. Fisher event, Gloria had been barred from future opportunities to earn points toward Nationals—at least at Fisher's. She must have come to Eddyville to get even. Kill or injure one or all of the horses—do something to really hurt Oletta. It's not like she wasn't capable of it. Oletta already suspected her of being the one who let the horses out in the storm.

But whatever Gloria had planned to do that night, she never had a chance to do it.

"The cops are going to find out about their fight," Logan said. "I mean, there must have been a police report filed and Monson saw Oletta's black eye. And when they do discover the connection, Oletta will be their number one suspect. But that still begs the question—how did Oletta know Gloria was there that night at the stables?

"Her son's trailer, the one I was staying in, is closer to the arena and I didn't hear anything. Dixon might have, but I didn't. Lane and Oletta's house is at least twenty yards farther and sort of back behind a cinder-block wall. She had no way to know Gloria was there. And if she did, how stupid would she have to be to shoot someone she had recently threatened—and do it on her own property?

"You would think she would admit to catching her trying to harm or steal a horse or something, then she could claim some kind of self-defense . . . what's Oregon law say about defending your property? Are horses property?"

"I'll have to look that up, but you're right," Sam said. "Lying about it afterward, hiding the gun or getting rid of it, then pretending you'd never seen her or even knew her—none of that is going to help her claim innocence."

"Did you hear anything at all that night?" Sam asked.

"I woke up once when Dixon barked at something. I went outside to check and listened, but didn't hear anything. I asked if anyone was there. Nothing. So I went back inside," Logan said. "Dixon settled down and I went back to bed."

"What time was that?" Sam asked.

"0-dark-thirty," Logan sighed. "I don't know. I was super tired and half-zonked from Oletta's margaritas. I didn't look at my phone to see. Now, I wish I would have. If what woke Dixon up was Gloria making noise in the barn before someone shot her, and if I had gone down to the arena, maybe I could have stopped her from doing whatever she was planning on doing and scared away whoever shot her . . . kept her from getting killed. It seems like Gloria was an awful person, but even awful people don't deserve to be murdered."

Sam paused her typing and Logan signaled to Kathy to get Ben's burrito started. Fifteen minutes later, Sam made Logan promise to let her know if she heard anything more from Oletta and then watched as she crossed the 101 with Ben's breakfast in tow and Dixon at her side.

✳✳✳

Sam's phone buzzed. It was her editor. A man of few words, he got right to the point. They were down a reporter, so he needed her to go to this afternoon's Planning Commission meeting—not her regular beat—plus cover the school board meeting tonight. All that in addition to following up on the homicide out in Eddyville.

"Sure, no problem," Sam said, wishing she could wring his neck. But this was par for the course in her job.

Her mind ran quickly through how she could rearrange her schedule. She had planned on going home for lunch to get some play time in with Magnolia, who was on the verge of taking her first independent steps. Sam didn't want to miss it. But it was almost time for Mrs. Horvat to put her down for her afternoon nap. She'd see her tonight.

Mrs. Horvat, a widow with three grown children—two doctors and a lawyer no less—loved watching Miss Magnolia and was used to her parents' frequent schedule changes. Tim watched her when he was home, but he was often out fishing for days at a time and Sam's hours were anything but predictable. Weekends and odd hours were the norm. Knowing how lucky they were to have an on-call sitter who lived next door, Tim made sure to keep Mrs. Horvat well supplied with fresh salmon, halibut, and crab.

Sam checked Google Maps. It was a two-hour drive to J. Fisher Training. If Julie Fisher was available, she'd just barely have time to make it out to Veneta and back before the Newport Planning Commission meeting at 3:00 p.m.

She might even beat the cops.

30

There was roadwork on the 20, but Highway 99 was clear, so Sam arrived on time at J. Fisher Training for her appointment with Julie, the owner. She had been surprised when the woman herself answered the phone when she called earlier in the morning. And even more when Julie said if she could get there before lunch, she'd be happy to talk with Sam. The police had apparently not discovered Oletta and Gloria's fight—yet.

Since no arrests were made, maybe the cops responding to the 911 call hadn't filed a report. She'd have to follow up with her contact at the Lane County Sheriff's department. They probably would be the ones to be sent out to a Veneta address, but it could have been Oregon State Police. She'd have to check.

Sam hadn't exactly lied to get this interview. She *was* interested in doing a story about the women who participated in trail riding competition events, she just didn't specify which women. Sold it as background research for a human-interest story she was working on. She would be featuring J. Fisher Training Center and wanted to see it in person, interview the owner, get some photos, etc.

Sam's phone took adequate pictures, but she always kept a professional-looking camera in her car, just in case. People took her more seriously when she pulled it out versus snapping pics with her phone. It was resting on the passenger seat so she wouldn't forget to take it in.

Julie told her to look for a large wooden sign with a silhouette of a horse and rider and the name of the place carved into it in relief. When she spotted it, she slowed down, turning into a small parking lot facing a long, low ranch-style building. Beyond that were multiple outbuildings, a camping area, and what looked like an obstacle course.

A wiry, no-nonsense woman clad in boots, jeans, and jacket, with shoulder-length, brown hair topped with a baseball cap, came striding toward her, hand extended.

"Julie Fisher," she said, "You must be Sam. Nice to meet you."

They shook and Julie said, "Well, you've got me for a whole hour, Sam. Where would you like to start? There's the indoor practice arena, the outdoor courses where we set up the competition events, and the stables. I can show you how we train our own horses, how the clinics and events work, and what the competitors are judged on when they come. I got you a blank scoring sheet for that. Your choice!"

Knowing she needed to ease into the questions she wanted to ask, Sam let Julie steer the first part of their visit.

"You know what's best. How about if we take the first half hour and you give me an overview of what you do here," she said. "Then we'll go back and take some photos of you with your horses, maybe doing one of the courses."

That was fine with Julie. She spent the next thirty minutes giving Sam the grand tour. Sam found herself genuinely interested in the whole process. Being a city girl, she had never been around horses, but she appreciated learning how much knowledge and skill this sport required. A natural competitor herself, she identified with the dedication it must take to be successful. She'd cut her teeth on hard stories in Olympia when she began her career as a journalist.

And she'd run into her share of backstabbing Glorias along the way. Getting back to the reason for her visit, she started looking for the opportunity to sprinkle in a few closer-to-the-bone questions.

When they got to the outdoor courses, a woman on a large, chestnut brown horse with a black mane and tail was having her horse pick his way through a section of downed logs, then up and over a little bridge crossing a small stream.

"Nice work, Janice! Samson's getting better at that one!" Julie said to the rider, who smiled in return and continued around the path to the next obstacle.

Sam got the woman to pose for several photos. She was happy to show off her horse.

"So you mentioned you hold several competitive events throughout the year?" Sam asked Julie after Janice went back to practice. "Is that right? When do you have them? I imagine they take a lot of effort to set up."

"Well, you're right about that," Julie said. " And, of course, we change the obstacles for each event. The competitors have no idea what order the challenges will be in. Gotta keep 'em on their toes! We just had one about a week ago, our spring event April 5 – 6," she said, "and we have two cowgirl events coming up this summer. One in July, one in August. And we also give clinics to help them prepare for these events."

"It'd be great to interview some of the horsewomen who do these. I don't want to wait until summer. I'd like to get this story out sooner. Any chance you could put me in touch with some of the women from your last event?"

Sam kept her face open and innocent.

Julie hesitated, then said, "Sure, I'll see if any of them are interested. Some have to travel quite a ways, but a few are local. I'll get back to you on that. In fact, I'll do that right now. I didn't realize what time it's getting to be. If you don't mind, we'll call it a day. I have some stock photos I can send you from events we've had in the past and you can go on our Facebook page—if you see any you like, let me know and I can usually get you a higher resolution one if I took it."

Sam nodded and because she had no other choice, followed her host back to the parking lot.

She thanked Julie for the tour and opened her car door. Disappointed she hadn't found out more about Oletta and Gloria's fight, she turned back and gave it one last try. "I forgot to ask you what a horsewoman gets for gathering enough points to win Nationals? Is it just a certificate or are there actual prizes?"

"Oh, yes," Julie said. There are cash prizes, buckles, and ribbons. Depends on what category you're competing in. But the real value is in establishing your reputation. People then hire you to train their horses and there can be stud fees if your horse becomes well known. That's where the money is. All these women know each other."

"Wow, sounds pretty competitive," Sam said. "Anyone ever take it too seriously? You know, fight over the results of an event?"

Julie stopped and leveled her gaze at Sam, considering her question. Then without answering it, she smiled brightly and said, "Thanks so much for coming out, Sam. I'll send you those photos and will look forward to reading your article!"

Here's your hat, what's your hurry?

It was obvious she'd hit a nerve. Julie wasn't telling her everything.

31

THURSDAY

APRIL 11

LINCOLN COUNTY JAIL

Whenever a death required criminal investigation, the Lincoln County Major Crimes Team was activated. The team consisted of personnel from the Lincoln County District Attorney's office, medical examiner, sheriff's office, Oregon State Police, the police departments from Newport, Lincoln City, and Toledo, and the FBI. Unless they had an active case, which fortunately only happened a few times a year, the Major Crimes Team only met on the last Wednesday of every month at the sheriff's office.

Because this homicide had occurred outside city limits, the sheriff's office would take lead. Monson could have made the callout last night, but because the clock started ticking from the minute he made the first call, he waited until six this morning to activate the team.

Each of the team members was only on loan from their home agency for five days. Five days to find and stop a killer. After that, the team would be disbanded and the unsolved case would be dumped back onto his desk for the sheriff's office to deal with, without the manpower, skills, experience, and resources of the rest of the team. Five days. From experience, Monson knew just how fast those five days flew by.

Today was Day 1.

He'd set the meeting for 8:00 a.m., but he and Grant had been there since 7:00 a.m. setting things up. Conference Room B at the jail was the only room large enough to accommodate the whole team plus computers, phones, and a fax machine. Besides the large conference table that seated fifteen, there was a wall-mounted TV monitor, a whiteboard, and a blank pad of chart paper set to the side on a folding easel. Hopefully, all of these blank surfaces would soon be filled with valuable information leading to the apprehension and conviction of their killer.

Grant walked in from the hallway with markers for the whiteboard and chart paper, plus a mug full of short pencils without erasers, like the kind elementary school teachers always seemed to have a supply of, although he wasn't sure why. Didn't kids need to erase things?

Someone had already set up a side table with coffee and sugars, plural—people needed fifteen kinds now. When he was a kid there were only two packets: a white and the pink one his mother liked that they now say causes cancer and you can't find anymore. This actually may have been true, since his mother had died of cancer at a relatively early age. There was still just one kind of creamer. The jail's generosity did not go so far as to spring for real cups, just a stack of Styrofoam ones. Monson was glad he'd brought his own, a large mug his wife gave him for Father's Day last year. It had the smiling faces of his two grandchildren, Decker and Darcie, four and two respectively, on both sides.

"Everything working okay?" he asked Grant.

Monson had mastered his smart phone and could write reports up on his laptop, but anything beyond that, such as hooking up computers, projectors, monitors, and printers so they could talk to each other, he left up to Grant.

"Yep," Grant said, tapping a few keys, watching the sheriff's logo come up on the wall monitor, then graying it out. "We're good to go."

Lincoln City PD was first to arrive. Gary Smythe was well-liked and a valued member of the team. Nobody could produce a search warrant as quickly or as well as Gary. If Gary wrote it, most judges signed it without argument, trusting he'd done his homework.

Newport and Toledo came in together. The Newport guy was a new hire from San Diego. Seven years in uniform. Just made detective. Patrol officer Fred Davies, not a formal member of the team, was standing in for Loretta Grieg, who was out on maternity leave. Toledo only had one other detective and they opted to keep him where he was for now. A tall, thin, bandy-legged man with stooped shoulders, sixty-two-year-old Fred's most noticeable feature was his watermelon-sized beer belly. He also came with a full '70s mustache, which Monson noticed he stroked often. Probably nervous. He'd have to make sure the man felt welcome.

The FBI representative was a short, thirty-something brunette named Barbara Bianchi whose only piece of jewelry was a thin gold chain with a simple, gold cross. Since this case didn't involve drugs or counterfeiting, it wasn't likely her agency would be involved, but she was sharp and could always pull in resources they didn't have. The FBI was much better funded than any local law enforcement agencies.

Grabbing coffee and an old-fashioned glazed, Barb took a seat next to Gary. Team members called out greetings, caught up on the news, then settled in, opening laptops if they had them, placing phones on the table face up, but on silent.

They knew for the next five days this case would take priority. Over soccer games and bedtime stories. Over overflowing inboxes back in their offices. They would see the faces around this table more than the faces of their wives and children. Their families understood. The allotted five days for a Major Crimes Team homicide investigation often ran eighteen to twenty hours long. As everyone knew from watching CSI or Bosch, the chances of homicides being solved dropped dramatically if the killer wasn't identified and arrested in the first twenty-four to forty-eight hours.

Monson lost no time in getting right to it. Grant queued up the PowerPoint.

32

"**Y**esterday morning, at 6:17 a.m., Willamette Valley Communications Center in Salem received a call from fifty-three-year-old Depoe Bay resident, Logan McKenna. She was visiting Oletta Hartley at her home and place of business, a daycare place for dogs called Adventurous K9, located at 98612 Highway 20, Eddyville, Oregon for a couple of days and when she went to clean out the horse stall—apparently she's not a very good card player . . . she lost and that was her consequence (a few chuckles from the team)—she discovered the body of a woman she did not know.

"After checking for a pulse and assuming the victim was deceased, Ms. McKenna called Ms. Hartley and then 911. The victim was IDed as forty-three-year old Gloria Merrick of Philomath through the wallet and phone found in her vehicle which had been pulled into some brush along the highway. It is presumed she walked in from there, although the reason is unclear.

"Ms. Hartley identified the victim also, but said she knew her only from seeing her in town at the feed store. Naturally, we'll be verifying all of this, but the driver's license photo matches. The ID seems accurate.

"But first, let me show you what we're dealing with."

The first slide showed the entrance and the front of the property.

Here Monson paused, then continued.

"As those of you who were part of Major Crimes a few years back know, Ms. McKenna was a person of interest in the 2019 Depoe Bay homicide of charter boat captain, Adam Hosteler, found dead on his boat, the *Mary Ann*. Ms. McKenna was later cleared of any wrongdoing—in fact, in a roundabout way, she helped us catch the guy by getting herself kidnapped."

A few heads nodded. Eyebrows were raised by those not employed in Lincoln County law enforcement in 2019, but they held their questions. They'd get the scoop later from the head-nodders, or when they could get on a computer and look up the case.

Monson moved on with a review of yesterday's events and a tour of the scene as Grant clicked through the slides, which included graphic crime scene photos of the victim's body.

"Pullman says Birdwell will verify and the bullet will have to go through ballistics, but it looks like it was from a .380. No weapon found."

"Any brass?" Gary asked.

"No such luck," said Grant.

"You'll find the initial statements from each of the four people on scene included in the packet in front of you, along with photos of the victim. Grant will also send you all of the files digitally. Send me your reports as you can, I'll be putting everything together in the murder book as we go."

Monson brought up the lights and asked for questions. Fred, who had been leaning back, balancing on the back legs of his chair, brought it forward, landing with a thud.

"You said the owners of that place knew the victim, right?"

"Not well, but yes, the wife said she knew who she was," said Grant.

"I'll bet this Gloria knew the husband a little too well! Like in a biblical way. Jealousy is a pretty strong motive for murder," Davies said.

"Anything's possible at this point," Monson said, acknowledging Fred's theory without agreeing with it. The rest of the team knew better than to make assumptions prematurely.

Monson continued, speaking now to the whole group, "What we need is information. Let's start with the people on site when we arrived. Grant's already started on the victim's phone. Gary, you want to start a warrant request for access to Ms. Merrick's property and vehicles? The address is in your packet."

Gary nodded and opened his folder.

Monson continued, "The victim had an acre and a half out in Philomath. Hopefully she lived alone. But could be a boyfriend or girlfriend. Roommate, maybe. Look for paycheck stubs, find out where she worked, talk with her neighbors, get any credit card statements, checkbooks. We need her bank records.

"We need to know who these people are, what their relationship with Gloria Merrick was. Hopefully Birdwell will narrow down the time of death. Then we can see who has alibis. And we need to know a lot more about Gloria herself. Why was she there? Who would want to kill her? Even if you think it might not be important, I want you to cast a wide net. Where did she shop? Eat? Do her banking? Security cameras, everything.

"So let's start with the people we know—we've got Paulette Lewis, the mother. Lane Hartley, husband, former military police with the Air Force—you know he has guns—and Oletta Hartley, his wife. And Logan McKenna."

"What about Mrs. Hartley's black eye?" Fred interrupted again. "You said she claimed she took a fall off her horse. Any chance her husband gave it to her? He the violent type? Maybe he was putting it to Gloria, promising to leave his wife and marry her. Then the girlfriend calls the wife and rats him out, says they're in love, he's going to leave you, that whole line—trying to force Lane's hand. He could have arranged a meeting with her down at the arena and put a bullet in her head to shut her up. Ditch the weapon. We couldn't prove anything!"

"Let's not get ahead of ourselves, Fred," Monson said. "But it wouldn't hurt to check hospitals and any domestic disturbance calls over the last year or two. You want Lane?"

Fred nodded.

Monson handed out the rest of the assignments.

"I want to know everywhere they went, who they called or met with. Everything they said or did in the last week. Get what you can. Call if you need me before then. We'll meet back here at 3:00 p.m."

<h1 style="text-align:center">33</h1>

The aroma of strong coffee and sizzling bacon warmed the cozy kitchen and steamed up the windows. Any other morning, Keegan would have enjoyed it more.

Keegan loved mornings. Breakfast and barbecue were his two specialties, although Suzie made better coffee, he had to admit. But today, she'd have to put up with his. Having been up with Aiden for several nights, it was her turn to get sick. She'd chugged some Nyquil last night and was still in bed. He knew she would have gotten up if he'd asked, but he didn't have the heart to wake her. He'd get the older two off to school after breakfast, then clean up Aiden and deliver him to his mom before he had to leave. He'd taken yesterday off, so he needed to go in to work at the Hartley's today.

Their fourteen-year-old, Mandy, was still upstairs getting ready, he could hear her blow dryer, but her little sister, Allison, only limping a little, made it to the bottom of the stairs all by herself, proudly throwing her arms up like she'd just stuck the landing at the Olympics. Allison had a great attitude.

"Daddy! Daddy! Minnie cake! Minnie cake!" she shouted, putting in her order as she climbed into her chair at the table. A spasm of pain flashed across his daughter's face and Keegan automatically flinched. He felt it in his bones. Due to a car accident a couple years ago, Allison had worn a transtibial (below-the-knee) prosthesis since she was four. She did okay with it, but it didn't fit all that well and certain movements caused her a lot of pain.

Keegan didn't rush over to coddle her, but it made him more grateful than ever that Allison would soon be getting a better prosthesis. She had been approved to participate in a new study. As part of the program, she would get a state-of-the-art computerized prosthetic, which was far superior to the basic model she had now. The doctors told them it would give her much more flexibility, stability, and strength, and best of all, their sweet little girl would experience a lot less pain.

Normally, this new leg would cost upward of $70,000 and was not covered by insurance, but because Allison was participating in the study, they were getting it at a deep discount—only $12,000. That was still a fortune, but with the extra gig he had taken on, they could swing it.

He had never done that kind of work before, but Allison needed that leg. At least it was over. Things hadn't gone exactly as planned, but he'd improvised. Oletta's neighbor had already paid him, and he'd paid the doctor yesterday. That money was long gone.

It was his responsibility to take care of his family and that's what he was doing. With this top-of-the-line prosthetic, Allison would have a new life.

Keegan looked over at his younger daughter again to make sure she was wearing something besides her Hello Kitty pajamas. Allison liked to dress herself for school. Thankfully, Mandy had already gotten her ready. Aiden, three-and-a-half, was in his booster seat, banging his spoon, smearing mashed bananas onto his pancakes—and everything else within reach.

"You got it, pumpkin," Keegan smiled at his daughter, "One Minnie Cake coming up."

The griddle sizzled as he poured one big pancake with two small pancake ears on top. Minnie Mouse. They'd gone to Disneyland two years ago and Allison swore she remembered, although she'd only been four at the time. He didn't contradict her.

After he served Allison her 'Minnie Cake', he got Mandy's short stack started. Then he yelled up the stairs. "Kitchen's closing in five minutes! Your Uber's leaving in ten!"

He slid Mandy's pancakes in front of her as she sat down, and then joined his children at the table.

"Thanks, Dad," she said, before pouring maple syrup on and adding two bacon strips on top.

Two simple words, but Keegan was grateful his sweet girl hadn't hit the 'I-hate-my-parents' stage yet. According to his best friend at work, who had two teenagers, that time was coming. But maybe not, he thought, getting himself a coffee refill before sitting at the table with his own food.

Watching Allison as she polished off her breakfast and excitedly told her little brother about the unicorn she'd seen in her room last night—

"Some people have monsters in their closet; I got a unicorn! When you're older you can have a ride on him, but you're too little now. You have to be six before he'll let you see him . . ."

—it seemed impossible that she had been through so much in her short life.

As Allison instructed Aiden and Mandy on the finer points of unicorn care, Keegan allowed himself to enjoy the moment. He never thought he would have this life. Things had been hard after his mom died. He'd taken some wrong turns and could easily have wound up in prison or worse. If it wasn't for his mom's best friend, Oletta, who folded him into her family without a second thought and had always been there for him, stuck by him even when he was wrong . . . well, he didn't know where he'd be now. He owed Oletta and her family everything.

He just hoped he could make it up to her.

The girls were finishing their breakfast just as Mrs. Donavan's dark brown Ford Explorer, their carpool ride, honked out front. Keegan kissed the girls as they ran out the door, then made short work of the dishes and poured a mug of coffee for Suzie. He didn't have time to give Aiden a full bath but wiped him down and changed his shirt before taking him up to his mom.

He woke Sleeping Beauty with a kiss on the forehead and handed her her coffee.

"Sorry I can't let you sleep longer," he said, "but I promised the Hartleys I'd get that exercise area finished today. You going to be okay to watch Aiden? I can see if Mrs. Valdez will watch him for a few hours."

"No, I'm good, hon," Suzie said, swinging her legs out of bed, taking a grateful sip of the hot coffee. Scooping up her son, she lifted Aiden into his playpen by the bathroom door with some of his toys and turned on the shower. "I can see him from here. I'll be fine, hon. Just need to wake up."

Keegan hesitated by the door.

"Don't worry," she said. "You go to work. I'm fine. It's just a cold. After a nice, hot shower I'll be good to go."

Reassured, he gathered his car keys and work jacket and trotted down the stairs.

Suzie yelled after him, "Don't forget Mandy's got soccer practice. Home by four-thirty, okay?"

"Four-thirty?" he yelled back.

"Yes!"

"Got it! Home by four-thirty at the latest. I'll be here!"

He smiled as he started his truck. Soccer practice meant pizza night and pizza night meant no dishes. He was all in for pizza night.

34

After a very long day, Monson finally let Oletta and Lane know that Gloria's body had been removed and they were releasing the scene. He reminded her that she, Lane, and Paulette were not to take any trips but were free to put their horses back in their stalls and resume their normal dog daycare business.

As if anything was ever going to be normal again.

After the cops left, she and Lane tore down the crime scene tape and mucked out the stalls, removing every last bit of dirty straw, then scrubbed out the feed bins and water buckets before refilling them. They washed away every trace of Gloria. Who knows what she was up to before someone shot her. They didn't stop until everything smelled of clean, fresh hay.

Then Oletta grabbed a shovel and marched toward the back door. This was her mess to clean. But when she got there she began to shake. She could not get her legs to take her outside. The body may be gone, but the blood wasn't.

Oletta didn't believe she'd ever forget what happened here. But she had to. She could do this. She was a grown woman. She'd had three kids, helped foal many a mare, set broken bones, and stitched up more torn flesh than she cared to remember. It's not like she'd never seen blood before—but this was different. Her feet remained rooted to the ground.

Lane came up behind her and gently took the shovel from her hand. Without saying a word, he grabbed a trash bag and pushed softly past her. She hated herself for letting him.

A minute later, the sharp sound of the shovel biting into the ground made her flinch. This was followed by the sound of dirt and what she knew must be dried blood being tossed into the bag. Bite . . . Toss . . . Bite . . . Toss . . . the steady rhythm continued until finally it stopped.

Scraping noises . . . a heavy thud of the now full bag being deposited into the trash barrel. A lid being secured was followed by the singular sound of a jet nozzle washing off the shovel. Then her husband's heavy footfalls walking back in. He hung the shiny, clean shovel on the wall.

Oletta let out a strangled sob and allowed herself to be engulfed in Lane's arms. It was only a matter of time before the cops found out about her fight with Gloria at Fishers. She should never have lied to that detective about her black eye, but he'd asked about it directly and she had to say something. Now she wished she could take it all back.

Once she had her emotions reasonably under control they went to get the horses. It was therapeutic to call them down and tuck them safely back into their new, clean digs, complete with a late dinner with extra berry treats for Hondo. When she explained to the police that she needed to limit Hondo's movement due to his recent broken leg, they had let her keep him in his stall but hadn't let her stay with him. She was sure all the stress and commotion had not been good for him.

LOOK AGAIN

Lane had pushed himself beyond the limits of his Lyme disease, so he went up to the house ahead of her. Oletta fussed over her babies for a while, then once she was confident they were okay, dragged herself up the hill and climbed the stairs to their bedroom.

Stripping off her clothes, she deposited them all into the hamper, then took a hot shower, pulled on sweats, and crawled into bed next to Lane, who was already asleep. She was so tired.

What was it the Bible said? "Sufficient unto the day is the evil thereof."

They got that right.

She tried to stop thinking and worrying about Gloria's murder, but sleep eluded her until she thought of Scarlett O'Hara's famous line from *Gone With the Wind.* "Tomorrow, I'll think about that tomorrow. Tomorrow is another day!"

Like Scarlett, Oletta had done what she needed to do. She would deal with the consequences tomorrow.

PRESENT DAY

After breakfast, Lane announced that the best thing they could do was to get back to their regular routines. Routines comforted dogs and horses and people were animals, too. Business as usual would work for everyone.

In the light of day, Oletta agreed. After taking care of the horses, she and Paulette spent the next couple of hours making calls to their customers letting them know Adventurous K9 was open for business. She decided not to deliver the news to Keegan over the phone. He was due in to work before lunch. She'd fill him in when he got here, or if he arrived before she saw him, Lane would talk with him.

She answered her customers questions briefly and with a positive spin. Yes, someone had died on the property, but nowhere near the outdoor area and pond where the dogs exercised and played. Yes, the police were investigating the cause of the woman's death. They had been told it was a physical injury. Neither of them mentioned the word 'murder.'

Oletta knew they were just kicking the can down the road. Eventually, it would be all over the news, but until the medical examiner officially declared it a homicide, the less they said, the better.

When they finished the calls early, Oletta realized she had the rest of the day free. There was always a long list of chores, but what she really needed was some equine therapy.

Calling Hawk, she headed toward the arena to saddle up Reign. Storm clouds hovered on the horizon, but if she hurried, she'd still have time to fit in a ride before the rain hit.

She waved at Keegan and Lane as she passed the carport. Keegan was already up on the John Deere but hadn't left yet. She almost went over to join the conversation, but it looked like Lane was handling it. Probably for the best. Lane would deliver the news but keep it short and sweet—just the facts. If Keegan needed to talk later, she'd be here for him. For now, she'd let Lane handle it.

She was giving the cinch on Reign's saddle a final tug to tighten it when she heard the front gate open and tires crunch on the gravel. Lane must have let someone in, but they weren't expecting anyone. Maybe Logan forgot something in the trailer and came back to get it. Things had been pretty chaotic yesterday. But she would have called first, probably, to make sure it was there before driving out.

When the car rolled by the arena, Oletta's blood froze. It was a dark vehicle with a sinister-looking, black grill aggressively sticking out in front. Blue lettering and the gold badge painted on the side said Toledo Police.

Shit.

Why was Toledo PD here? The only law enforcement she'd seen yesterday were the two Lincoln County Sheriff's deputies,

Monson and Grant, the trooper from the state police who'd guarded the gate, and the M.E. and crime techs. Maybe this guy's visit had nothing to do with the murder.

Fat chance.

No. Her heart sank. They were here for her. They must have found out about her and Gloria's fight.

Trying not to panic, Oletta quickly unsaddled Reign and led him back into his stall, then went out to face the music. Maybe they weren't here to arrest her, maybe they would just ask her to come to the station and give a statement. She wanted to kick herself for not telling them everything yesterday. What was she thinking? This just made her look guilty!

A police officer with salt and pepper hair and a thick, Starsky and Hutch mustache unfolded himself from the front seat, stood, and stretched. Adjusting his gun belt, the officer took a breath and looked around.

He looked familiar. Where had she seen this guy before? Before she could place him, he walked right past her, heading toward Keegan, who was about to head out on the John Deere. She could hear the engine and see it vibrating. Lane must have gone back up to the house.

Confused, Oletta followed the cop, a sense of impending doom mounting inside her.

"Toledo PD! Get down from your vehicle . . . show me your hands!" the cop shouted.

Turning around in his seat, Keegan took one look over his shoulder at the police officer and jumped. Moving faster than Oletta had ever seen him move since he sprinted thirty yards down the field to make that touchdown for Toledo in his senior year.

"Stop!" the cop yelled. "Stop or I'll shoot!"

"Keegan!" Oletta shouted, panicked now. "Stop!"

For a split second, she thought Keegan would keep running and there was nothing she could do to keep this cop from shooting him down. For a long second, time seemed suspended, and Keegan's life hung in the balance. Then Keegan slowed and turned around. He put his hands on his head and waited. The expression on his face was difficult to interpret. She just hoped she'd done the right thing. She'd never forgive herself if Keegan was physically harmed, possibly killed, until she could figure out what the hell was happening.

Hoping her heart would stop hammering in her chest, Oletta introduced herself calmly to the officer and asked why he wanted to talk with Keegan. If *she* was reasonable, maybe *he* would be reasonable. Everyone just needed to calm the hell down!

Instead of answering her question, she watched in horror as the officer crossed the field, and roughly handcuffed Keegan. Marching him back to his patrol car he stuffed him into the back seat, behind bars—essentially in a cage.

Rushing forward Oletta yelled, "Wait! What are you doing? We need to talk about this! Who are you? What's your badge number?!"

Ignoring her, the Toledo police officer got into his vehicle and engaged the automatic locks.

Keegan's face was drained of all color. Leaning forward, he shouted out as the officer rolled up his window. "It's okay, Oletta. Don't worry! It will be okay!"

Furious, Oletta banged on the hood of the car as it backed out, then barely missed having her foot run over as the car made a three-corner turn, spraying gravel on its way out.

This couldn't be happening. But it was.

35

Still half in shock, Oletta ran back to the house to let Lane and Paulette know what happened. They both loved Keegan as much as she did—and knew his history.

Right now she wished Lane was still a cop. He could call someone. Lane had been an MP in the Air Force, but that was years ago. He had no current contacts with law enforcement. He didn't even go to the gun range anymore. When his neuro-Lyme disease got worse, he had Keegan help him set up a practice range at the far end of their property, behind the house, away from the horses and dogs. They had cleared a small path from the house to the range which would accommodate his mobility vehicle when he needed it. Otherwise, he walked. It was good exercise.

Oletta burst into the kitchen. Paulette was cleaning vegetables for a salad and Lane was pouring the remainder of this morning's coffee into a thermos. Both stopped what they were doing. After she filled them both in, Lane took her in his arms and said, "Keegan's a big boy, now, and he's been clean for years. I'll call Toledo and see if I can find out what's going on. It will be okay, Oletta. Trust me."

Oletta's ever-practical mother made more coffee and set out mugs and a plate of cookies in the middle of the kitchen table, instructing everyone to sit. "Brain food," she said.

"I just can't believe they think he had anything to do with Gloria's murder," Oletta said.

"Maybe it's not about that," her mom said. "Maybe he's got unpaid parking tickets or something."

Lane looked up the ten-digit non-emergency number for Toledo PD and dialed. He told the receptionist who answered what had happened and asked where their police officer had taken Keegan and why.

The receptionist was pleasant enough, but said she didn't know anything about it. She also informed him that even if she did know, she would not be at liberty to share that information.

Lane patiently explained he was former law enforcement himself and that Keegan was a good man, like a son to them. They just wanted to find out where he was so they could help. There must be some misunderstanding.

He must have been convincing, because the young woman finally relented and said, "Give me a minute, I'll see what I can do," and put him on hold.

A few minutes of annoying on-hold music later, she came back on the line.

"I checked with the watch commander. He sends all the cars out and he has no record of sending anyone out to your place. Are you sure it was a Toledo patrol car, sir?"

"Yes, I'm sure," Lane said, "my wife saw the car."

"Can you describe the car your wife claims to have seen again? Maybe it was . . ."

Oletta put her head in her hands, "Keegan wasn't even here the night Gloria got shot. He had nothing to do with this!"

Lane thanked the woman and hung up. He turned to Oletta and took her hand. "Let's not panic. We don't even know why he was picked up. Maybe he got into some other kind of trouble.

I know we don't want to think it's possible, but he could have fallen off the wagon. People do. We only see him a few times a week. Think. Have we noticed any change in his behavior recently?"

Oletta jerked her hand away, "Keegan's been straight for over sixteen years! Ever since Mandy was born. He's married, has a family, a good job, a house—there's no way he would backslide now or start hanging with his old friends. I would *know*, Lane. He's here almost every day he's not working his other job or with his family. I know the signs. Keegan is clean."

"I agree, Letti," Lane said. "I'm just trying to keep an open mind. There must be an explanation. Cops don't pick someone up for no reason. And why did he run?"

The room got quiet as they all tried to think of what to do next.

"There's another possibility," he said. "Keegan and Suzie have had a lot of expenses with Allison. All those doctors and hospital stays. Maybe he didn't do drugs again, but he needed money for Allison's care. Maybe he did a job for one of his old buddies for some extra cash, just to help them get through the winter until better weather and he gets more work. One of them could have gotten picked up and fingered Keegan to get a deal with the DA."

Paulette got up and started clearing the table. "Keegan is a good boy—a good man. He wouldn't go down that road again."

Lane asked, "Do any of your clients know anyone in law enforcement in Toledo?"

Oletta shook her head no. Then her eyes lit up and she pulled out her phone.

"I do know one person. Well, not an Adventurous K9 client, but what about Logan? She seems to know Detective Monson, or he knows her. And her brother is a cop."

"What makes you think she knows Monson?" Lane asked.

"Yesterday he looked right at her and called her by name before I introduced them. I was curious how she knew him, but with everything going on, never asked her about it. And then after we gave our statements, she went home."

Lane shrugged his shoulders, "I don't see how she would know Monson, at least not very well. She's not law enforcement and Monson doesn't strike me as a big socializer. I doubt they're in the same bridge club. She probably met him at some fundraiser or city event. But give her a call—you never know. It's worth a try. If she can get him to find out where Keegan is, that'd be a start."

Oletta scrolled through her recent calls and tapped a number, "I'm probably grasping at straws, but . . ."

Her call was answered on the second ring.

"Logan?"

"Hi, Oletta," Logan said. "Wait, let me get inside. It's kind of noisy out here. Ben's using the leaf blower."

Oletta heard boots on wooden steps, then a door shut, then quiet, then Logan's voice again. She could hear her much better now.

"How are you guys doing?" Logan asked. "Are the police still there? Have you heard anything? I didn't want to call and bother you, but do they have any leads yet?"

"We're okay, thanks for asking," Oletta said. "They took down the crime scene tape last night and said we could put the horses back in, but that's not why I called. I wanted to ask you a question. I noticed Detective Monson knew your name yesterday. How well do you know him? Well enough to ask a favor?"

Silence met her question for a few beats.

"Oh, uh, well, until yesterday, I hadn't talked with him in a while, but I did have dealings with him a couple of years ago. Ironically enough, I met him during another homicide investigation," she said. "In fact, two different ones, about a year apart."

Logan proceeded to explain how she had first met him at a crime scene where her half-sister had discovered a young woman drowned in a hotel pool and later been questioned by him. He was very thorough. Since she'd been instrumental in helping to solve those crimes, they'd parted ways with a kind of grudging, mutual respect, but weren't bosom buddies.

Oletta considered this.

"If you called him, do you think he'd talk to you?" she asked.

"About what?" Logan said. "I mean, I don't know. Is everything okay? Why do you want me to call him?"

"I don't want to involve you in any of this, Logan, but I don't know who else to call. It's about Keegan," Oletta said.

"Oh," Logan said. She remembered the easy smile of the relaxed young man she'd met yesterday. He'd gotten up to get her another can of Coke when they had lunch up at the house after their trail ride. Nice guy.

"Sure, shoot," Logan said.

"This morning, a Toledo cop came here and picked him up. Yelled at him to get off the tractor. Keegan ran, but then he stopped. I thought the officer was going to shoot him, so I yelled at him to stop, and he did—then he handcuffed him and drove away, without telling us where he was taking him or why."

"Oh my god, Oletta!" Logan said. "Do you have any idea why?"

"That's what we'd like to know. Lane called Toledo and the watch commander said they never sent a car out here. I can't imagine an imposter driving around impersonating a Toledo police officer, arresting random people."

"Have you called back? Was he officially arrested?" Logan asked.

"I think so, but I don't know, it all happened so fast. He was cuffed and put in the back of his car. Can they do that if they don't arrest you?"

"Either way, it doesn't make any sense," Logan said.

"No, it doesn't," Oletta said. "I know Detective Monson and Grant were from the sheriff's office, but Lincoln County is a small place. We didn't have anyone from Toledo PD out here yesterday. I would have seen the car, and this car had Toledo PD emblazoned on the side. Monson was in charge, so we're hoping he either knows or can find out where Keegan is and why he was taken in. Keegan's a good kid. We can't help him if we don't know where he is. Can you help?"

"Of course," Logan said. "I don't know if he'll tell me anything, but I have Monson's card in the office. I'll call him right now. Did you happen to get the license number on the patrol car? What did the officer look like? Anything you can remember may help."

Oletta described the officer.

"I'll call you back as soon as I know anything," Logan said.

As soon as she disconnected the call, it dawned on Oletta where she had seen this guy before. Of course! His hair and mustache were darker twenty years ago and his pot belly less prominent, but it was the same guy, she was sure of it. Officer Fred Frickin' Davies. Mom didn't allow swearing in the house, but if she did, Oletta had a string of more accurate adjectives to describe this piece of dog crap who'd taken Keegan who knows where.

36

Detective Monson glanced at the clock, then got up to use the facilities before everyone arrived at 3:00 p.m. He received updates from most of the team members during the day but was anxious to hear their most recent reports and bring everyone up to speed. There would be a lot of information to sort through, most of it discarded as they eliminated possibilities, but for now, they needed to consider everything. He was hoping someone had come up with something they could use.

They were still filling in the blanks, learning more about the murder victim, setting up a timeline for her activities and whereabouts the week before her death. That's how the job was done. Making calls, knocking on doors. Fact by fact, patiently building a solid case. You never knew what scrap of information would prove valuable.

Monson headed toward the men's room at the end of the hall. On the way back, he saw Fred Davies coming out of Interview Room 1, looking very pleased with himself.

This wasn't Davies' home station. Why would he need an interview room? He wasn't a detective. Was someone having him work two cases at once? This one and something that overlapped with Newport? He'd have to talk with Toledo. Impress upon them that he needed every team member to be 100 percent focused on this homicide investigation while they were assigned to the team.

A growing feeling of unease rose in Monson's gut. Maybe he should talk with him after the briefing. See what's up before he called his boss.

By 3:00 p.m. everyone had arrived. Davies sat in the back, arms folded, a smug grin on his face. Monson started with OSP and worked his way around the room, asking everyone to share what they'd learned so far.

"Vehicle registration for the 2007 silver Chevy Tahoe found on the side of the road about a half-mile west of the Hartley property on Highway 20 is valid. The vehicle belonged to the victim, forty-three-year-old Gloria Merrick, black hair, brown eyes, 5'6", 135 lbs., 81137 Abbey Lane, Philomath, Oregon."

FBI agent Barb Bianchi and Jay Vallik, the DA's investigator, were up next. After giving the Benton County Sheriff and Philomath police a heads up, they had driven out to the address listed on the victim's registration.

"Warrant?"

"Yep. Had 'em in hand. Gary obtained search warrants for the house and any structures, computers, or vehicles on the property. Phone records are on the way."

Everyone gave Gary a silent round of applause. Since the dead have no expected rights to privacy, they didn't really need search warrants, but it was always better to have them than not. Didn't want a case thrown out on a technicality.

Monson nodded for them to continue.

"Rural property, zoned for horses, about three-quarters of an acre. Most of the properties out there have horses. House in the front—small one-bedroom, single-car attached garage, back half is fenced, with a makeshift wooden stall. Not a full stable, but somewhere for the animal to get out of the rain. Water pump, barrel, salt lick. Older, reddish brown horse on one side with feed bin, storage on the other. We put in a call to animal control. They're sending someone out for the horse."

"Tell us about the house," Monson said.

"Simple lock, no security system," Barb said. "Key was under the mat."

"Roommates? Boyfriend?"

"Looks like she lived alone and if she ever had any romantic or family ties, we didn't see any evidence of that or any other visitors. Nothing recent anyway," Jay said. "No men's clothes in the closet."

Barb continued, "Ikea desk with one file drawer contained what records we did find. She banked in town, Citizens, on Main. According to her check register, she made mortgage payments, so didn't own her house outright. Going back a couple of years, looks like she was current for a while, wrote a check on the second of each month, but this year she's gotten behind. Last one January 2nd, 2024."

"Okay, follow up on that. Find out why. Computer?"

"Yes, an older model HP, but it's password protected," Barb said. "We're working on it."

"But we've got her phone," Jay added. "Found out where she worked, Jackson's Feed & Supply, also on Main. Manager's been off this week, but they said he'll be in tomorrow. Gloria worked in the back, so the salesperson in the front didn't know her well and wasn't sure exactly what her hours were last week. She thought she might have had a trail riding event. She took time off for those."

"Right, get her schedule, try to nail down her coworkers. See how they got along and if they know of any jilted boyfriends or ex-husbands. Also, track down where those trail-riding events are held."

Monson looked up at the whiteboard where Grant had been adding notes. In the center he'd taped a picture of Gloria enlarged from her driver's license, her address and phone scribbled underneath. On the left was a map encompassing all of Lincoln and Benton Counties, including marks for Gloria's residence, bank, and place of work in Philomath to the Hartley's property in Eddyville where her body was found. Not much, yet, but he hoped it would be filled with connections and other leads over the next twenty-four hours.

"Good work," he said, then turned to Grant, "Oh, and we need to get out to that Adventurous K9 employee. He wasn't there yesterday, but we need his statement. He should be home later. We can swing by tonight. You have the address?"

Grant nodded and scrolled through his phone.

Monson was pretty sure Fred's attention had not fully been on this case today, but on whoever was in Interview Room 1, but he asked for his report anyway.

"Fred, you have anything on the husband yet? Lane? Any domestics, hospital records for the wife, or other reason to look at him more closely?"

Fred cracked a huge smile, "Nothing on the husband, boss, but I can help you find that Keegan fellow. He's cooling his heels across the hall." He jerked his thumb toward the door. "Picked him up this morning out at the Hartley's when he showed up for work. Tried to run, but I got him. He's been in there a while, so he should be softened up and ready to talk by now . . ."

The looks of disbelief on everyone's faces were totally lost on Fred.

"You're welcome. he added, smugly.

37

The entire room went silent. All eyes were on Monson, who was staring at Davies. Seconds dragged into a full minute, which seemed much longer than that to everyone present. Then Monson rolled his shoulders and unclenched his jaw.

Placing the black marker in his hand back onto the table, he looked Officer Davies directly in the eye and said, "You have Keegan Shaw in Interview Room 1."

It was more of a statement than a question.

"Officer Davies, you are on loan from the Toledo Police Department to work with the Major Crimes Team for five days, standing in for Loretta Grieg who is on maternity leave. Is that correct?"

Davies nodded, looking a little less sure of himself.

"And who are you to report to during that time? Who is your immediate supervisor?"

"You, I guess," Fred said. "Whoever is in charge of the team . . . we're all working together to solve this thing."

"And what were your instructions this morning, Officer Davies, your assignment? How were you supposed to spend the first full day of the precious few we have to catch whoever killed Ms. Gloria Merrick?"

Fred looked a lot less sure of himself now. "Well, you asked me to check up on Lane, the husband, but . . ."

Monson cut him off.

"This young man, Keegan, the one who was not on scene the day the body was discovered and whose initial statement has not been taken. I'm afraid to ask, but why did you drive out to the Hartley property this morning? Did you attempt to talk with him first, before the situation escalated? What did you say, exactly?"

Fred relayed the sequence of events, leaving out the part where Oletta got Keegan to stop, not him.

"He ran!" Fred all but shouted. "Innocent people don't run. I had good reason to pick him up. It was good police work. It took me a minute, but I remembered this kid. Keegan Shaw. Toledo High. Ran with a bad crowd. Drugs, car theft, you name it. He was trouble then and he's trouble now! These guys never change, they just get better at not getting caught."

"Is that the reason you gave him when you came to his place of employment and treated him like a criminal in front of his boss without trying to talk with him first? At any point did you tell him he was under arrest or read him his rights, Officer Davies?"

"No! I didn't have to read him his rights. I wasn't arresting him, just bringing him in . . ."

"Did you in fact do *anything* you were instructed to do, or trained to do, or did you go off on a wild goose chase of your own, with no authority, opening us up to lawsuits, and possibly poisoning the well of this investigation in the process? If this young man is guilty, he's going to be so busy covering his tracks we'll never be able to prove it. And if he's not guilty, he'll clam up out of fear, or just to spite you, Davies, and then once he recovers, he'll turn around and sue you and the department."

Monson stopped to get his temper under control.

"Officer Davies, I want you to go home for the day," he said. "You're dismissed."

"And Fred . . . ," Fred stopped and turned back, hand on the door, "you better hope we can undo the damage you've just done."

Fred looked like he might argue, then thought better of it and stomped out.

Monson ran his fingers through his hair, then told everyone to go get some dinner before getting back to work. Barb and Jay said they were returning to Gloria's neighborhood to finish canvassing. Catch those who weren't at home earlier. Gary was working on the computer and phone. He was also their go-to tech guy when Grant wasn't available. OSP was going to do the background on Lane and Oletta's domestic situation that Fred should have done.

Monson shrugged on his suit jacket and smoothed his tie. Grant did the same. They weren't getting dinner anytime soon.

Asking Grant to go into the observation room first, to take advantage of the two-way mirror, Monson opened the door to Room 1 and walked in.

The heater had been cranked up. A very sweaty Keegan was seated on what Monson knew to be a purposely uncomfortable chair, his forearms resting on the small table, opposite two other plastic bucket chairs.

Monson introduced himself but remained standing.

"Am I under arrest?" Keegan asked, looking around behind them, probably for the officer who'd left him there.

"First, Mr. Shaw, we are very sorry for the misunderstanding today. You were mistakenly detained this morning. As you probably know by now, a woman was found dead Wednesday morning at one of your places of employment in Eddyville and we are investigating that homicide. As part of that investigation, we're talking to everyone who worked at Adventurous K9 or had access to and was familiar with its operations and layout.

Again, you are free to go. Would you like to use my phone to call home? Your family is probably worried about you."

Keegan pulled out his own phone. "No, thanks, I already texted my wife. Told her I was working late. Didn't want to worry her until I knew what was going to happen. Davies made it sound like I was under arrest, although he never booked me. You're sure I'm not under arrest? "

Monson wanted to say, 'Should you be?' but instead said, "No, sir, as I said, you are free to go, but we will need to stop by tomorrow morning to take your statement. Again, just one of many we are collecting. We doubt you'll have much to add since you went home early and don't live on the property, but we need to speak with everyone."

"Sure," Keegan said. "I can do that. I don't work my regular job tomorrow, but can I meet you someplace else besides my home? I don't want to upset Suzie or the kids."

Restaurants were too public, and Monson didn't want to put Keegan on the defensive by asking him to meet at a police station, so after stepping outside to make a quick call, he came back in, followed by Grant, and asked, "How about Siletz Public Library? They've got a small room in the back they said we can use tomorrow morning. Shouldn't take more than a half hour. Nine o'clock okay?"

Keegan said that worked for him. As long as he was out of there by 10:00 a.m., he could still make it to his oldest daughter's game.

"What sport?" Grant asked. He and his girlfriend were looking for a sport for their six-year old. Right now it was a toss-up between soccer and gymnastics. They were also looking for a piano teacher. Never too early to start. Tiffany, his first child—now a teenager he hadn't seen in years—lived back east with his ex-wife, took ballet when she was little. He used to get pictures now and then of her recitals. He had no idea what she was into now.

"Soccer," Keegan said. "Midfielder."

In addition to the apology, Monson gave Keegan a cold Mountain Dew from the vending machine, a voucher for the pizza place, and a ride back to his car. Keegan had been a surprisingly good sport about it. He didn't mention the word 'lawsuit' once. Monson doubted that he himself would have been so accommodating if he'd been hauled in by Fred Davies and left to sweat bullets in an overheated room.

Without being obvious about it, Detective Monson observed Keegan Shaw in the rearview mirror as he downed his soda and talked sports with Grant. No need to put the young man on the defensive tonight, but tomorrow he'd ask him why Davies was jonesing for him.

There must be some history there.

Just because Davies was an idiot didn't mean Keegan was automatically innocent. They needed to find out a lot more about Keegan Shaw before nine o'clock tomorrow morning.

38

After leaving a message on Monson's line—she wasn't surprised he didn't pick up—Logan called Sam. Sam had connections all over the county. If anyone could locate Keegan, she could.

Sam was in town finishing up a story on annual gray whale migrations and why this year's migration had been delayed. After Logan gave her the bare facts about what happened that morning, she said she'd check her sources and call right back. It didn't take long.

"Well, he wasn't booked anywhere," she said. "I called Toledo, Newport, Lincoln City, sheriff's office, the jail . . . nobody has him. Are you sure it was a Toledo cop that picked him up?"

"That's what Oletta said. It said Toledo right on the side of the car," Logan said. "I can't think of anyplace else to try, can you? I hate to leave Oletta hanging. She loves that kid."

"Not off the top of my head, but I'm free for a couple of hours, how about I bring lunch, and we can brainstorm," Sam said. Logan did not object. She and Sam were on the same wavelength when it came to food. The greasier and saltier, the better.

While she was waiting, Logan updated Oletta with what little good news she had. At least Keegan didn't seem to be in jail anywhere.

An hour later, Logan and Sam were licking their fingers and gathering up fast-food containers. Fish and chips from the Horn. Always a good choice.

Once the kitchen table was cleared, Sam pulled out her laptop. Logan went into the office and got a large pad of chart paper and some markers Ben had used to design the layout of his raised bed garden. She put the pad on the counter, leaning the top against the cupboards, anchoring the bottom with the toaster. *Good enough.*

"Where should we start?" Sam asked.

"How 'bout with who's who?" Logan said, creating a five-column grid with a black marker on the chart paper. Across the top, she labeled the first column "Names," the next three were "Motive," "Means," and "Opportunity." The last column she left blank. Then she started filling in the chart.

"Oletta Hartley . . . Lane Hartley . . . Should we include him?"

"We should list everybody, eliminate later," Sam said, starting a matching Excel file on her computer. Recreating Logan's grid digitally, she tapped in the names as Logan continued.

"Lane Hartley . . . Paulette something . . . I don't know her mom's last name, we'll have to get that . . . Keegan Shaw . . ."

"Don't forget Julie Fisher at that training center," Sam said.

Sam pushed her glasses up her nose. "Uh . . . full disclosure, I drove out and nosed around Fisher's already. Told her I was working on a story about horse training, wanted to feature her place. I wanted to see if she'd mention the fight. I hinted, but she clammed up at the end."

"Do you think she knew about Gloria's murder or that it happened on Oletta's property?" Logan asked. She didn't mind

Sam not telling her—Sam didn't know Oletta. She could be more objective.

"No, I don't think so. I'm guessing she probably didn't want to shed a bad light on the sport, not necessarily protect Oletta," Sam said. "But they are friends. If she doesn't know, I wonder how she's going to react when she finds out."

For the next hour, they filled in what they knew or what they could find out through social media posts and other sources online about each of the people listed. Anything not fitting in motive, means, or opportunity went in the miscellaneous last column labeled "Notes."

Logan stepped back to take in the information as a whole. The names they had only took up the top half of the chart. She made extra rows, leaving room to add other people of interest if they discovered any.

After a few minutes, Sam said, "The one connection they all have is Oletta. Unless we're missing something or someone."

Logan hated to admit it, but looking at it in black and white, Sam was right. Gloria was murdered on Oletta's property five days after getting into a physical fight with her. She almost caught her cutting off Reign's mane and tail. She suspected Gloria of letting the horses out in the storm a few days before that, which could have resulted in Hondo's death.

Oletta had plenty of motive. As for means, although the murder weapon had not been found, Oletta had been raised around guns and her husband was ex-military. She probably had access to one. She didn't want to make assumptions that she knew how to use a gun, but she probably did.

Everyone else on the chart was either family or as good as. They were all loyal to Oletta.

"So either Oletta shot Gloria and everyone else is covering for her, or one of her trusted family members—and Keegan could be included in that—got rid of Gloria for her." Logan said.

She stared at the chart. It was like trying to untangle a Gordian knot. Any one of them could have done it. But having met all of these people, Logan had a hard time picturing any of them as killers. But then, that's what people always said, right? 'He was such a nice man—I can't imagine him killing anyone, he wouldn't hurt a fly!'

It still didn't solve the problem of how any of them could have known Gloria was at the arena in the middle of the night.

Her head hurt.

Sam's phone buzzed. She held her finger up for Logan to wait.

Logan saw from Sam's screen that it was Bailiff Nichols from the courthouse. She'd only met him once, but Sam knew him from covering crime for the paper and he'd grown up with Tim.

Sam listened intently for a few minutes, then said, "Thanks, Nichols, I owe you one!"

He said something and she laughed, "Lunch, yes, but Local Ocean? Nice try! I was thinking McDonalds . . . Yeah, yeah, don't call me, I'll call you . . ."

"Found him!" she said.

"That's great!" said Logan. "Is Keegan okay? Where is he?"

"Well, the good news is that he's fine," she said. "He's down at the Lincoln County Jail, but not *in* jail," she said. "A Toledo PD officer assigned to the Major Crimes Team parked him in one of the interview rooms, but when Monson found out, he raised holy hell. He hadn't told the guy to do that."

Logan tried Monson's number again. This time he picked up. She could hear road noise in the background. She explained that Oletta and Lane were concerned about Keegan. They knew he was at the jail, but no one would tell them anything.

He wouldn't tell her anything, either, except to verify that Keegan was not under arrest. He was fine and, in fact, he and Grant were giving him a ride home right now.

LOOK AGAIN

Logan immediately dialed Oletta to give her the good news, or at least as much as she had. Maybe Keegan would be able to tell her more.

39

Carl added three sugars and took his second—*or was it his third?*—cup of coffee into his office. He could use the extra caffeine; he only managed a few hours of sleep last night.

He flipped on the light, set his cup on his desk, and sat down, not bothering to open the blinds. The view of the forest did not enthrall him like it did John. Besides, light coming in from that direction made the wall map difficult to see. And it was worth seeing.

Astrid Meadows. Staring at the map, he could see the horses, stamping their feet, the bright silks of the jockeys, the betting windows, and above it all, his luxury private suite overlooking the track. He could taste the cold crab cocktails and a long pour of his favorite, Macallan 18. And the money. He could taste the money.

He was so close. He could *not* lose this!

The leather captain's chair squeaked as he leaned back. He closed his eyes and ran through the last twenty-four hours.

Nothing had gone as planned.

The timetable had been tight before, now it was almost impossible. He checked the calendar again. Tomorrow. He had until tomorrow to nail this down, but after last night there was no way he could get it done that quickly.

Amateurs! That's what he had to work with out here in the boonies. His Jersey guys were pros, but he couldn't use anybody from the old neighborhood. Paulo would find out. And he didn't want Paulo interfering with the agreement he had with Louis. Louis had given him his word, but Paulo didn't owe him anything. And Paulo was blood. Louis' son.

No, he would not accept defeat. He still had time. If he handled this right, nothing could be traced to him. What he needed was information.

And John was going to get it for him. He just didn't know it yet.

Carl realized his chance earlier, after breakfast, when John said he was going into town for groceries. There hadn't been anything on the news yet, but news traveled fast in a small community. Especially bad news. If there was any gossip to be had about the murder last night, Carl knew John would hear it in town.

Sure enough, when John returned about an hour ago, he was full of the latest neighborhood gossip. Did he know that a woman had been killed on the property next door? There was even a YouTube news video. The cashier at Naturals had it. John powered up his computer, turned the screen so Carl could see it, and hit play.

Carl kept a straight face while watching, but he almost did a fist pump in the air when the reporter mentioned the name.

Thank you, John! That's the information I needed.

When the video ended, Carl kept his face neutral and shrugged his shoulders at the senseless violence in the world before heading out to the patio for a cigarette. None of their business. Nothing to do with them. It was all he could do not to rush into his office right then, but he remembered how to play it cool. This reminded him of the do-si-do with the Feds years ago. This was a game he knew how to play—and win. He doubted John would ever rat him out—after all, he paid his salary—but better safe than sorry. Carl knew that given enough incentive, no one was loyal.

As John put away the groceries, Carl noticed a light was blinking on the cradle for the kitchen phone. He came in and hit play. There was one message. A young man's voice.

"Uh, Mr. Muller, I just wanted you to know I finished that job. Once I got into it, I had to do things differently, do more work than we agreed on, but don't send any more money. What you sent already is fine. I hope the job is okay, because I can't take on any more projects right now. I'm kind of swamped. Okay, thanks."

Carl grunted and hit erase.

John asked if he wanted Black Forest ham or roast beef for lunch. Carl said the ham would be fine.

When the interminable meal was over, Carl finally escaped to his office, leaving John to do whatever it was John did to keep the household running efficiently. That was not something he concerned himself with.

He did not notice John's eyes following him as he left the room.

Once inside his office, Carl lowered his shoulders. Every cell in his body buzzed, every sinew pulled taut. Around John, he'd kept up an appearance of calm, but it was a strain. Lifting the delicate teacup to his lips, he took a measured drink and set it carefully back on the saucer. He tried to slow his racing heart.

All was not lost. A murder next door might even work in his favor. He'd paid good money to get this done. The important thing was getting Astrid Meadows and Cedar Lodge built and launched so he could start recouping that money, most of which he hoped to borrow from Louis. Of course, that loan was contingent on his obtaining that last piece of property. He promised Louis he'd have his hands on the Hartley's place by tomorrow night. And he would.

Now was not the time to panic.

But in spite of his best efforts, that is exactly what Carl's body was doing. Panicking. He couldn't stop. His pulse quickened. His heart fluttered. His chest tightened. He struggled for breath.

Willing himself to focus, he flipped open his laptop, almost knocking over his coffee. Waiting impatiently for the search engine to load, when it did, he typed in the woman's name with shaky hands.

He needed to clean up this mess, silence this woman so none of this could be traced back to him. He'd bought the other properties through shell companies from the Cayman Islands to Wyoming, so he'd covered that angle, but he was making offers on the Hartley place directly. Faster that way. The realtor had no idea he owned the rest of the ones she'd sold. The purchases had been made over the last couple of years, not all at once, and under different names.

But now, this woman with the barking dog could unravel everything. Forget the loan from Louis—if she could identify the man at the barn, he was looking at jail time at the very least and probably the death penalty. And Astrid Meadows would never get built.

Astrid was the love of his life. Now this McKenna woman was the only thing keeping him from giving Astrid all she deserved! And all he deserved. He never got rewarded for all those years stuck in Switzerland. Never ratting anybody out. Living that boring life. It had been a long time since he'd felt like himself.

But what if he couldn't get this done in time to call Louis tomorrow night? He looked at the map again. Would Louis still honor their deal? No, Louis wouldn't forget a faithful soldier. Louis wouldn't pull the deal if it took an extra day or two to make it happen, would he? Yes, Louis was feeling a little under the weather, but no heart problem was going to take out that hard-nosed SOB.

Carl took a deep breath.

No. He had time. He just needed a plan. Do his homework. Make a plan. Execute the plan. He typed in the name.

Logan McKenna.

If you wanted a job done right, you did it yourself.

40

Monson asked Fred Davies to come in at seven, an hour before everyone else was set to arrive for the morning briefing. No sense embarrassing the man further. Everyone makes mistakes. Now that he'd given the man the night to calm down, he hoped the Toledo officer would realize the mistakes he had made and be ready to accept his role as a team member, not a wild card. At least he wanted to give the man the opportunity.

But from the way Davies came in, resentment and defiance oozing from every pore, Monson knew there wasn't much chance of that happening. Still, he had to try.

"Officer Davies," he said, nodding at the chair across the table from him. "Take a seat."

Davies sat. He started to lean his chair back to balance on its hind legs, but seeing the look in Monson's eye, thought better of it.

"Yesterday afternoon, you shared some pretty strong reasons with me about why you took the actions you did with Mr. Shaw," Monson said. "We also spoke about adhering to the chain of command. I want you to know I have not yet written a report or contacted your supervisor."

Davies just glared at him.

Monson's eyes were kind. He tried again.

"We all sometimes do things we later regret. Now that you've had a chance to sleep on it and before I write that report, I'd like to give you the opportunity to modify the statements you made yesterday."

He leaned back slightly, giving the man the floor.

Davies defiantly stuck out his chin and smoothed his mustache.

"I'm a good cop," he said. "And I was right to bring in that kid. I don't know how long you've been wearing suits, but I've got twenty-two years in uniform. All of those years were in Toledo. I know that town inside and out. I know those kids. I know who knows who, who works for who, and who's done how much time where."

Forgetting to be respectful, Davies folded his arms and rocked his chair all the way back, balancing perfectly.

"You know what these losers do the minute they get out?" he asked.

Monson remained silent.

"I'll tell you what they do," he said, lurching forward, causing his chair to land on all four legs with a bang. "They go *right* back to what they did before," he said, stabbing the table with his finger to make his point. "It's called reci . . . re . . . recivism— that's it! I took a course on it. Fancy name for repeat offenders. And they're *all* repeat offenders."

The word was 'recidivism', but Monson didn't bother to correct him. He watched as all the meanness, all the small, petty thoughts and resentments running around this man's tiny brain poured out of his mouth.

"With all due respect, *sir*," Davies said, "Keegan Shaw was bad then and he's bad now. The bottom line is this: People. Don't. Change."

Inwardly, Monson sighed, then took an axe to Fred's ego.

"It's a shame you feel that way, Officer Davies. I was going to give you a second chance, but after talking with you, I think maybe you're right. People don't change. At least some people. You're off the team. Report directly back to your supervisor."

He got up from his chair, but did not reach across the table to shake Fred's hand.

"That's directly back. I'll give your supervisor a call and let him know you're on your way. I recommend you not stop for coffee. He'll be expecting you."

A vein at Davies' temple bulged and his face turned scarlet, but he said nothing as he got up and stomped toward the door.

"Oh," Monson said to his back. "And when you get there, let him know my report will follow. Should be on his desk by tomorrow."

People in the jail heard Davies slam the door.

A few minutes later, Grant came in.

"What'd you do to Davies?" he asked. "He's going to have a coronary before he gets to the parking lot."

"Nothing he didn't bring on himself," Monson said. "I sent him back to Toledo."

Grant was fine with that. It would mean more work for the rest of them, but he knew and trusted the others. Davies he could do without.

It was already almost eight o'clock. Their appointment with Keegan wasn't until nine. The Siletz Public Library was only twenty minutes away, but Monson had a thing about people being late. He liked to arrive early.

Monson was curious what Keegan would have to say for himself—what information he would volunteer and what he'd have to drag out of him. Grant agreed to stay and run the morning briefing, get the autopsy report and phone records as soon as they came in. Monson said he expected to be back by eleven. He'd call to see what everyone wanted for lunch.

41

Monson pulled into the library's gravel parking lot ten minutes before nine. He smoothed his tie as he got out of his car. He was still grumpy from his meeting with Davies.

His long legs carried him up the walk past a large, white wooden sign. Marine blue lettering outlined in black assured him he was in the right place. Siletz Public Library. At the top of a bright white flagpole twice as high as the modest, single-story dark brown library itself flew an American flag large enough to grace the state capital.

Monson approved.

He noted the recently-mowed, bright-green lawn and neatly trimmed junipers that anchored the front entrance. Nothing fancy, but it was obvious the community took pride in its civic buildings.

After checking in with the librarian at the front desk, he made his way past the children's section and stacks of fiction until he got to a small room on his left. The door was already open. Keegan was inside, waiting for him, looking a little nervous.

The librarian had thoughtfully left two bottles of water on the table and turned on a Keurig next to a spinning rack of Costco K pods with two mugs upside down on some paper towels.

After the usual morning greetings, Monson popped in a Starbucks dark roast and placed a mug under it. When it was done, he doctored it with cream until it was a creamy khaki. Just right.

Keegan already had his.

He looked around the room. Besides the counter with the Keurig and a conference table that seated four, a small window overlooked the gravel parking area. A wall clock was the only break in the anonymous decor. 'TIME TO READ' was printed across the face, with the hour hand at nine, the minute hand at twelve.

He checked his phone. At least it kept accurate time.

Monson pulled out the chair opposite Keegan and sat. He placed his coffee to his right. Removing his notebook, pen, and phone from his pocket, he lay the phone on the table to the left and the notepad in front of him. Then he got started.

"So Mr. Shaw, thank you for coming down today. I'll try and get you out of here by ten, in time for your daughter's game, so let's get right to it. Do you mind if I record this?"

He gave Keegan a self-deprecating smile and tapped the side of his head, "I'm afraid my memory isn't what it used to be. Recording saves time and me having to call you back to repeat things.

"Sure," Keegan said, sitting up straighter, scooting his chair in, warming his hands on his coffee mug. The picture of cooperation.

"Let the record show that . . . ," Monson went through the usual spiel, verifying date and time, the two people present, Mr. Shaw's voluntary participation, etc.

"Now, Mr. Shaw . . ."

"Call me Keegan."

"Okay, Keegan," said Monson, "Did you know the deceased, Gloria Merrick?"

"No, never met her," Keegan said.

"What about know *of* her? Did you ever hear your employer, Mrs. Oletta Hartley, her husband, Lane, or her mother, Paulette, or any other employees at Adventurous K9, talk about her or mention her name?"

"Uh, well, yeah," Keegan said. "Not really. I mean, they might have mentioned her, but if they did, I don't remember it. Like I said, I never saw her there or anywhere."

Next, Monson asked him a few softball questions like where he grew up, went to school, and how he knew Oletta and her family. How long he'd known them.

Warming up now, Keegan answered, "As long as I can remember, my mom and Oletta were friends. When Mom died, Oletta pretty much raised me. She's like a second mom to me. She and Lane are good people. So's her mom. I call her Granny just to piss her off. But not as an insult. She's really active for her age. She's really old, like seventy or something, but she still rides. Draco is her horse."

Monson asked a few more questions, then threw a curve ball.

"You mentioned that Mrs. Hartley—in your words—pretty much raised you after your mother died. That must have been hard, losing your mother so young. A lot of kids go off the rails when something like that happens to them. Did you have any trouble during those years, Keegan? Any run-ins with the law?"

Keegan set his jaw. Monson could see the kid wasn't stupid.

"Yes, I did, but that was a long time ago. I straightened up. Got clean and stayed that way," he said.

Monson waited.

"I admit I made some bad choices in high school. The Hartleys saw that I was hanging with the wrong crowd, so they encouraged me to join the football team, thinking athletes would be straight arrows. Some of them were, but most of those guys were the biggest users on campus. They're the ones that got me into drugs.

"Anyway, the details aren't important, but one night, senior year, we were on our way home from a party at Kyle's house where we were celebrating our big win against Newport. We stopped at the QuickMart in Toledo for some more beer. My buddy, Sean, used his older brother's ID and scored some vodka, which was even better. I was the most sober, so I was driving. But I'd already done a couple of lines before we left the party, and I had another baggie in my pocket when we got pulled over."

"Oletta went to bat for me, but only on the condition that I go to rehab, get a sponsor, go to meetings, submit to random drug tests—the whole nine yards," he said. "She and Lane were tough. Nine o'clock curfew, making sure I deleted all those guys' numbers from my phone, putting me to work so I didn't have any time to get in trouble. They went with me to court. I pleaded guilty and got six months in juvie.

"Anyone who tells you juvie is kiddie jail has never been there," Keegan added. "I swore I'd never go back. And I never did."

"But some people won't let that go—your past," Monson said softly. "Isn't that right?"

He had a feeling Davies had been Keegan's arresting officer.

"You're talking about Officer Davies?" Keegan said.

"Why didn't you tell me about him yesterday, or file a complaint?" Monson asked.

"No way," Keegan said. "No offense, but I stay as far away from the police as I can. And I've learned not to argue with cops. I knew he had nothing on me. I just had to wait it out until he let me go."

"Why do you think he picked you up?" Monson asked.

"Because he can," Keegan said. "He hasn't bothered me for a long time, but for a while, he wouldn't leave me alone. He saw me as that same jerk I was in high school, a druggie loser heading for prison. What's funny is that Officer Davies was the DARE officer for a while at our school, but he hates kids.

Especially the guys. He thought every boy between the ages of ten and twenty was doing drugs or thinking about doing drugs or robbing old ladies.

"With me and my friends, he was right. At least about the drugs. We were high half the time," he said. "But I cleaned up my act. After high school I enlisted. Army.

"And no, I didn't come back with PTSD. People think everyone who goes over there does, but I went over in 2009, during the drawdown. All I did was pull patrol and help pack up boxes. One tour."

"The point is, I grew up, but Davies doesn't buy that," he said.

It looked like Keegan had more to say about Davies, but then thought better of it. Probably assumed cops stuck together against him—which they probably had in the past.

Monson asked a few more questions to establish a timeline of Keegan's whereabouts the night of the murder, then thanked him for his time and let him go.

As he washed out the two mugs and put them upside down to drain on a fresh paper towel, he considered Keegan's inflection and body language as well as his words.

He came to two conclusions. One, the man had no real alibi. He left work early Tuesday to take his daughter to the doctor. They verified that already with the doctor's office.

The rest of the evening he claimed he spent with his family. Monson knew he could have sneaked out during the night and come back. Another possibility, of course, was that his family did know, but were covering for him.

Which brought Monson to his second conclusion. Keegan had no motive. According to him, he didn't even know Gloria, so what possible reason would he have to drive out to Oletta's place and shoot her?

Still, as much as he liked the kid, they needed to nail down his story.

42

Logan got her morning chores done early so she and Sam could get to work on their investigation for a couple of hours before Sam needed to be home. Mrs. Horvat had agreed to watch Miss Magnolia as long as Sam got back by eleven-thirty sharp. She had a hair appointment in Newport at noon.

Ben was slow-roasting a mess of ribs for dinner. In the battle of wet versus dry, Ben definitely fell in the dry rub camp. *'Sauce ribs are lazy man's ribs.'* He even had his own secret blend of bold spices.

Right now, Ben was looking at the chart paper grid Logan had taped onto the cupboard.

"You know," he said, pointing with his BBQ tongs as he opened the oven door. "The one person you forgot to put up there is Gloria. I mean she's obviously not a suspect, but . . ."

Sam and Logan looked at each other.

Jeez! We forgot the murder victim!

Unabashed, Sam clicked away on her keyboard to insert a row in her Excel spreadsheet and Logan put up a blank piece of chart paper next to the suspects' grid and in neat, block letters printed out their murder victim's name, Gloria Merrick.

"Thanks, hon," Logan said, shaking her head at overlooking something so obvious. "We need a picture."

Ben gave Sam the WiFi code, and she located and sent Gloria's driver's license photo to the printer. Logan cut it out and taped it in the center of a blank piece of chart paper.

Logan didn't ask Sam how she accessed the DMV database. Plausible deniability.

From Gloria's driver's license Logan added her address and vitals below her photo, which Sam had cropped. Driver's license photos were notoriously awful, but Gloria's wasn't bad. Long, black hair—a little stringy and dyed from the look of it—framed a long, sharp face. Physically, her lips curved up slightly, but the smile didn't reach her eyes. Pale blue, they glared out and challenged the world. This was one angry woman, or at least one with a huge chip on her shoulder. Logan wondered what life experiences made her that way or if it was genetic.

Who are you? And why did someone hate you enough to kill you?

She and Sam took over Ben's kitchen, but he was a good sport about it; as long as they stuck to the table and didn't block his access to the pantry, it was all good. He'd just cook around them. Logan's only assignment for later today was de-silking the corn on the cob (leaving the husks on—Ben put them right on the grill), cutting up the watermelon, and tossing a green salad. That she could do.

Normally, Max would have been underfoot tripping everyone up, but at least some of his training was taking. For the moment, he was happily chewing on a puppy toy.

Dixon, the better behaved of the two canines who ran their lives, was napping at Logan's feet. He'd had his morning run—a nice, long one to Fogarty Beach, including a surf swim, so he would be good until around 2:00 p.m. when he would require either a thirty-minute game of catch or another run.

Logan studied the two pieces of chart paper on their murder board. There were still a lot of empty blocks where vital information and leads would go as soon as they had any. And Gloria's face was still floating in a sea of white. Their murder victim was still a mystery.

Logan decided to remedy that right now. After counting the names on the suspects grid, she drew that number of straight lines out from the pic in a spoke pattern and held up her black marker. They needed to figure out what the connections were between the suspects and Gloria. Oletta she knew about, but only from what Oletta had told her. There may be more.

Oletta Hartley—fellow National Trail Riding competitor

J. Fisher—Owner of J. Fisher, held competition event Gloria attended.

The other names had no relationship with Gloria that they knew of, so she left those blank.

Then with the fine end of the Sharpie marker, she drew cross connections: Keegan Shaw to Oletta to Lane to Paulette. It was starting to look like an imbalanced spider web a kid had taken a swipe out of.

She needed to fill in some blanks.

"Okay, who should we start with?" Logan said. "How about J. Fisher, since you went and talked to her already?"

"Okay . . . ," Sam said, opening up a Word file while Logan added the basics to the chart. "Julie Fisher, forty-nine, owner/ manager of J Fisher Training, 24662 Vaughn Rd, Veneta, Oregon. Her services include training young horses, riding lessons, etc. She hosts clinics—sort of training trail rides—and events where participants can win points toward Nationals."

"Yeah, Oletta was telling me about that," Logan said. "I don't know how many places host these events or where all of them are, but she goes to these every month or so with her horse, Reign, to compete with other horsewomen who do trail riding to bank points. At the end of the year they tally up the totals and prizes and awards are given out."

"Is there big money? They always say, 'Follow the Money!' What are the prizes worth?" Logan asked. "Oletta showed me a big belt buckle she won with her old horse, the one she had before this one. It was gold and silver. She showed me a picture. His name was Diamond. Beautiful animal, white with reddish blonde markings—I think she called him a palomino pinto. Movie star horse."

Sam nodded. "There are other prizes, too, but they benefit for the most part indirectly by building their reputation. Bragging rights. If they win, people bring their horses to them to train and if they have a great horse, people will pay for breeding rights."

"I think Oletta does it for fun," Logan offered. "She described the women she rides with as good friends. They are competitors, but also share a lot of tips and cheer each other on."

"Except for Gloria," Sam pointed out.

"True," Logan said. "Except for Gloria. Doesn't sound like anyone was friends with her. And vice versa."

Ben had gone outside to work on some shelves he was building in the garage for canned goods. Logan stared at Gloria's driver's license photo.

"Where did she come from?" she said.

"Her address is right there," Sam said.

"No, I mean originally?" Logan mused. "Was she born here, or did she move from somewhere else? She's not married, but does she have family here? What's her story?"

"That I can find out," Sam said. "Just give me some time. I can work on it when Magnolia goes down for her nap."

After Sam left, Logan decided to drive out and see Julie Fisher herself. She needed to hear from someone other than Oletta what went down last Sunday. And she'd take Dixon. Max would need a potty break soon and Ben had a hard enough time walking one dog, let alone two.

43

Logan decided not to call ahead. She didn't want to give Julie the opportunity to turn her down. Better to take her chances and show up unannounced. If she left now, she'd get there just after lunch. The thought of lunch made Logan's stomach growl. She'd have to drive through McDonald's on the way.

The gamble almost paid off.

Logan followed her GPS and soon saw the wooden sign with the horse Sam had described. Parking next to a green truck in front of the main building, a low-slung ranch house, she got out and stretched. The sun emerged from behind a cloud, and everything stood out in bright relief. Logan left her jacket in the car with Dixon, cracked the windows, and hit the clicker to lock it.

A small sign above the door said "Office" so she headed in that direction to find the owner. As if summoned, a woman in jeans, ball cap, and boots came around the side of the building, unhooked a ring of keys from her belt and fitted one into the keyhole.

"Excuse me, Julie?" Logan said, striding up the path. "Are you Julie Fisher?"

The woman turned and squinted out from the shaded porch at Logan, who was still in the sun.

"Yes," she said, "That's me. How can I help you? If you're coming for the clinic, I'm afraid it was yesterday. We're just wrapping up this morning. There'll be another one next month, though . . . ," she said cheerfully, popping the door open with a nudge of her hip. "This thing always sticks. If you want to come in, I have some flyers in the office."

"Um, no, I'm not here for a clinic," Logan said. "I wanted to talk to you about one of your regular attendees, though, a Gloria Merrick?"

Julie Fisher backtracked out to the porch and stared at Logan suspiciously, closing the office door behind her.

"Gloria Merrick?" she said, raising her eyebrows a bit. "Why do you want to know about her?"

"Well, that will take some time to explain. Can we talk in your office?" Logan asked. "My name's Logan. Logan McKenna. I'm a friend of Oletta's."

She decided to be up front and honest with this woman, since she probably wouldn't buy another cover story excuse like Sam's.

Julie seemed to consider her for a minute, then said, in a much more formal, cooler tone, "I'm sorry, I don't know who you are, but I'm very busy right now. I don't talk about any clients or former clients—and if you're from the media, I'm not saying Gloria was either. If you would like to find out more about future clinics, please call and make an appointment . . . the number's on the sign . . ."

With that Julie Fisher turned and went inside. The decisive thunk of a deadbolt being clicked into place made her position very clear.

Well, okay, then.

It was a long shot anyway, Logan reasoned, walking back to the parking lot. It had been worth a try. She'd give Sam a call from the car and see if she turned up any more information on her end. If Gloria participated in clinics and competitions, she had to have a job to pay the rent and keep a horse. They could start there to learn more about her.

Lost in thought, Logan was startled when a woman came up behind her and said, "Don't worry about Julie, she's a stickler for the rules. Julie never gossips."

When Logan turned around, a woman about her age stuck out her hand, "Hi, I'm Denise, nice to meet you."

"Oh, uh, thanks," Logan said, unsure where this was going. "I'm Logan, nice to meet you, too."

The woman's handshake was firm and solid, like the rest of her and she had a ready smile. A 'Let's Get Wild' t-shirt with bucking broncos cavorting across it topped well-worn jeans. A blue flannel shirt was tied around her waist. Dusty boots and ball cap. A western version of Logan's own wardrobe.

Removing her aviator sunglasses, Denise said. "I decided to come over and introduce myself when I heard you say you knew Oletta. Any friend of Oletta's is a friend of ours. Come on back and meet the girls. We'll tell you whatever you want to know about Gloria. Who *none* of us are friends with!"

They must not have heard.

Logan accepted the offer and followed Denise back to an RV area where about a dozen other horsewomen, probably the ones who had participated in this weekend's clinic, were packing up, dousing campfires, or checking tires and jiggling doors on their campers to make sure they didn't fly open on the road. A few vehicles were shiny and new, most were average, and some were held together with duct tape and bungee cords.

Denise cut in between the third and fourth horse trailers, where two women were sitting on folding chairs, drinking coffee—or whatever was in those cups—in no hurry to leave.

"Donna, Jan," Denise said as she pulled up another chair. "This is Logan McKenna. She's a friend of Oletta's and wants to know all about Gloria."

"Hi, Logan," Jan said, straightening her large, blue-framed glasses, which were slightly askew. Her broad smile pushing into her cheeks, gave her face a friendly, elfin look. "Julie doesn't kick us out of here for another hour. Ask away!"

Donna, a woman with intelligent blue eyes and even features sported a brick-red cowboy hat and a southwestern print shirt with quilted black vest. Logan guessed she was in her sixties or seventies—it was hard to tell—and looked comfortable in her own skin.

Denise threw herself down in the only other empty chair and got right to the point.

"Is this about what happened at the event two weeks ago? Gloria was 100 percent at fault for that fight, no matter who started it! If she's talking smack about Oletta . . ."

Without saying anything, Donna quietly reached over and gave Denise's wrist a quick squeeze, then withdrew her hand and smiled. Denise took a breath and reined herself in, waiting for Logan to tell them what she wanted to know.

44

Logan wasn't sure how to tell them what had happened, so she just came right out and said it, "No, that's not it. Gloria's not talking about Oletta—or anybody. Gloria's dead."

"What?! Are you sure?"

"Yes, I was actually the one who found her. I was visiting Oletta out in Eddyville and found her body Sunday morning, just past the arena."

"Gloria's dead?"

"OMG!"

Denise was first to zero in on the critical point.

"So Gloria was found dead on Oletta's property." She looked at the other women. "That means if those yahoo cops filed a report about their fight, the police are going to think Gloria was out there to mess with her horses again and Oletta caught her at it and delivered on her promise."

The woman did know how to cut through the crap.

Logan hated being the bearer of such awful news, but now that they knew, maybe they could help fill in the gaps.

"I think you're right. And I think the only way to help Oletta is to learn more about Gloria so we can figure out who would want to kill her," Logan said.

"How did she die?" Donna asked. "Could it be suicide?"

"No," said Logan, "I don't think that's possible. She was shot . . . in the back."

For the next hour, the women shared what they knew, including a detailed account of the fight they had witnessed two weeks ago, just a few feet away from where they were now sitting. They talked so fast, Logan couldn't keep up, so she pulled out her phone and recorded the conversation.

"I know Oletta can't prove Gloria let her horses out that night in the storm in Eddyville, but did anyone see Gloria hack off Reign's mane and tail here at Fisher's? Or even see her coming back to her camper?" Logan asked.

"No," Denise said, "but Gloria's sneaky. We all know she's done things—bad things—but no one has ever been able to catch her at it. Or if they do, it's their word against hers, like Oletta catching her climbing out of Reign's stall in the barn. She saw that part at least. She was obviously up to no good. What else would Gloria have been doing in Reign's stall?"

Donna narrowed her eyes and added, "She's like a slippery eel."

"There was that one time," Jan said, "out in Arizona. Before her family moved here."

She turned to Denise and said, "Remember Rhonnie? She moved here from Tucson. She was the one who told us about it."

"That's right," Denise said. "I forgot about that. They couldn't prove that one, either, but Rhonnie said everyone knew it was Gloria."

She summarized the story for Logan.

"This happened back in the late eighties. Gloria would have been high school age, I think. She did rodeo back then, not trail riding. There was a rodeo queen competition in Tucson and Gloria didn't win. The new rodeo queen, Cindy something—I forget her last name, lived in a little town called Sierra Vista, which was about two hours south of Tucson. Near a military base. And guess who lived in the same town?"

"Gloria," Logan guessed correctly. "So what happened?"

"Well, she didn't do anything there, but a few weeks later, back in Sierra Vista, Cindy was supposed to do some training for cowgirls as part of her rodeo queen duties. She woke up one morning and both her horse and trailer were gone. They found the trailer way out off some back road, burned to the ground."

"Yikes," Logan said.

"That's not the worst of it—her horse's tendons had been cut and he was staked out in the desert and left to die."

"That's awful!" Logan said. "Did he survive?"

"No," Jan said. "They had to put him down."

Logan was stunned. How could anyone want to hurt an animal or make it suffer like that? For a minute, no one said anything.

Then Denise spoke up. "As much as I loathed that woman— and no one would put it past Gloria to do something that horrible—the police had no evidence. No way to prove it was her."

"Well . . . that's true," Jan said, "but obviously she did it! You've got to look at the timing. She moved here right after that. After Rhonnie told us that story, I looked it up. Gloria started school in Toledo that fall. That has to be the same Gloria. The article said Cindy was well-liked. And we all know Gloria has a jealous streak almost as wide as her mean streak."

"Well, she must have finally pissed off the wrong person," Denise said. "Someone shot her, but it wasn't Oletta. If it was me Gloria was harassing, I'd have no problem sending her to hell, but Oletta? Oletta doesn't have a mean bone in her body. But, if this goes down like I think it will, they're going to blame her anyway."

They were all quiet for a minute, thinking about Gloria's inglorious end and the danger Oletta was facing. Whatever demons haunted Gloria in this life and made her act as she did, she was beyond pain and punishment now. It was the living—the one who would be accused of killing her—that needed help.

Donna, who had been quietly listening, looked directly at Logan and said, "There's something else you should know. It gets worse. Oletta threatened to kill Gloria if she ever came near her horses again—Gloria made sure the cops wrote that part down. Oletta did say that, but she didn't mean it literally. She just said that in the heat of the moment, right after what Gloria had done to Reign and what she suspected her of doing the week before—letting her horses out in that storm. She almost lost Hondo in that storm."

Logan looked around her at the good-hearted women with weathered faces and kind eyes. Oletta had some very good friends. She'd earned their trust. But the police would only look at the facts stated in the police report. Oletta had gotten into a physical fight with Gloria, and she had threatened to kill her.

Jan reminded them that they needed to vacate the RV camping area by 3:00 p.m., so after Denise walked her over to show her the barn where Reign's mane and tail had been cut off and the window Gloria scrambled out of, Logan snapped a few pics and thanked them all for their time and openness. She promised to keep them posted and yes, if there was anything they could do to help she'd let them know. As she walked back to her car, Denise was already on the phone to Oletta.

Driving home, Logan left the radio off and cracked open a window. The sun slid behind the clouds again and the temperature dropped ten degrees. Which was okay with her. The cold air helped her think.

She gave Sam a call to find a time when they could get together to share what they had learned. Sam had to work most of the weekend, and they were going to Jean's Sunday night.

LOOK AGAIN

Sam promised to pump her sister-in-law for information over dinner. They agreed to meet at Pirates on Monday morning.

Speaking of dinner . . . Ben's BBQ ribs should be done by now. Watching for the highway patrol, Logan inched the speedometer up just a few more miles per hour.

45

Monson stopped to pick up a prescription for his wife at Walgreens and gas up his car, so it was almost twelve-thirty when he pulled into the parking lot of the jail in Newport and went inside. The familiar aroma of pizza filled the hallway. Made him realize how hungry he was. He hoped they'd saved him some. They had, but all that was left was one with artichokes and black olives. He preferred pepperoni, but he slid two slices onto a paper plate anyway. With enough red pepper flakes and parmesan cheese, it would do. He grabbed a Dr. Pepper from the cooler and sat down.

Barb was giving her report.

"The computer was password protected, but once our guys got the warrant—thank you, Gary—they used their software to bypass it and gain entrance. We're still going through it, checking the cloud for deleted emails, but so far, nothing significant has turned up. Looks like she does her banking and bill paying online. Everything looks current, except for being behind on the last few mortgage payments—that looks a little hinky, we're checking into that—no other late notices or anything out of the ordinary. Few personal emails. If she has family living, they're not close.

"I also got into her social media. Instagram and Facebook." Here she tapped on her own computer and it projected Gloria's Facebook page onto the screen.

Monson wondered how she did that.

Barb scrolled through several areas.

"Not in a relationship and hardly anyone ever comments on her posts. If I didn't know better, though, I'd think she was a very successful, happy horse woman. Lots of pics of her in western gear on beautiful horses. Not her horse, though, unless they're ones she used to have. These look expensive. Her horse is not as good. "

Barb knew horses, her daughter rode English and took lessons somewhere in Corvallis.

Next, she opened the photos. Several soft-focused selfies of Gloria in suggestive poses, wearing revealing clothes, looking almost cartoonish.

A couple of the men in the room hooted, and Gary said, "There's an app for that!"

Monson looked confused. Grant leaned over and explained there were contouring apps that could take inches off your waist and then bump up the size of your breasts, or if you were a guy, another body part of your choice, which Gloria had obviously done with some of her photos.

How sad. But it told them something more about Gloria. *Insecure.*

Jay Vallik, the investigator for the D.A. was next. Monson was relieved to have the photos off the screen.

"Finished canvassing the neighbors," he said. "Mostly, she kept to herself. When she wasn't working or out at night sometimes, she was home. They didn't know much about her other than that she had a horse. She lived alone. Mrs. Blakely, a widow who lives across the street, said other than bringing the occasional man home—who usually left before morning—Gloria didn't seem to have any visitors. Every month or so, she would trailer her horse and go somewhere, but she never stayed long. Other than that, she assumed when she left for the day it was to go to work, although she didn't know what she did for a living."

"Any disagreements with neighbors?" Monson asked. "Anyone not like her?"

"It would be harder to find someone who *did* like her," Jay said, "At work or in her neighborhood. Mrs. Blakely said she had a low-level, ongoing feud with a man whose property shares a fence with hers along the west side, to the right if you're looking out of Mrs. Blakely's living room window.

"Neighbor's name?" Monson asked.

"A Mr. George Hanson. Said she's heard them yelling several times. Arguing about water. He claimed she stole his water to fill her horse's barrel by reaching through the chain-link fence and grabbing his hose. Gloria yelled back at him she didn't do it, but Mr. Hanson got a camera installed and it stopped happening, so he is pretty sure it was her."

Monson reached for the last slice of pizza and slid it onto his plate. The artichokes weren't bad.

Jay said he'd follow up on Lane since Davies wasn't there. Military records, registered weapons, any domestics or trouble with the law since he'd been discharged from the Air Force years ago. Word must have gotten around about Davies, even though Monson hadn't said anything yet to the team.

While Barb and Jay got into their computers, Grant came over and updated Monson on what he'd missed before he got there.

Birdwell's autopsy report had come in. She couldn't get much closer than Jean for TOD, putting it at between one and three in the morning. As they already pretty much knew from the size of the hole in the victim's back, she was shot with a .380 auto.

If and when they had a possible murder weapon, the OSP Crime Lab up in Portland could compare the striations on a bullet shot from it to the one Birdwell retrieved from the body and see if they could get a match. The ME aged the victim's multiple abrasions and contusions to about a week ago, which would be two or three days before she died. No defensive wounds and no tissue or blood under her nails. So no struggle. Just point and shoot.

Monson had the report copied and Grant sent it out electronically to all members of the team. Then, for the next hour they strategized, deciding next steps in the investigation. Around 2:00 p.m., Monson got up to get a bottle of water from the cooler.

"Anything on Lane, yet?" he asked as he walked by Jay, who was still working on his computer.

"Not yet," Jay said, "Honorable discharge, nothing showing up locally, but he has guns. Five registered, currently. Couple of rifles."

"Any three-eighties?"

"One," Jay said. "But if he shot anybody with it, he wouldn't be stupid enough to keep it around. And if he did, he'd clean it, maybe shoot a lot of rounds so we couldn't match the bullet easily."

"True," Monson said. "But we should check. Why don't you and Barb go see if Mr. Hartley is missing any of his weapons? See if Gary can get you a search warrant for it before you go. If he's guilty and knows we're looking, he'll ditch it, but maybe we'll get lucky, and he won't be so smart."

Jay made the call and after some back and forth, gave Monson a thumbs up.

"Good to go, boss," he said. "Gary's sending it over."

He started to close his laptop when his computer dinged with an incoming email. He opened it and quickly scanned the content and the attachment.

"You're gonna want to see this," he said. "I sent some feelers out to see if Mr. Hartley had any recent domestics. He was clean, no police reports on him, but guess who *does* show up?"

He leaned back and grinned, pointing at the screen.

"His *wife*, Oletta Hartley," he said. "Sunday morning, April 7 incident report, 24662 Vaughn Road, Veneta, Oregon, a place called J. Fisher Training. Guess who else was in their report?"

Jay looked up from his computer and paused for effect.

"Our murder victim, Ms. Gloria Merrick."

Asking Jay to scroll down so he could see it all, Monson read the report, then had him print it out, then read it again. It was all there. What Gloria had done, or what Oletta Hartley accused her of doing. Hacking off the mane and tail of her horse that morning and releasing all of her horses out of their stalls a week before. Oletta claimed to have caught her in the act that morning, but the deputies found no direct evidence, so no one was charged.

Mrs. Hartley hadn't been exactly forthcoming about how well she knew their murder victim.

"Yes!" Grant said. "We've got motive, and a demonstration of Oletta's capacity for violence. It clearly stated Oletta was the one who dragged Gloria out of her trailer and started the fight."

Jay jumped in, "As for weapons, one of her husband's handguns is a three-eighty auto, which she almost certainly had access to. And Gloria was shot on her property."

Monson tried to remain objective, but he couldn't argue. The cherry on the sundae was Oletta's threat. The report clearly stated she said she would kill Gloria if she ever caught her messing with her horses again. Most of the witnesses must have been friends of Oletta's, because only one, a young woman new to these events, backed up Gloria's claim. But she did, so it went into the report.

A report dated less than a week before Gloria's murder.

Monson rocked back on his heels. He started to feel a mixture of excitement and relief. It was rare, but sometimes you just got lucky. This report pretty much wrapped up their case and delivered it with a big, shiny bow.

He didn't want to be guilty of rushing to conclusions as Davies had done, so he'd make sure they followed procedure on this. Get a warrant. Do it right.

Still, it felt good. He clapped Jay on the back and looked at Grant.

"Let's go find us a judge!"

46

Friday afternoons were pretty quiet at the courthouse, but they got lucky, and Judge Henderson was still in his office. After reading the report and hearing them out—he said he'd be happy to sign the search warrant for Lane's .380 auto as soon as Gary could get it to him. It took another two hours for Grant to write it, but by six o'clock they were on their way to Eddyville to hopefully find and collect the murder weapon.

They didn't expect trouble, but took two cars anyway. Better safe than sorry. Monson and Grant were in the lead—Grant was driving—followed by two uniforms in a black-and-white. With a cage, it was better equipped and safer for transporting a suspect should they need to take anyone in.

Wide awake even without the caffeine infusion from the Dr. Pepper, Monson ran through the various scenarios they might encounter when they arrived. He decided the best approach was for him and Grant to go in first. Do this calmly and without drama. But they had no idea how many people were up at the house or how the other family members might react. It could get messy very quickly, so even though he didn't want to tip the Hartleys off prematurely, both cars had to get through the gate.

No one was visible when they pulled up. Monson hoped they hadn't made the trip out here for nothing.

Grant pressed the button on the intercom. The man of the house answered.

Grant identified himself and said he and Detective Monson just had a few more questions to ask him and his wife. He apologized if he was interrupting their dinner, but they needed to clarify a few points before the weekend. It would just be a few minutes.

Lane said no worries, they were just finishing up dinner. He buzzed open the gate and said someone would come down to get them. He didn't sound happy the police were here again, but neither did he sound unduly alarmed.

Monson wondered what his reaction would be when he saw the black-and-white. As a former MP, Lane would surely know this wasn't a friendly visit. He hoped someone else would come down to get them.

The gate swung open electronically and they drove in. Grant assessed the layout and parked between the carport and the house, preventing or at least slowing down anyone trying to hop on one of the work vehicles stored there. After the gate shut, Monson had the patrol unit directly in front, blocking any exit to the highway.

It was as good as they were going to get.

Monson and Grant got out of the car just as Lane came out of the front door of the house and started toward them. He was walking but was using a cane. Before he came around the corner and saw the patrol car, Monson waved at him to stay where he was.

"We'll come to you!" he called out, as if being considerate.

Lane seemed relieved and turned to go back into the house. Monson discreetly signaled the uniforms to stay with their vehicle and he and Grant followed their host.

Oletta held the door open and took them into the living room. She indicated the detectives should sit on the couch. She and Lane took the two recliners. Lane gratefully sank into his chair. It looked like it had an electronic lift feature, which made sense with his neuro-Lyme disease. A Michael Connelly hardback lay face down on the wooden coffee table. But no coffee or cookies—an indication they wanted this to be a short visit.

The rest of the room was lined with wooden bookshelves, framed photos, and a large TV. Other than crackling and popping sounds of the wood stove the only other sound they could hear was someone in the kitchen doing dishes.

Needing to find out who else was in the house, Monson jerked his thumb back and asked, "Who got stuck with K.P.?"

Oletta answered, "That's my mom, Paulette. She has her own place but joins us for dinner most nights."

Folding her hands in her lap, she asked, "So how can we help you, Detective? Lane said you had some questions for us."

"Why don't you ask your mother to join us?" Monson said. With eyes on everyone he would have a better chance of controlling the situation.

Oletta looked at her husband, who nodded. She went and got her mother. They heard someone turn the water off and Paulette came in, drying her hands on a dishtowel. Oletta offered her the recliner, but she said she'd stand.

Monson got to the point. "First, Mr. Hartley, we're just covering our bases here, but do you own any guns? In particular, a three-eighty auto?"

Lane frowned, but said, "Yes, I have several guns. All registered. And one of them is a three-eighty. I was military police."

Monson continued, ignoring Lane's mention of their common law enforcement backgrounds. There were good cops and bad cops. Lane being a cop didn't mean anything one way or the other.

"Do you keep your guns in the house?" he asked.

"Yes," Lane said. "I have a gun safe in the back."

"When was the last time you fired that particular gun?"

"Last month? Last week?" Lane said. "I can't give you a precise date. I have a practice range out back. I try to rotate through them, keep them cleaned."

"I'd like to see the .380," Monson said, keeping his voice even.

This was the deciding moment. Either Lane would cooperate, or not cooperate.

Lane did neither.

"I don't like the direction these questions are taking, Detective," he said, pressing a button on his chair to start the lift. "I think you and your partner need to leave now."

Things happened quickly after that.

Grant produced the search warrant. Lane read it over, then called Kraken over to brace so he could get to a standing position. He was having trouble with his cane. Frustrated, he gave his keys to Oletta and she walked Monson down the hall to a back bedroom, where she opened the gun safe for him.

The .380 auto was there. Monson, who had already pulled on gloves, reached in and lifted it out of the case with two fingers, sliding it into an evidence bag he had in his pocket. He recorded the collection with his phone, noting the address, location in the house, time, and persons present, then slipped the bagged gun into his other jacket pocket.

Now for the hard part.

47

After dinner, Logan and Ben decided to walk off the ribs by taking the dogs down to Depoe Bay. Max now trotted and pranced happily beside Ben without lunging and pulling. Not a perfect heel, but their work with the positive reinforcement trainer down in Newport, Pike (pronounced Peeka) Bremer, had done wonders. Oletta had recommended her for one-on-one training. They'd only had two sessions, but were very pleased with the results.

Dixon kept his usual perfect heel on Logan's left. She kept the leash on for appearances, but he didn't need it.

Warm with a cooling breeze, it was a perfect evening. The sun sank lazily toward the horizon, streaking the clouds pink and orange along the way. When they got to Ainslee's, Logan handed Dixon's leash to Ben while she ran in to get two bags of caramel corn. Tonight was movie night. They hadn't decided between *Hunt for Red October* and *Jaws*.

They had just walked in the door back at the house when Logan's phone rang. She didn't recognize the number.

"Hello?"

"Logan, it's Paulette, Oletta's mom," she said. "Have you got a minute?"

Unloading the two bags of caramel corn on the kitchen counter, Logan unsnapped Dixon's leash.

"Of course," she said, wondering what else could have happened at the Hartley place. "Is anything wrong? Did they pick up Keegan again?"

"No," Paulette said. "Keegan is home as far as I know. But those two detectives, Monson and Grant, were just here. Monson had a search warrant for one of Lane's guns. They got that and we thought they were going to leave, since that's what they came for, but once he got the gun, he took Oletta with them for questioning."

Several thoughts ran through Logan's mind, the most basic was something she'd learned from Rick—cops didn't get search warrants without probable cause. They must have found out about Oletta and Gloria's fight. Would that be enough to justify taking Oletta in, too? She had a lot of questions, but first things first.

"Did they arrest her?" Logan asked.

"No," Paulette said. "Thank God, she went voluntarily. I think she didn't want to cause any more stress for Lane. Stress aggravates his neuro-Lyme disease, and he was already having a bad day with that. He couldn't even get out of his chair tonight without Kraken's help."

"Okay," Logan said. "I understand, but Oletta really needs an attorney. Do you have one?"

"No," Paulette said. "But Lane's looking for one, now."

"Good," said Logan. "Did Monson say where they were taking her?"

"No," Paulette said. "It all happened so fast, I didn't think to ask."

"If it was an arrest it would be Lincoln County Jail for sure, but even just for questioning, that's probably where they would take her. The sheriff's office is in the same building. I'll see if Sam can find out for us," Logan said. "But I want you to really hear me, Paulette. The sooner you can get someone down there, the better. If they let her call you, tell her to stop talking and ask for a lawyer and tell her not to talk with the police without that lawyer present."

"Okay, of course. We're hoping she knows that," Paulette said. "I hate to ask, but do you know of a good attorney on the coast to call? We're not rich, but I have some money saved. We can pay them upfront. Lane says it would be best to get someone whose office is out there. They'll know their way around with those cops and judges and we need someone to get out there and help her as soon as possible."

Logan racked her brain. Patricia Haggerman's name came to mind, an attorney in town Logan respected, but Haggerman dealt only with immigration cases. Then she remembered Mike Witcomb. Of course! He helped out one of Sam and Tim's former employees last year when he was falsely accused of murder. She gave Paulette the man's name, then scrolled through her contacts to get his office number for her.

"I hate to ask another favor," said Paulette, "but would you mind calling him? I'll take my phone with me, but I've got to get down to the barn to feed and water the horses, then get back to help Lane. Cell reception isn't the best at the barn and I've got my hands full here."

"Of course," Logan said. "I'll call right now."

She dialed the number and got the law firm's voicemail, but then remembered she had the attorney's private cell number, too. She called that one.

"Hello," Witcomb answered on the first ring. There was a background buzz of clinking glasses, music, and conversation. Probably interrupted him at a Friday happy hour or dinner out. She forged ahead, anyway.

"Mike, this is Logan, Logan McKenna," she said.

"Yes, I can see that," Mike said, obviously seeing the caller ID. "Haven't talked with you in a while," he said. "How can I help you, Logan? Been robbing banks again? Are you in need of a good defense attorney?"

"No, not me," Logan said, "but a friend of mine needs one."

Mike listened without interruption as she explained the situation. After asking a few pertinent questions, he asked for Paulette's number. Logan gave it to him, then heard gravel crunching footsteps and a car door open.

Yes! He was going to help!

Next, his car engine started up. He said he'd call Paulette on the way to the jail. He wouldn't make any promises until he spoke with Oletta, but he agreed with Logan that she needed an attorney. He was on his way.

Good man.

Knowing Paulette or Mike would call her as soon as they knew anything, Logan went into the living room to update Ben. Whatever happened next, at least Oletta would have good representation. She wondered why the police had taken Lane's gun. They couldn't have gotten a search warrant without connecting it to Gloria's murder. Or maybe they could. She didn't know what the requirements were.

They must think Oletta used Lane's gun to shoot Gloria because of their history, but if that was the case, why would Oletta keep the murder weapon in the house? She had plenty of time to get rid of it.

Logan still couldn't wrap her mind around Oletta being capable of killing anyone, but for that matter, anyone with access to her and Lane's house could have gotten that gun and used it to kill Gloria. Without more evidence, Lane, Keegan, and even Paulette were still on the suspect list.

48

Slumped in his chair, Carl stared straight ahead. Morning light, filtering in through the slats in the blinds accentuated the large pores on his nose, turning them into miniature black craters, stark against his pale skin. The air was stale.

His phone lay face up on the desk in front of him. It was ringing. He was ignoring it. There was only one reason Paulo would be calling him.

He had hoped to have more time, but last night's deadline had come and gone. Carl finally swiped the screen to answer the call but refused to pick up the phone. The more distance, virtual or otherwise, between him and Paulo the better. He couldn't stand the boy.

He tapped the call on speaker.

"Hello," he said.

Paulo's greeting was just as cryptic. "Louis's dead."

"I'm sorry for your loss," Carl said, his voice dripping in sarcasm he knew would go right over Paulo's head.

The punk didn't seem at all upset about his father's death. Not that this came as a surprise. Carl did wonder why Paulo made the call himself. He could have had an underling do it. He would have heard the news from someone eventually. Paulo's next sentence answered that question.

"The old man said you wanted money," Paulo said.

Of course.

"No," Carl replied, sitting up straighter. "We had a business arrangement. Louis was going to *invest* with me—in an enterprise which would have made him a lot of money in return."

"Whatever," Paulo said. "My father wasn't exactly thinking straight recently. Whatever he promised you, he didn't know what he was doing."

Carl waited, although he knew where this was going.

"I just wanted you to know I'm in charge now and I will be using the Family's resources elsewhere," Paulo said. "So no money."

Click.

Carl sat there staring at the silent phone in impotent rage. His fingers curled into a fist, which he slammed down hard onto the desk—once, before regaining control. That little prick *enjoyed* delivering every syllable of that message.

In the old days, this kind of behavior would result in Paulo being disciplined or even taken out—and not quickly, either. He'd be made an example of, but things were different today. All the young Turks were loyal or at least obligated to Paulo in one way or another. The boy wasn't completely stupid. While his dad was alive, he had used his time wisely, setting things up—banking favors, making threats. Paulo put everything in place so the transition of power would go smoothly. Carl grudgingly admired him for that.

For another few minutes, Carl sat perfectly still, willing his fury to subside.

It was so quiet he could hear the crows battling the jays in the trees outside the closed window. He looked around the room, taking in the map on the opposite wall, the blueprints on the table, the filing cabinet with the records of all the property he had obtained through his shell companies. All useless now.

It had been so thrilling to get all those deals so fast. *Bam!* *Bam!* *Bam!* Every win a trophy to throw at Astrid's feet. As if that would keep her cancer at bay. He hadn't realized how fast he was burning through his money.

He'd been obsessed. Even after she died he kept buying properties, convincing himself he was building all this for her. Astrid Meadows.

And it all would have gone through if the guy he'd hired to torch the Hartley's barn so they would sell hadn't screwed up. Royally.

Amateur! He should have known.

Carl channeled the rest of his anger into ripping down the map, stuffing it along with the blueprints and anything else referencing the project, into the trash. Then he sat back down at his desk to marshal his thoughts. Astrid Meadows had been his focus, his goal. Now what?

He could survive financially. Sell the properties, start over. Buy a nice place downtown Detroit or Chicago. Somewhere fresh. New identity. Lay low. Eat out every night. No need for a private chef. Actually, that would be simpler. John always wanted to talk menus, and he had no interest in the planning; he just wanted his meals good and on time.

But before he left, he had one more mess to clean up.

The dead woman was no longer a problem, but the woman who came out of that trailer to see what her dog was barking at was.

His guy said he wasn't sure whether or not she got a good look at him or not. The night was dark and there was little moonlight. But if she did see him and could identify him . . .

Carl knew the guy would fold under questioning for sure—or give his name up to make a deal with the DA. The police hadn't come knocking on his door yet, so maybe he was safe, but he couldn't afford to leave anything to chance. Hiring someone to commit arson wasn't a capital crime, but once the cops started digging, well . . . they'd find plenty from his past. Enough to put him away for life or worse.

He needed to shut this woman up. Thanks to John's inadvertent reconnaissance, he knew her name. Logan. Logan McKenna was the woman who stuck her head out that door when her dog barked and looked out toward the barn—sealing her own fate.

Carl opened his laptop and clicked on history in the menu bar. He had Googled her name yesterday after John showed him the news report. The first hit was a local events calendar.

Pianist Michael Dane will be performing as usual at Gracie's Sea Hag in Depoe Bay from 6:00 to 9:00 p.m. Saturday night, April 13. Joining him will be local musician, Logan McKenna.

There was no image of either musician on the calendar, so Carl clicked around some more and found a short music video of a Logan McKenna, surrounded by swirling mist, playing a violin. Taken from behind and to the left, you couldn't see much of her face, just a mass of long, auburn hair falling halfway down her back. A black t-shirt topped form-fitting jeans. Lean arm muscles moved as she played.

He watched the video again. The music was ethereal and sad all at once. Eyes closed, lost in her playing, the woman seemed unaware of her audience.

Carl's pale blue eyes ran over the woman's form. Under other circumstances, he would have stripped off those jeans and nailed her, but now all he wanted to do was kill her. And the sooner the better.

Pulling up Google Maps he plugged in directions to Gracie's Sea Hag in Depoe Bay, and then sat back in his chair. It would be close—he had some things to do—but he'd be ready by tomorrow night.

He was in the mood for a little live music.

49

With everything that had happened this week, Logan almost forgot she was playing at Gracie's tonight. If it hadn't popped up on her phone, she would have missed it completely.

Logan was becoming known in the area and was frequently invited to sit in with local musicians. On performance days, she came in early to help set up. Eli Ritter, the day manager at Gracie's and a talented cook, always made band members a free breakfast. Logan's favorite was the Hangtown Fry, A Sea Hag specialty consisting of a fluffy three-egg omelet with freshly shucked Yaquina Bay oysters, bacon, green onions, homemade hash browns, and a biscuit. He didn't even bother to ask if she wanted to switch out the biscuit for fruit.

Sam came in and Logan nodded while making last-minute adjustments to the mic. The *Sara Lynn* was in for repairs, so Tim was home for a daddy/daughter day with Miss Magnolia. Sam gave Eli her order. He waved away her offer to pay, so she sat at one of the tables in the lounge and pulled out her computer.

A few minutes later, Logan joined her. She and Sam had a lot of information to sift through and time was not their friend. Every second this case went unsolved was torture for Oletta and her family. While Sam got set up, Logan finished with the mic, then gave Oletta a quick call to see how she was doing. She caught her just before she left on a trail ride with Reign.

Now that the word was out that a murder had occurred at the camp, Oletta said their Adventurous K9 business had all but dried up.

"Even that obnoxious realtor doesn't call anymore. The buyer must have lost interest. Not that we ever want to sell, but I couldn't give this place away now."

Logan wanted to know if she had savings to fall back on or other sources of income, but felt it was inappropriate to ask. People were more private about their finances than their sex lives. She let Oletta take the lead.

"We'll be okay for a while," Oletta said. "We've got some savings. I had to cut back Keegan's hours, though. I hated to do that, but hopefully he'll be okay. He told me last week he picked up some extra work. A one-time job, but it was going to pay well and the guy even paid him in advance."

They disconnected as Oletta was about to lose cell service on the trail. Logan felt somewhat better, but she knew from her own lean days after Jack died, that savings only lasted so long. And of course, Oletta was still in the cops' crosshairs.

Logan knew how this worked. The DA wanted convictions. Unless she and Sam could find the real killer, the police would patiently build a case against Oletta, brick by brick, making the facts fit if necessary. She respected Monson, but by the very nature of his job he had tunnel vision on this, she was sure.

The restaurant side of Gracie's was open and hopping with customers, but the lounge was still fairly empty. Once they had hot coffee in front of them, Logan and Sam got to work.

"Okay," Sam said, "What do we know?"

First, Logan filled Sam in on what she had learned from Oletta's friends at Fisher's. It had been too late to give her a call last night.

"They are adamant Oletta could not have done this," Logan said. "And nobody's crying over Gloria being killed, either."

She told her Jan's story about the incident years ago in Arizona—the rodeo queen's horse trailer being torched and her horse mutilated and left to die. They were almost certain Gloria was guilty, although she'd never been charged.

"Where was that?" Sam asked. "And what year?"

"I think she said late eighties, maybe early nineties?" Logan said. "Gloria was high school age. It was on the southern border, near a military base. Sierra Vista, I think."

"I'll find it," Sam said.

Next Logan told her about Monson and Grant showing up at Oletta's with a search warrant for Lane's gun and Oletta's subsequent field trip to the jail. Luckily, Witcomb had agreed to take Oletta's case if she was arrested, but Monson got in at least twenty minutes of questioning before he could get there and put a stop to that.

"Who knows what Oletta had said before he got there," Sam said.

Since Oletta was not under arrest, she left and was now at home, although until they could clear her name, she'd have a shadow of suspicion hanging over her and her business. The story of her connection to Gloria, the murder victim, was already circulating.

The thought of the real killer getting away with murder and blaming it on her friend lit a fire in Logan. More than ever she wanted—no needed—to find the truth. She tried to think back. What was it Oletta said? Something about . . . damn! It was right there, but now it was gone. Maybe it would come to her later. For now, she'd follow the threads she could remember.

"Let's focus on Gloria," Logan said. "Somebody killed her. Lots of people disliked her, but we need to find out who hated her enough to murder her. We've got to get back to learning more about her. Who she was."

The server brought them their food and refilled their coffee. Sam moved her computer over, then doused her pancakes in marionberry syrup and dug in.

"Well," she said, between mouthfuls, "I have a good candidate for you. This turned up in my data dive. Well, actually Huey's."

50

Sam was good, but she was a baby hacker compared to Huey Nguyen.

Huey was the computer guru for the New School in the Dundee Hills area. Logan met him a few years ago when he helped her implement and refine *Fractals*, a music/math program she had created and directed before her music career took off. She had become friends with him and his sister, Than, a talented chef in Portland. They got together whenever she was in town, often at *Vietnam Pearl*, Than's restaurant in Old Town.

Huey could hack into anything. Often not legally. But that was okay. Whatever Huey found out, Logan would pass along to Mike Witcomb or the police, who could officially subpoena the records. It just had to be done carefully, so as not to point the finger back at Huey.

Huey only used his powers for good and Logan always protected her friends. When she was younger, Logan was a dot your i's and cross your t's kind of girl. Later in life she learned that rule-following was not always the best measure of morality.

"I'm listening," Logan said, feeling hopeful for the first time since all this happened. "Shoot."

"Well," Sam said. "I hope you don't mind, but I thought we could use Huey's help."

Her mouth full, Logan gave her the 'hurry-up-get-on-with-it' rolling hand signal.

"Gloria has an ex-husband," Sam said, pushing her glasses up on her nose. "An angry one. Mark Ott."

Logan gave her two thumbs up. This was great news!

"Yeah," Sam said, "Gloria wasn't particularly tech savvy, but somewhere along the line she synched her phone and laptop, so all her emails were saved to the cloud. No physical computer necessary to access it."

Logan wondered if the cops had this information yet. It depended on how strict a rule-follower Monson was.

"The emails started a few weeks ago," Sam said, "Huey found a slew of them between him and Gloria. It's all in here. Basically, they're arguing over the property where Gloria lived out in Philomath. She and Mark married in 2012, then divorced almost eight years ago in December of 2016. They owned that property together. Mark moved out, but Gloria got the house— or the right to live there until it sold. She was supposed to sell it and split the profit with him, but never did. She claimed she tried, but there were no buyers. He didn't believe her."

"Couldn't he get a court order or something to force her to sell? Eight years is a long time," Logan said, gesturing with her fork. "Why did he wait until now to fight about it?"

A couple of men came in and sat at the bar. Logan wondered if they served alcohol this early. Probably. People ordered Mimosas and Bloody Mary's with their Sunday brunch. Why not whiskey or a shot of tequila with your eggs? Funny how some drinks were more socially acceptable than others.

Logan pulled her ADHD mind back to what Sam was saying.

"Well, he may have tried, the emails don't go back that far. And maybe he couldn't afford a lawyer," Sam said. "Or just didn't need the money until now."

"So what were the emails about?" Logan asked.

Sam angled her screen so Logan could scroll through and read them herself. While Logan read, Sam finished her pancakes.

When she was finished, Logan looked up, incredulous.

"The police should have this! Why are they hassling Oletta when they have an ex-husband to investigate?" She pushed the computer back to Sam, "Mark Ott is one angry man."

"From what I can gather in the emails, his patience was used up," Sam said. "Looks like he was threatening to force her to sell."

"Which begs the question of what he means by force. Was he unhappy enough to kill Gloria for it?" Logan asked. "It's not a huge property; it can't be worth that much, right? And they were only married a few years, couldn't have had much equity in it."

She tapped her phone and dialed Huey. He picked up on the second ring.

"Huey, it's me, Logan," she said. "Thanks for Gloria's emails . . . could you do me one more favor?"

She waited while Huey said yes.

"Could you find out if Gloria and Mark's names were still both on the deed for that property—the land and house where Gloria lived? If she died would he automatically get it? . . . see if either of them had a will. No, I don't think they had any kids . . . but they may have had some from previous marriages or kids outside of marriage, I guess.

"Also, I want to know if there were any domestic violence callouts on this guy? Did he ever come after Gloria physically or threaten to? Were the police ever called out to their house? Some of these emails are pretty nasty, but I'd like to know if he ever did more than yell. Something concrete I can take to Witcomb. Maybe he can get the police to focus on someone else besides Oletta."

Logan listened and then wrapped up the call.

"Thanks, Huey," she said. "I owe you one."

Logan offered to pay her debt with a homecooked meal, but Huey politely declined. He'd had Logan's cooking before.

Fifteen minutes later, Huey called back.

That was fast.

"Still checking on the deed and if Gloria had any kids, but I did find a restraining order. 2016. Gloria got a restraining order on him in December. Several domestics the previous year. They divorced a year later. I'll send over the details and his current contact information."

Logan thanked him and disconnected. When the text came through, she saved Ott's information and before she could change her mind, dialed his number.

As she waited for him to answer, she tapped her foot, a sudden surge of impatience filling her body. They needed to find something soon, before the police stacked up enough circumstantial evidence to arrest Oletta, or someone trying to protect her.

<h1 style="text-align:center">51</h1>

Mark Ott's voicemail was direct and to the point.

If you got this recording, I'm either at work or on the can. Leave a message and I'll get back to you.

He didn't sound like an angry killer. Logan left a short message.

A few hours later, her phone rang.

"Hi Mark," Logan said. "Thanks for returning my call."

"Sure," he said. "I don't recognize your name. You said this was about Gloria. Are you with her divorce attorney's office or the bank? "

"Neither one," Logan said. "I didn't know Gloria, just knew of her through a friend."

"Didn't?" he said.

Logan hesitated, then said, "I gather you haven't heard the news."

"What news?" he asked. "I've been working double shifts this week. And I never watch the news. It's all garbage, anyway. What's going on? Why are you calling me about Gloria? Are you thinking of buying the property? I can answer any questions you have about it. It needs a new roof, but we can give you an allowance on that."

"No," Logan said, "that's not it. I am sorry to have to tell you this, but Gloria's dead."

There was silence on the other end of the line, then Mark let out a loud Whoop! Logan held the phone away from her ear.

"Woohoo!" Mark crowed. "Finally! How'd the witch die?"

"She was shot," Logan informed him. "Murdered."

That ought to tone him down.

"What?" he said in a much more sober voice. "When?"

"Sometime very early Wednesday morning, out in Eddyville," Logan said. "I don't know much more than that. The police are still trying to figure out what happened."

"Wow," he said. "I had no idea. Sorry for what I just said, but Gloria and I are divorced. She was giving me a hard time about selling the house . . ."

"That's what I wanted to talk to you about," Logan said, trying to segue smoothly into what she wanted to know.

"I'm sorry, who are you again?" he asked.

"Logan," she said. "Logan McKenna. I'm the one who found her body."

"Oh." He didn't ask for more details.

Maybe because he already knew. Maybe because he was in shock. Even though their recent emails back and forth were angry and sometimes downright hateful, Gloria had been his wife for over five years. They'd probably loved each other once.

Logan only had a few hours before she was due at the Sea Hag for tonight's gig, so she didn't have time to drive out to Philomath to meet Mark in person. It wasn't ideal, but she'd have to have this conversation over the phone.

"Look, Mark," she said. "I know you just got off a long shift. I'll make it quick. I only have a couple of questions."

To her surprise, Mark agreed without asking her what she wanted to know or why. Again—either very confident or still in shock. Either way, she was going for it before he changed his mind.

"Okay," she said. "I know you guys divorced in 2016. Gloria got to stay in the house, but she was supposed to sell the property with the two of you sharing the profits after paying off the loan, is that right?"

"Yeah," Mark said. "But she refused to sell. Said if she did she couldn't afford to buy another piece of land where she could keep her horse. She did trail riding stuff. But it was no longer my job to support her useless horse habit. She wasn't even very good."

"Why now?" Logan asked. "You two divorced years ago. Why wait until now to try to get her to follow through on the sale so you could get your half?"

"Because Gloria's a mess, alright?" he blew out a frustrated breath. "We didn't have a lot of equity in that house, and I didn't need the cash right away, so I didn't push it. But then a few months ago I got a late payment notice on the mortgage, which didn't make sense. Before we split I made every payment on time and as far as I know, she had never been late before.

"I found out from the bank that Gloria hadn't paid the mortgage for over three months! Typical Gloria. I took time off work and went down to the bank to straighten it all out. I showed them the divorce settlement where it clearly spells out that my *ex*-wife was responsible for making those payments, since she is living there, not me, but they told me it didn't matter. My name was still on the deed *and* on the original loan, so if Gloria didn't start paying and they had to foreclose on the property, that would go against *my* credit for up to seven years! Seven years! I finally have enough money saved for a downpayment so I can buy a house of my own and she goes and screws it up."

"I have heard that Gloria could be really difficult to deal with," Logan prompted.

"You don't know the half of it," Mark said, "she ran up credit cards, was a falling down drunk half the time. What I ever saw in that woman . . . well, she was hot when she was younger, I mean . . ."

Logan ignored that and stuck to her mission of trying to get information out of him.

"I heard the cops even got called a few times to your place," Logan said. "Before the divorce. She even got a restraining order on you."

There was dead air on the line as the penny finally dropped.

"What? How do you know about that? You think *I'm* the bad guy?" Mark said. "*That's* why you're asking all these questions? That restraining order was bullshit! BULLSHIT! *Gloria* was the violent one, not me. Gloria attacked *me*, but when I tried to defend myself, she got a tiny scratch on her cheek. The cops took one look at that and threw my ass in jail. I had blood running down my face from a beer bottle she threw at me, but they believed Gloria. They always believe the girl. I have nothing to say to you, I don't need this."

If his phone had been a landline, Logan was sure Mark would have slammed the receiver down in her ear.

The domestics, combined with the restraining order, plus the fact that Gloria was about to ruin his credit for years, gave Mark Ott plenty of motive. With Gloria dead, unless she had children they didn't know about, the house would automatically be Mark's. He could catch up on the mortgage payments, sell it, and be done. Still easier than dealing with Gloria.

But was that enough to push him over the edge and commit murder? And if he did kill her, how did he know she would be at Oletta's that night?

52

Like everyone who was anyone in the Family, Carl kept a go-bag with cash, a passport, and travel visas to Brunei and Vietnam, countries without extradition treaties with the U.S. But he hadn't looked at it in months. He was retired, after all. And, he had to admit, since Astrid died, he'd let a lot of things slide.

When he did finally check it, his passport was out of date. Renewing it online was faster, but you had to know how to navigate the site—upload a new photo, etc. Carl hated dealing with computers, so he'd had John take care of it. He even had John pay extra to put a rush on it. The new one should have arrived by now.

He checked the entry table where John usually put the mail every morning, but it was empty. He checked the mailbox outside, but it was empty, too. It wasn't a holiday. There should at least have been some junk mail.

Then he remembered. John had taken off after lunch for a drive down the coast. Again. Said it relaxed him. Carl knew it was John's afternoon off, but he needed him to do his damn job before he left. What was so great about the coast, anyway? Water, rocks, and a two-lane highway that went nowhere. Not his cup of tea.

Irritated, Carl went up to John's room to see if in his hurry to see the god-damned ocean, he left it there. Logically he knew the mail wouldn't be there, but he needed that passport.

Once he had it in hand, he would sell this big empty barn of a house and all the properties, take the cash and go. Maybe even go first and collect the money later. Nothing was keeping him here after tonight. No Astrid Meadows, all that was gone—all gone to shit.

He had rebuilt before, and he'd do it again. He just had to tie up one loose end, make sure there was no trail for the cops to follow. Then he was out of here.

He opened the door to John's room. Bed made, fresh air and sunshine streamed through the open window. Neat as a pin. He quickly scanned the surfaces of the dresser, nightstand, and small desk. No stack of mail.

Carl cursed under his breath and looked around. Knowing it was probably pointless, he walked over and rifled through the few papers on John's desk, hoping it was there. Nothing. He doubted it would be in the drawers, but irritated, he jerked them open one by one anyway, spilling their contents on the floor.

Then for good measure, he started on the nightstand. That's where he found it.

Not his passport, which of course would never have been in John's room in the first place, but a five-by-seven portrait of Astrid, smiling out at him lovingly from an expensive scrolled, silver frame.

For a second he stared at it, not comprehending. What was John doing with a picture of Astrid?

He searched his brain for all possible explanations. Had he stolen it, or had she given it to him? They were always laughing and talking in the kitchen. Had John had an affair with her right under his nose? Carl's blood pressure slowly began to rise, then he thought again.

No. John wasn't stupid. He wouldn't have risked that. Carl would have had him killed. No, this didn't look like a stash of forbidden memorabilia from a torrid affair. He checked all the drawers in the room and under the mattress—anyplace he may have hidden anything, but he came up empty.

No nudie shots, no notes, no love letters. He flipped the photograph over. Not signed. No, Astrid hadn't given it to him. He recognized the portrait. It was one Astrid had taken before she started her chemo, before her hair fell out. John dealt with the portrait studio. He must have kept an extra copy and had it framed. This was a one-way crush. What a sap. Still, John needed to pay. Those were the rules.

Carl carefully put everything back as it was and did the same with the contents of the desk drawers. By the time he exited the room, quietly closing the door behind him, Carl knew exactly how he would pay back his trusted employee's disloyalty.

Johnny boy, you fell in love with the wrong man's wife.

7:00 P.M.

GRACIE'S SEA HAG LOUNGE

DEPOE BAY

Carl entered the bar and let his eyes adjust after being outside in the bright sun. It was early, but the place was already hopping. The Hawaiian piano player was delivering up Boomer standards that went down well with the crowd, mostly tourists with a sprinkling of working-class stiffs. Spotting an empty stool, Carl took a seat at the bar and ordered a double whiskey, neat. He didn't bother asking for Macallan's. This place didn't look like it had anything better than Jameson's.

He sat in the shadows, even though he knew that with the spotlights on them, the two performers probably couldn't see beyond the first few tables in front of the stage. No sense risking it.

From his seat at the bar, Carl had a good view, but he wasn't here for the music. The woman he'd come for was standing to the right of the piano on the small stage, in front of a microphone, her violin down at her side. She was smiling at the pianist, letting him do his thing, waiting for her cue to come in. Carl allowed his gaze to travel slowly down her body and back up again. Such a lovely neck. White and creamy.

She was every bit as striking as she was in that YouTube video. Five eight or nine, tight body. He wanted in the worst way to wrap his fingers around that neck. But that wasn't the plan.

Over the last twenty-four hours, he'd done his homework, scripted his moves. He knew where she lived, what car she drove, and from one of the dishwashers who didn't realize why he wanted to know, the crucial bit of information—that she often walked home after a gig instead of driving. And Logan McKenna only lived a few blocks away.

Perfect.

All he had to do now was sit back and enjoy the show.

Carl watched as Logan tapped her foot and raised her violin, tucking it under her chin, holding her bow at the ready. Hard to believe this one puny woman could take him down, but on the plus side, she had no idea who she was dealing with.

It felt good to be back in control. He remembered Jersey when the families were still in charge—the power they'd had— lords of the neighborhood, the city, hell, the whole damn state!

The bartender set his drink in front of him—sooner than he'd expected, given the crowd. He took a sip. Not bad. It wasn't Macallan's, but it went down smooth.

As Logan began to play, Carl thought back to this morning, when he made the discovery of John's infatuation with his wife, the discovery that required a slight adjustment to his plans—one that included a very satisfying twist of revenge. John hadn't suspected a thing when he asked to borrow his car tonight. Carl's Porsche was always in the shop. Such a temperamental beast.

53

Logan arrived at the Sea Hag early and offered to help Michael set up, but he joked that he'd been doing this for so long, he could do it in the dark. Which, of course, was exactly how Michael did everything. Michael was blind—had been since the age of eight. But that hadn't kept him from enjoying a long and successful music career.

After going over the set, they started right on time. Sitting in with the silver-haired Hawaiian was fun, as always. He knew his audience and played many of the old standards, segueing smoothly between numbers, talking with the crowd. Tourists returned to see him every year and local fans ranged in age from young fishermen to old geezers. That night, one of his loyal followers was celebrating his ninetieth trip around the sun with a cold beer, tuna melt, and fries. Michael had everyone join in to sing him Happy Birthday.

Several men offered to buy her drinks during the night and on her break, but all took rejection in good-natured stride. Clary, the owner, didn't allow obnoxious drunks. No one hassled her.

At the end of the gig, after tucking Bella back into her case, she joined the night cook and some of the servers for a drink at the bar. It took a while to unwind after a performance, even a small venue like this.

Around nine-thirty she said her goodbyes and let herself out the back door, waving at the kitchen crew as she passed. Clouds of steam rolled out the open screen door, which was propped open with a metal mop bucket. The unmistakable smell of commercial floor cleaner common to every food establishment she'd ever worked in, wafted up from the soapy water.

White aprons tied around their waists, the two remaining dishwashers and the manager turned the music up loud. Razzing each other, they danced across the wet floor, scrubbing, wiping down every surface, putting the kitchen back to rights.

There is beauty in honest labor, she thought.

Only three cars were left in the parking lot. It was dark and the moon had not yet risen. One of the servers offered her a ride. She thanked her, but said it was a nice night, she preferred to walk.

Like any woman walking alone in the twenty-first century, Logan automatically scanned the parking lot. Nothing unusual popped out. No one hiding behind the hedges or lurking in the shadows. After exiting on SW Conway, she headed toward Collins, planning to zigzag over to Williams Ave. From there it was a straight shot home. Streetlights were intermittent and the east side of the street was thick with the typical Oregon coast mix of salal, ferns, blackberry brambles, and ivy. She used the flashlight on her phone as needed, where the shadows were too deep to walk safely.

She was only a couple of blocks away when she spotted Ben up ahead, walking toward her, Dixon on a lead. She had to smile. He did this every time. And every time he pretended it was a coincidence. No, he wasn't being overprotective, he just *happened* to be taking Dixon for a late-night potty walk about the time he expected her to be walking home. Whatever his reason, she was always happy to see him. The man was a gem.

LOOK AGAIN

With only a few houses nearby to lend ambient light, she picked up her pace. She could see Ben, but he probably couldn't see her yet.

Suddenly, she saw Dixon yank his lead out of Ben's hand and bolt toward her. Growling and barking, he shot right past her, his leash trailing wildly behind him. Confused, she turned, trying to grab the end of the lead, wondering what he was going after. Must be a deer or something, she thought.

She turned to look. Not a deer.

A man. He must have been right behind her, but now he was running for his car, Dixon snapping at his heels.

She tried to make good observations—height, weight, what he was wearing, but she only saw him from the back and only for a few seconds. It all happened too fast.

When the man got to his car, he yanked open the door and launched himself into the driver's seat, kicking savagely at Dixon as he did so. Blocked by the car door, Logan couldn't see what was happening, but there was a flurry of motion, then Dixon let out a sharp yelp and landed on the pavement.

The car door slammed, and the man gunned the engine and peeled out, leaving a furious Dixon behind, barking his head off. Dixon started to chase after the car, but Logan called him back.

By the time she remembered the mini flashlight in her pocket—the one Ben insisted she carry in every jacket—flicking it on and aiming it at the receding vehicle, the car had already rounded the corner. She couldn't make out much of the license plate.

She would have taken off after the car herself and tried again, but just then her very out-of-breath and worried husband arrived and took her in his arms.

It was over almost as fast as it began. Although shaking with adrenaline and licking his lips, Dixon came immediately to her side when called and stayed in a sit while she checked him for injuries. Nothing seemed to be broken, but there were some flecks of what might have been blood around the right side of his mouth.

Once he knew they were okay, Ben wanted to call the police, but Logan talked him out of it. Tonight's events could just as easily be interpreted as Dixon being a crazy, out of control rescue dog attacking an innocent stranger vs a complete stranger coming after her for no reason at all. Ben finally relented and hustled everyone home. They kept a sharp lookout all the way back in case the car returned, but the rest of the walk was uneventful.

If Ben had seen the flash of metal in the man's hand, he'd never have let Logan out of his sight. It might have been a gun, but it could have been a phone. Until she was sure, she wasn't about to call the police or worry Ben any more than he already was.

54

Looking past Dixon to a rolling wave, glistening jade green in the morning sun, Logan went over it all in her mind again.

Had the man been following her, or did he just happen to be walking down the street minding his own business when Dixon came after him? But then why did Dixon attack and maybe even bite him? And if he did bite him, why didn't the man stop and demand to know if the dog was current on his rabies shots? Or get their contact information so he could send them the doctor bill?

If he was innocent, why had he run away?

That was not normal behavior.

And why didn't the dome light come on inside the car when he opened his door?

No matter how hard she thought, she came back to the same two questions:

Who was this guy and why had Dixon gone after him? Dixon had never shown aggression to anyone before.

She may not know the why, but she knew who might be able to help her with the who. Keeping an eye on Dixon, she called Sam. Cell reception was iffy, but they could hear each other okay.

After filling her in, Logan gave her a description of the car—sedan, four-door, dark—she wished she was better with cars—and as much of the license plate number as she had seen as he rounded the corner, speeding away. She started with the general and worked her way to the specifics.

"It wasn't an Oregon plate. Oregon plates are kind of light colored with a fir tree in the middle. At least ours are. This one was yellow with black letters and numbers. C57 then a squiggle and some other letters or numbers—he had turned the corner by then and I missed the rest. I think there was also some writing on the bottom."

"Are you sure it was yellow with black letters and not the other way around?" Sam asked. "California has yellow and black. There are a lot of Californians up here," Sam said with a little snark in her tone, forgetting that Logan and Ben were from California, too.

Californians were sometimes resented by the locals for moving here and snapping up all the real estate. A Californian could sell their high-priced house there, then pay cash for one here, often over what the seller was asking, pricing native Oregonians out of the market.

"No," Logan said. "I'm sure. It was definitely yellow with black letters."

There was a second or two of silence, then Sam said, "Got it. New Jersey. They're the only state with that color pattern for their plates."

"New Jersey?" Logan said. "If he was a tourist, that was a long road trip."

Logan stood up and called Dixon over. It was Sunday, so Sam wouldn't be able to get her contact at Newport PD to track this down for her until tomorrow, but she promised to call Logan as soon as she had anything. She'd also try Huey.

Before Logan could hook Dixon up for the return run, her phone rang.

Even Sam wasn't that fast.

Logan glanced at the screen and smiled. It was a Facetime call from Amy. She tapped the phone and Ian's happy face filled the screen, then the view jerked up toward the ceiling—Ian hadn't refined his Facetiming skills yet. Logan's mood immediately lightened. It looked like her five-year-old grandson was in an airport.

That's right. Amy and Ian were flying up from Orange County to meet Liam in Portland. Their flights were within an hour of each other, then they were all catching a flight to the Big Island of Hawaii for a family vacation. Liam, a marine botanist, had been up on a kelp restoration project in Alaska, and Amy was taking some time off from the Sea Otter and Marine Mammal Rescue Center back in Jasper, CA, where they lived.

Ian was holding the phone, jumping up and down, shouting, " . . . amma Logan! Gamma Logan! We're coming to see you!"

Laughing, Amy leaned in so her mom could see her face, "Well, only if Grandma is going to be home, Ian. Are you going to be around, Mom? We're thinking of making a quick trip out to the coast."

"Of course," she said. "I would love to see you! But I thought you were on your way to Hawaii. What happened?"

"It's a long story, but Liam's flight was delayed, and he had to reschedule. We have to head back tomorrow afternoon to catch an evening flight but thought we would come see you guys for the day if you're up for a last-minute, whirlwind visit."

"Absolutely!" Logan said. "What time can you get here? Ben's making brunch. I'm sure there'll be plenty."

Uber now came all the way out to the coast, so Amy said they didn't have to take the shuttle and could be there in two and a half hours.

"Perfect!" Logan said. "We can even fit in a trip to the aquarium this afternoon if you want. They just finished the remodel, and they have a new octopus. Ian would love it and I've been wanting to see the new Ring of Fire exhibit anyway."

They disconnected so Amy could get on the road and Logan grinned at Dixon, "Guess who's coming to visit, Dix? Ian and Amy! Yeah! Race you home!"

This is just what she needed. Tomorrow she'd meet Sam, and they'd tackle the case again, but right now, she could use some family time. Working on this case, wading through the dark side of human nature—all the ways humans could hurt each other—affected her psyche more than she liked to admit. For the rest of the day, she intended to surround herself with goodness and light.

Besides, sometimes to solve a problem, you need to get away from it.

55

While she waited for Amy and Ian to arrive, Logan made up the bed in the guest bedroom and ran to Chester's for kid food for Ian—mac and cheese, yogurt, apples, and strangely enough, prosciutto and melon. Ben made some once for the grown-ups, and Ian had polished off most of the tray himself. It helped that each bite was secured by a toothpick, which made eating them more fun.

She still had an hour to kill before they got there, so she lifted Bella out of her case and ran through some Scottish lullabies. The lilting melodies in a minor key brought back warm memories of her playing Amy to sleep when she was Ian's age. She always asked for the one about the Silkie of Sule Skerry.

Logan was lost in the music when the phone rang. It was Sam and she had news.

"Don't ask me how," she said, "but I dug up a couple of things. You got a minute?"

Logan explained that the kids were coming soon, but until then, yes, she was all hers.

"Okay, I'll be quick," Sam said. "First, the car. It's a 2017 Honda Accord registered to a John Carter, 798 Fordam Road."

Logan was disappointed. She didn't know any John Carter and had no idea where Fordam Road was. She was sure the man had been following her, but it must have just been a coincidence. Why would a complete stranger be following her?

She was about to tell Sam she'd call her back after the aquarium, when Sam said, "Guess who lives next door?"

"Wait—how did you get his address from Jersey plates?" Logan asked.

"He has Oregon plates, just hasn't put them on yet," Sam said.

"Oh, okay," Logan said, "So who does he live next door to?"

"Oletta and Lane," Sam said. "Fordam Road is in Eddyville, comes off Highway 20 and curves around behind their property. Not exactly next door, but they share a property line. I've got a plot map. There's a house on that lot, but it's on the other side of the trails and pond on Oletta's property. Doesn't look like they would be able to see each other's houses."

This made no sense at all, but it must be related; Logan just couldn't see how.

"Wait," Sam said. "Don't hang up yet. I'm also sending you John Carter's driver's license photo, see if it looks like the guy you saw last night. Do you recognize him at all?"

Logan put Bella back in her case and pulled out her computer. Sam's emails had just come in. She opened the one with the photo.

"Oh!" she said. "I have seen this guy, but only from a distance. He's almost always at the Farmer's Market in Newport when we go. I've never met him, but I'm pretty sure that's him. The white ponytail and all."

There was silence on the line as she racked her brain for any interaction she may have had with this man. She'd have to ask Oletta and Lane if they knew him and if he knew Gloria in any way.

LOOK AGAIN

Just then Logan heard crunching gravel as Amy's Uber pulled into the driveway and a few seconds later, Ian's excited chatter as he burst in the front door, looking for her.

"Kids are here, Sam," she said. "Thanks for getting me this information. I'll try to figure out who this guy is. We'll wear Ian out this afternoon, so hopefully he'll sleep in with his mom tomorrow. I'll call you back as soon as I can."

"Okay," Sam said, "I'm sending the plot map over now."

Logan promised she'd look at it and hung up just in time to brace herself for Ian's full bore frontal attack, leaping into her arms. Gathering him in close to her, she hugged him tight. God, she loved this little guy.

After brunch, which Ben made sure included honeydew melon wrapped in prosciutto slices, each chunk secured with a fancy toothpick—Ian liked the red ones—the four of them headed to the Oregon Coast Aquarium in Newport. The parking lot was full, but not packed, so they found a spot near the front and walked in.

Amy immediately noticed the beautiful new signage at the entry. White letters stood out crisply from rich jewel tones of royal blue and teal—an abstract wave pattern in the background. It practically glowed. Ben took several pictures of Amy, Logan, and Ian together in front of it.

They continued down the entrance walkway, which was paved in large part with memorial bricks. Most were tributes to spouses, parents, or grandparents who had lived long lives.

When they stopped to take a picture of Ian near a burbling stream where the path curved, the inscription on one of the bricks caught Logan's eye.

David Arthur Braun 1978—2022
Forever Loved

Only forty-four. She wondered what the story was behind that one.

Once inside, Logan pulled up the map of the exhibits on her phone. They caught the tail end of the Pelican Stage demonstration, then wandered through the seals and sea lions exhibits and Seabird Aviary until the next Sea Otter Feeding at 1:00 p.m.

The aquarium currently had three playful sea otters, Sadie, Sawyer, and Wilson. Ian pressed his nose against the glass so he could see the creatures better. While putting the otters through their paces, tossing shellfish as rewards, the docent shared interesting sea otter facts and history.

Beginning in the mid-1700s, the fur trade decimated the population of sea otters on the West Coast of America from hundreds of thousands to less than a hundred. Currently there was a stable population of about 3,000 in Monterey, California. Now and then, one or two lone males were spotted in Oregon, possibly searching for food or mates. The lucky few who survived sometimes found a home at an aquarium like this one. And no, you couldn't keep one as a pet. They were wild animals and very expensive to maintain, eating about $14,000 in shellfish every year!

Next up were the interior galleries, including the touch pool in the Rocky Coast gallery and the one housing the new octopus, the Ring of Fire, which Logan couldn't wait for Ian to see. Ian was fascinated with all wild animals, particularly owls, ever since his visit to the Raptor Center in Eugene, Oregon where Logan still volunteered when she could.

After poking and prodding a bit harder than he should—*"Gently, Ian, gently"*—at the brightly colored sea anemones, sea stars, and urchins in the touch pool, Ian wanted to know where the octopus was.

Logan informed him that Bunsen was not in the touch pool, but in her own special tank replicating her home in the ocean. In her photo the octopus was clearly visible, but Logan explained Ian may have to look several times before finding her, because she was very good at hiding.

56

The almost floor-to-ceiling viewing glass was tucked into a corner, away from the main flow of foot traffic. On the left, a colorful display board and bilingual video shared a plethora of facts about these mysterious creatures. Ian ignored the video and ran to the glass instead, pressing his nose against the cold surface, hunting for Bunsen.

The exhibit was set into a corner of the room. All but the front sheet of glass was lined with dark rock, mimicking her natural environment.

"Where is she?" Ian demanded. "I don't see her! You said her arms were so big they could wrap around a car, but she's not in there!"

Logan scanned the tank, hoping to find the wily cephalopod for him. This trip had been her idea. Grandma better deliver.

A docent nearby smiled at the child's insistence and came over to help.

"She likes to hide, doesn't she? Have you looked all the way up and all the way down?" she said.

Ian threw his head back and squinted, almost falling over backward. Logan unobtrusively steadied her grandson with a hand on his back and said, "See anything?"

After a second or two of intense scrutiny, Ian huffed out a sigh, totally dejected as only a five-year-old can be, dramatically dropping his shoulders.

"No, maybe she's taking a nap. Even octopuses get tired," he added, rationalizing his failure.

The docent just smiled and pointed toward the bottom right corner of the tank, just above where the rock met the glass. Logan stared where the docent was pointing and suddenly the outline of the octopus became clear, her shape forming right before her, emerging from the rock in all her three-dimensional glory, without ever having moved. Pressed against the wall, several of her tentacles stretched up and out, some curled beneath her. Her skin was an exact match, the same color and texture as the rough, speckled rock. Perfectly camouflaged.

Logan leaned down and whispered in her grandson's ear.

"Look again, Ian," she said. "Look again!"

Ian followed her gaze and when the shape of the octopus formed for him, his eyes lit up and he shouted, "There she is! I found her! I found her!"

Several other children came over to see what he was shouting about, and he proudly pointed the magnificent creature out to them, patiently instructing them in the finer points of octopus identification.

All in all, the aquarium was a hit.

Exhausted and happy, after visiting the gift shop for a stuffed octopus to take home, they piled into the car and headed back to Depoe Bay. When they got home, Amy decided a nap was in order and for once, Ian didn't argue. Logan helped them settle into the guest room. Since they had eaten a snack at the aquarium just before they came home, Ben said a late dinner would work fine. That gave them time for one more coastal adventure before dark. Ian voted for owl hunting in the forest.

While everyone else napped, Logan took her computer into the living room and opened her email. She wanted to look at the photo Sam sent her of this John guy to see if she could remember if she had ever met him. She also wanted to see where Oletta's lot connected with his in the back. Maybe they had fought over lot lines or water rights or who knows what. He had to be connected to all this somehow.

She knew how heated property disputes could become, but Oletta hadn't mentioned any problems with neighbors. Certainly none that would result in murder. Still, she needed to follow whatever leads she had. She downloaded the man's driver's license photo, then zipped Oletta a quick email, attaching her neighbor's picture. Maybe she would know how he tied into all this.

Next, she opened Sam's second email and downloaded the plot map. Sam had included sales history for the surrounding properties, which included prices for each sale date. Enlarging the image so it filled her screen, she took a closer look. As Sam had said, plots 42 and 79 (the lots matching the Hartley's and John Carter's addresses respectively) connected just beyond the pond. Buffered by a few acres of undeveloped land criss-crossed with trails, brush, and trees, where Logan and Oletta had enjoyed their trail ride before all this happened. Hard to believe that was less than a week ago.

She tried holding her laptop at arm's length, then pulling it back in, hoping different perspectives would help.

Nothing.

She looked again and there it was! Just like the octopus at the aquarium, a vague shape materialized right in front of her eyes. She didn't know what it meant yet, but excited, she printed out the map.

Forgetting that her daughter and grandson were down for naps, Logan yelled, "Amy! Did you bring Ian's colored pencils?"

A few minutes later, with a newly awake Ian parked at the kitchen table creating octopus masterpieces, Logan had Amy open Sam's email and read her the plot numbers of all properties that had sale dates within the last three years, then colored in those that abutted Oletta and Lane's land with Ian's 'pumpkin' pencil. Since he didn't need orange for his octopus, he generously shared.

Wow.

Once those lots were colored in, it was obvious. An island of white in a sea of orange, Oletta and Lane's place was surrounded.

She checked the history of the adjacent properties again. Prior to recent sales, these properties hadn't changed hands in years. So why now? She looked at the sale prices again. Most had sold at or above market value. That might explain it. She and Ben had bought their place just a few years ago, and they had looked at surrounding towns as well as the coast, so she was very familiar with the real estate market around here.

But what did it mean? Had John Carter bought up all these properties colored in orange? The listings Sam sent didn't include the names of buyers and sellers, so she didn't know. But if he did buy them, why? They weren't special in any way. As far as she knew there were no oil deposits or valuable minerals to mine around here.

She snapped a picture of the map and sent it to Sam. First, she'd see if Sam could do her computer thing and find out if John owned all the orange lots. Then they had to figure out what made Oletta's property worth killing for. Nothing made sense. Gloria had been shot, not Oletta. Even if John wanted that last property, how would killing Gloria have helped him get it?

57

Logan stared at the map a little longer, then briefly scanned Sam's email before logging out. Not much there but Sam had included the original listing for each property, which included bare-bones information like list price, county, taxes, and realtor.

Hmmm . . .

Getting the number from the listing while Amy took Ian for a bathroom break before they left, Logan dialed. This would just take a minute.

A crisp, cheerful voice answered, "Audra Branham of Branham Realty, how can I help you?"

Winging it, Logan introduced herself and asked if she had any rural lots available for sale in the Eddyville area, preferably along Highway 20, with or without houses already on them.

After asking a few pertinent questions to prequalify her prospective buyer, the realtor said, "Yes, there are some parcels available, but I've got to warn you this is a very popular area. They go fast. I've sold quite a few out there."

"What if I offered cash?" Logan said.

"Well, that always helps," Audra said. "But depending on the market there are always holdouts, people get greedy. I've got one now that is still turning down offers, even though the buyer has increased their offer twice already."

Logan managed to get off the phone without making an appointment to go out with the realtor to look at properties. Then Liam called Amy to update her about his new flight schedule, so Logan quickly called Oletta.

First, she told Oletta to pull up her email and take a look at John Carter's driver's license photo. Oletta did, but said she didn't recognize him.

"Who is he?" she asked. "You said his name was John? Do you think he had something to do with Gloria's murder?"

"I'm not sure," Logan said. "Just trying to fit some puzzle pieces together. In the meantime, here's another off-the-wall question. What was the name of that realtor that kept calling and bugging you and Lane to sell?"

"Oh, that was Audra. Audra Branham," Oletta said. "She's one persistent woman, but that's why she's the number one realtor in this area."

Another connection, but Logan still didn't see how it all fit. She promised to fill Oletta in when she knew more. Wishing she had more time, Logan began closing all the windows to log out. She now knew that all of the properties surrounding Oletta and Lane's ten acres had been purchased recently, through the same real estate agent.

Hopefully, Sam would be able to help her fill in that last piece of information—who bought all those places that surrounded Oletta and Lane's property? And why? She would check back later, but for now, she needed to focus on Amy and Ian, who were already at the door, Ian wriggling impatiently as his mom muscled him into his jacket and hat.

"Yes, Ian," Amy said, "You're wearing your beanie. The sun will go down soon, and it gets cold in the forest."

Ben was already in Corvallis with Clay. Their radio group had another dinner/training out there tonight. Since Max was better behaved now, he got to go with the guys. Since Ben wouldn't be home to cook, Logan planned on taking Amy and Ian to Mazatlán for Mexican. They had the best nachos in town.

Stepping outside, Logan stopped briefly to look down the hill and across the highway at the ocean and take a deep breath. She loved this time of day.

Not bothering to lock the door, they headed out for their owl hunt. Both Logan and Amy had their phones in case they should spot one, which was possible. The family of barred owls was back. Logan caught a glimpse of him (or her) last time she and Dixon hiked up the logging trail and Ben saw one in the back yard. Barred owls' territories were large, so it may even have been the same one.

After securing Ian in his car seat and they were all strapped in, Logan backed out of the driveway and headed south. She'd left Dixon behind because he got very excited whenever he saw an owl, raccoon, or deer and this was to be a stealth mission.

About a mile and a half later, she turned off the highway onto an unmarked road. A few yards in, the road widened into a small, ersatz parking lot surrounded by a tangle of blackberry bushes and salal. There were only a couple of cars, so they had plenty of room to park. The road then continued up the hill, disappearing into a dense stand of trees. That's where she'd seen the owl before.

Logan handed a pair of binoculars to Amy, but Ian insisted on carrying them. After adjusting them for Ian's eyes, Logan hung them around his neck and said, "Okay, we're off!"

Reminding Ian to be quiet, they followed the road up the hill. When they entered the forest, the temperature dropped, and they had to wait a minute for their eyes to adjust to the semi-darkness. Logan led the way. Many of the trees had been clear-cut over the years, but this section remained thickly forested. That's why she liked it.

Shadows grew long and animal sentinels warned of the strangers' approach. Douglas squirrels, invisible against the bark of cedars until they were inches away, frantically skittered up trees. Stellar jays scolded, their bright blue forms flitting between branches, leading them ever inward.

Then, amongst the other sounds, came a raucous cawing. Something was happening up ahead, off the path. Logan wasn't sure, but she had a good idea what it was. She motioned for Amy to follow and took Ian's hand.

A few tense minutes later, everyone holding their breath, Logan stopped and pointed straight ahead. About forty yards away, silhouetted against the setting sun, was the very recognizable shape of an owl. It sat perfectly still on a branch at its junction with the trunk. If it hadn't been for the sun sinking behind it on its daily journey to the horizon, they'd never have seen it.

But the owl wasn't the one making all the racket. It was the crows. Five or six of them were mobbing the stalwart creature, who continued to sit very still, ignoring them—or trying to.

Logan helped Ian see it up close with his binoculars. When he did, he shouted, "She's big!"

With that announcement, the owl abruptly swiveled his or her head toward the humans and gracefully lifted from the branch, winging silently away.

Amy managed to snap a picture, but it was so dark, it didn't show much except the amazing wingspan of the raptor in flight.

"Wow!"

58

It was almost eight o'clock, now and the sun was setting, so Logan told Amy she'd look at the owl pics in the car. Right now she wanted to get them all safely back to the parking lot before it got too dark to see.

All the way back to the car, Ian could not stop talking about the owl.

When they arrived, Amy got Ian into his car seat, then patted her pockets. Looking at Logan, she asked, "Did I give you my phone?"

"Nope," Logan said. "Don't think so." She checked her jacket to be sure, then shook her head.

"Damn it!" Amy said. "I must have dropped it. Do you mind watching Ian for a minute while I go find it? It can't be very far in, I had it just a minute ago."

Knowing she was more familiar with the paths than Amy, Logan said she'd go, but if she didn't find it right away, they'd have to come back in the morning. As it was, she doubted she'd be able to see much in the quickly gathering night. But ten minutes later, she emerged victorious from the forest, waving Amy's phone in the air.

"Got it!" she said. "Lucky for you, it was on the main . . ."

Then she saw Amy, one hand on the open car door, holding her head, blood dripping down the right side of her face.

Logan sprinted toward her, catching Amy just as she started to crumple.

"What happened? Where's Ian?!" she said, supporting Amy with one arm, checking her head wound with the other.

Quickly, Logan scanned the back seat, searching for Ian, then answered her own question.

Where her happy, chattering grandson had been just a few minutes ago, was nothing but a gaping hole. The child seat was empty, the seatbelt dangling out to the side.

"He took him!" Amy said. "A man took Ian! He pushed me down and just pulled him out of the car and drove off!"

Breaking away from her mother's arms, Amy started grasping at Logan's coat, stuffing her hands into one pocket after another, "Where are the keys? Where are your keys? We've got to go after them!"

Logan fished her keys out of her inside pocket but kept them in her hand. Steering her frantic daughter into the passenger seat, she tried to gather the facts, "What kind of car was it? What did the man look like?" she asked.

But it was hard to get anything out of Amy, who was dissolving into tears and self-blame.

"How could I let this happen? I was right here!" she wailed.

Logan gripped her daughter's arms and forced her to look in her eyes.

"You've got to focus, Amy. What did he look like? What kind of car was he driving? Think! Did you see anything?"

Amy shook her head, which started the bleeding up again, then scrunched up her face and concentrated.

"Kind of tall . . . older . . . white or maybe silver hair, curling at the collar . . ."

"How tall? Taller than me?" Logan asked.

"I think so, yes, yes, he was tall . . . like Ben tall, but thinner . . ."

"What about the car?"

"The car . . . the car was light gray, maybe dirty white, sports car, two-door . . . . I must have passed out after he knocked me down, then drifted in and out, but I did see him driving off."

So not the same car that followed Logan last night—but the description of the man could fit—she thought he was tall, too. Of course tall, white, or silver-haired men were a dime a dozen on the coast, which had a high percentage of retirees.

"You're doing good, Amy," Logan said, "This will give the cops something to work with. I'll call on the way. Right now, let's get you home."

Gently securing Amy in the car, she grabbed a towel from the back they kept for when they took the dogs to the beach. Not very sanitary, but it would have to do for now. She pressed it against Amy's head and instructed her to hold it there firmly until she could get her home. She'd take her to the ER later if she needed stitches. Right now, she needed to get the cops on this guy's tail and get Ian back.

Logan started the car and threw it into reverse. As she backed out, she grabbed her phone, intending to tap in 911, but it rang before she could. She tried to swipe to reject the call, but accidentally answered it instead.

Ian's voice come through loud and clear. "Mom!" he yelled, but he was quickly silenced.

Stunned, Logan's insides turned to water. She turned off the engine and put the call on speaker, gripping her phone like it was her only lifeline in a category five hurricane. Both women leaned in to hear better.

"Logan McKenna?" a man came on the line. "I assume you recognize this young man's voice."

"You need to bring him back," Logan said, stating the obvious, but she couldn't think of what else to say. "He's just a little boy and his mother is frantic. What do you want? Whatever it is, you can have it. Just bring Ian back."

"Ian!" Amy yelled into the phone.

"Now, now," the man said. "You need to control that daughter of yours, Logan. We don't want any hysterics, now, do we?"

"What do you want?"

"Well, now that you mention it," he said, with what could only be characterized as glee, "I do want something . . . *you*!"

Then his voice became serious again.

"And only you. No cops, no one else. I texted you the address. Come by yourself. And don't try anything, I'll know if you do. And definitely don't bring that hysterical mother with you. We want a clean, quiet exchange. You for little Ian here. Clean. Simple. Do you agree?"

"Yes, yes, whatever you say," Logan said, hushing Amy by squeezing her hand. "But what about Ian? How will we know he will get safely back home?"

"Oh, don't you worry. I've already made arrangements for that," he said. "I'll fill you in when you get here."

59

The man continued his instructions.

"When you arrive, turn off the engine but stay in your car. I'll text you what to do next when I see you are here and determine you are alone. I'll give you one hour," it sounded like he paused to look at the time, then said, "Did you get the text? Read me back the address."

Fumbling with the phone, Logan tapped on the message icon and opened the most recent one from an unknown number.

"798 Fordam Road, Eddyville."

That was John Carter's place, but the man she remembered from the Farmer's market was shorter and stocky, with a long, white-blonde ponytail. This guy was tall and thin. It was a forty-five minute drive to Oletta's place on Highway 20. She didn't know how long it would take her to find Fordam Road. She stalled for time.

"But it's already almost eight-thirty! It's a good forty-five minutes to get out there, even without traffic and I don't know where Fordam Road is."

"Well then, you'd better hurry. If you're not here by nine-thirty . . . well, I'll keep little Ian alive, but the longer you take to get here, well, let's just say he may have to forego piano lessons."

With that parting shot, he disconnected.

Mother and daughter gripped each other's hands, then Logan took charge. Her first responsibility was to see to Amy, take her home, point her toward the medicine cabinet, and convince her to stay put, that this was the only way to keep Ian safe. Given the fact that she was still woozy and bleeding, Amy reluctantly agreed, but said if she didn't hear from her mom by the time Ben got home, she was calling the cops.

Satisfied Amy would stay put for now, Logan checked her car to make sure it had enough gas. It did. Logan dashed back inside and ran upstairs. She needed one more thing. Unlocking the small, metal safe in their closet, she pulled out the small handgun Ben insisted she keep and learn how to use. It was a thirty-two. She knew how to load and point the damned thing, but she fervently wished she'd gone to the gun range more than the one time he took her.

Once in the car, she lay the gun on the passenger seat under her jacket and floored it out of there. She didn't know what she was going to do when she got there, but she felt marginally better with a weapon to even the playing field.

When she reached the outskirts of Newport on Highway 20, she wanted to floor it, but only pressed on the gas as hard as she dared without drawing the attention of the highway patrol. She could afford the tickets, but not the time if she got pulled over. And she wasn't sure what Oregon law was, but she was confident that having a loaded gun loose in the car would be a big no-no and might even result in a free tour of the jail, or at least further delays. No, she'd stay within five miles of the speed limit.

Logan glanced at the illuminated dial on the dash. Eight-fifty-five. She'd used voice commands to call up directions. She could see the map on her phone. There were only two turns off Highway 20. She'd make it by nine-thirty—but just barely—if there were no delays.

While she drove, she tried to focus on what she had learned in the last few days, so she knew what she was up against when she got there.

A car registered to a John Carter on Fordam Road was involved in the incident that occurred when she walked home from her gig at the Sea Hag Saturday night. But the man she'd seen jump in the car and drive away after Dixon went after him did not fit John's description.

John had no connections to Oletta or Gloria that they knew of, other than living in the property that joined Oletta's in the back. This man, the one who had taken Ian, drove a different car and was tall and thin with gray hair only as long as his collar, not hanging down his back, according to Amy.

Did the men live at the same place? Or maybe only John lived there and hired this other guy to come after her and then kidnap Ian.? But why? She kept coming back to that. What reason did anyone have for coming after her?

The only connection she had to any of this was discovering Gloria's body at Oletta's. She never knew Gloria at all. Had they inadvertently pissed off this neighbor on their trail ride in some way? She thought through everything she did. They had seen nothing and no one on the trail except Keegan, who was working that day. They'd had lunch, then dinner with everyone, then played cards, drank a little too much tequila, then went to bed.

Dixon woke her up that night, barking, but when she got up to investigate, there was nothing. Except for the security light out by the front gate on the other side of the arena, it was totally dark. Standing at the top of the short set of stairs outside the trailer door, she looked in the direction of Dixon's attention but couldn't see more than a few feet into the night.

But . . . she realized with a chill . . . with the light from inside the trailer shining brightly behind her, anyone standing near the arena would have been able to see *her* very clearly, including Gloria's killer, even though she could not see them.

She didn't understand the rest of what was going on, but at least this piece of the puzzle made sense. The killer must think she could identify him.

The cars weren't the same, but if that flash of metal she saw in his hand was a gun, that man outside Gracie's Sea Hag wasn't taking an after-dinner stroll and Dixon didn't randomly attack a stranger. Dixon saved her life last night.

And he wasn't giving up. He must have done his own Google search and discovered her home address, staked out the house, waiting for an opportunity. He must have followed them to the logging road and waited until they returned from their hike.

What she didn't understand was why he drove two different cars and why he just didn't shoot her there in the parking lot or even in her driveway. He must have had plenty of opportunities to pick her off. Waving Amy's phone in the air, she made a perfect target. Why kidnap Ian?

Maybe he was just stupid. No, he must have a reason, but his reason didn't matter. What mattered was getting Ian back safely.

Checking for cops, Logan pressed on the gas and inched up the speedometer.

Grandma's comin', Ian, Grandma's comin'!

60

John held the large-bowled, red wine glass up to his nose and took a deep sniff. Satisfied, he took a tentative sip, rolling the fruity pinot noir around in his mouth.

Excellent. He'd have to take a bottle to the owner of the little French bistro he had discovered next time he went to the coast, see if she liked it as well as the cab he took over this morning. Lauren. Wonderful woman. He pictured her now, efficiently waiting on customers, greeting everyone with a bright smile and welcoming spirit. Diminutive, with a headful of springy brown curls that simply radiated energy, he'd rarely seen the little dynamo stand still—or stop talking!

He met her when he stopped in one day to see if she had any good croissants. They got to talking and he'd recommended a Chablis that might go with her limited, but excellent menu offerings. Lately, he had taken to bringing her a different bottle to try whenever he was on the coast, stopping by near the end of her busy times. Sometimes she would take a break and join him at one of the small tables. And sometimes, to extend the conversation, he'd help her prep for lunch.

He realized he missed this, this female companionship. It was what he and Astrid used to do. Looking back, he probably filled that gap for her, as well, giving her conversation and attention Carl never did, in fact, probably couldn't.

Yes, Astrid was safe, but Lauren wasn't. No guard rails there. Lauren wasn't married to a mob guy. Was he willing to act on his feelings and risk a real relationship with her? Was fifty-five too late for love?

A loud noise at the front door broke John's reverie. Carl, making more racket than usual. Must have been a package on the porch and he was wrestling it inside. John sighed and put his glass on the counter. He'd catch hell for that one. It was his job to bring in the mail.

He went to help, but before he got there, Carl entered the kitchen, dragging a wide-eyed, terrified little boy, about five or six years old, still soft with baby fat, with him. White-blonde hair fell across the child's forehead and a wide piece of silver duct tape, one end frayed, was taped tightly across his mouth, encompassing most of his lower face from ear to ear. Tear-filled, sky blue eyes darted from one man to the other.

"We've got company for dinner, John. John, meet Ian. Ian, John. Why don't you whip us up something to eat? This one may not have an appetite, but I'm starving!" Carl announced. Shoving the terrified child roughly by the shoulder into the bench seat by the window, he added, "Keep an eye on our guest here while I make a quick call."

What in the hell?

Carl tapped the front of his phone a couple of times, then put on a big smile, as if whoever he was talking to could see him, but he wasn't on video.

"Logan," he said brightly. "How's your trip coming along? Almost here? . . . Well then you'd better hurry. You've got eight minutes. And don't forget—no cops."

He held the phone away from his ear, then laughed and said, "Such language, Ms. McKenna! My Astrid would never have talked like that."

Tossing his phone on the counter, Carl pointed to the open bottle next to John and said, "Get me a glass of that, why don't you, John, while I go drain the snake. Been sitting in that damned parking lot for hours."

Trying to act as if all this was perfectly normal, John lifted a stemmed red wine glass out of the cupboard and gave Carl a generous pour. The little boy sat stock still, staring at him in fear, fighting tears. He had scootched around to the back of the bench seat, getting as far away from Carl as he could.

When John heard the bathroom door shut, he rushed over to the kid. He didn't dare remove the duct tape, but making what he hoped were comforting sounds and gestures, he whispered, "It will be okay, Ian—it's Ian right?"

Ian nodded.

"Okay, just stay right where you are, okay, Ian? I'm going to figure this out," he said. He read somewhere that repeating someone's name calmed them. He hoped this was true. Carl had said Logan. That was the name of the woman that reporter mentioned had discovered the body at their neighbor's place.

Checking at the door to make sure his boss was still in the bathroom, John picked up Carl's phone and hit redial.

When a woman answered, he whispered, "Hello, Logan? This is John, you don't know me. I don't have much time, but Ian is okay. Yes, I'm looking at him right now. Okay, but talk fast. Carl will be back any minute."

Ever since his unsuccessful prostate surgery, Carl's urine stream barely dribbled out, so John knew he had a couple of minutes. At least he hoped he did. He needed to know what was going on so he could help.

He listened intently as Logan summed up the situation, explaining how Carl had kidnapped Ian at the logging road and was holding him hostage until Logan came.

"Carl kidnapped Ian because he thinks I saw him shoot a woman named Gloria last Friday night. I didn't, but that doesn't matter now. It's my life for Ian's. A straight trade."

"But why kidnap Ian? Why not just shoot you in the parking lot of that logging road?" John asked.

"I don't know, but I am coming to get Ian. Carl said no cops. I am coming alone as instructed."

They whispered back and forth for another thirty seconds, sketching out the beginnings of a rough plan while he rummaged through the kitchen's junk drawer for a minute until he found what he was looking for. He needed an edge. Something to slow Carl down until he could think of something. Then John heard the bathroom door begin to open and he quickly hung up. There was no way Carl was going to let Ian go once he had Logan. He would kill them both. He plopped a small pill into the glass of red wine and hoped for the best.

John signaled Ian to be still and smoothly pushed Carl's glass of red wine toward him by the footed stem as he came into the kitchen.

Carl took a long drink and smacked his lips. "Got any of that lasagna left?" he asked, completely ignoring the fact that there was a terrified child three feet away. "Warm some of that up for me. Be right back."

Not knowing if Carl was still in hearing range, John could only give Ian the universal calming signal with both palms pressing down in the air, then the 'shhh' signal with his finger on his lips. His heart was pounding, but he tried to smile reassuringly while he got the lasagna out of the fridge for his boss and put a plate of it in the microwave to warm it up.

The plan he'd made with Logan had so many holes in it, he doubted it would work, but he had to do something. She'd be here any minute. Logan thought Carl would honor their agreement—a life for a life, but John knew he could not be trusted.

Carl was very capable of killing, but why would he shoot Gloria? Whatever the convoluted reason, John was sure it had something to do with trying to get that property for his horse track. The one he'd named after Astrid. Sacrilege.

The man had to be stopped. Tonight.

Carl reentered the kitchen, holding his gun, making sure it was loaded. When he was satisfied, he unclicked the safety, and gesturing with the barrel, told John to stay and guard the boy, make sure he didn't move.

John's heart sank. Carl had no intention of trading a life for a life. He was going to kill Logan, then come back for the kid and probably him. This was happening too fast. There wasn't going to be time for their plan to work. Even if he could call the cops, they would never get here in time, they lived too far out in the country. They were on their own.

He had to buy some time, but before he could think of anything, both men heard Logan's car pull up outside. With curt instructions to stay where he was, Carl gave John a manic smile and went out to greet his guest.

John racked his brain for some way to stop what was about to happen. He had no gun.

That's when he heard the shot. Louder than he expected. Very loud.

It was too late.

Then Carl sauntered back in, pointing the gun directly at his chef's chest, who had started toward him.

"Where do you think you're going?" he growled.

61

Back in the kitchen, Carl forced John to slide onto the bench seat in the breakfast nook from the right side, joining Ian, keeping his eyes and his gun on both. Carl pulled out the chair on the end, flipping it around to face his captives and straddled it, resting his hand on the back, keeping the gun pointed at John.

"We can't have a murderer running loose on the property, can we, Ian?"

Ian squeezed his eyes shut and buried his head into John's shoulder. John pulled him close, comforting the child as best he could, patting him reassuringly on the back, then leveled his gaze at Carl.

"You didn't have to do this," he said quietly. "She never saw you."

Carl gave John a quizzical look, "What did you say?"

John spoke quietly, "Logan. I talked to her on the phone earlier. She said she never saw you that night. She was no threat to you. She was never any threat to you." A tear rolled down his cheek. "You didn't have to do any of this."

Carl threw his head back and let out a huge laugh. "That wasn't me, you idiot, it was that incompetent Toledo cop. He had one simple job to do—set that barn on fire to soften up those people to sell, but then he goes and shoots someone, bringing way too much law enforcement attention my way.

"I don't care if the McKenna woman saw him or not, she needs to be silenced. And her sacrifice, as it turns out, will not be in vain."

Carl gloated, a big smile on his face. When John didn't ask what he was talking about, he said, "I found your little shrine to Astrid. How sad for you. I thought I'd deal with you later, but then I realized I could kill two birds with one stone! With only a slight change of plans. Listen up, this is what I'm going to tell the cops when they show up.

"Logan wasn't going to testify against Fred for that woman's murder. She saw *you* from her trailer, not him. *You* were the one who shot Gloria. You went out there to set fire to the arena that night, to force the Hartley's to sell, but then Gloria showed up. She just got in the way. Collateral damage."

"But how would getting the Hartleys to sell benefit me? I don't own this place or any of the other properties you bought," he said. "Yes, I know about Astrid Meadows, Carl."

"No, but you knew about the will," Carl said, his eyes glittering. "I'll make sure I leave a copy of it laying around where you could find it. That gave you a reason to be there and kill Gloria, even if it was not your original intent."

"What will?" John asked, thoroughly confused now.

"The one that I now intend to update. It leaves you everything if Astrid and I should both die."

"What?" John said, "that's ridiculous!"

"I agree, but it was Astrid's idea. Near the end I did whatever she wanted. I just wanted to make her happy. We didn't have any kids to leave it to, so she said we should leave it to you. For all your loyal years of service, which we now know were not so loyal, were they, John?

"Of course it would all go to me first, when she died, but if I got hit by a truck or something and you were still living—the will stipulated that you would get everything. You were probably planning on killing me next!

"The chemo made her crazy. I was humoring her, but I fully intended to change it back; I just hadn't got around to it. Now, I'm glad I didn't. Gives you plenty of motive."

John just stared at him, "But . . ."

"Do I have to spell it out for you?" Carl sneered. "We trusted you. I trusted you. I hired you when your restaurant went belly up. Took you into my *home*. Paid you well. You had access to everything . . . including my wife."

He waited for that tidbit to sink in.

John blanched, then said, "Astrid was always faithful to you, Carl. You know that."

"Well, I can't ask her now, can I?" Carl said. "But I think you're right. You were the one who betrayed me, not Astrid. So I've already sprinkled a trail of crumbs for the cops to follow, buddy boy," Carl said. "I took your car last night in case anybody saw me. This was all supposed to be over with last night and it would have been, but that dog came after me."

He grimaced at the large bandage on his left wrist. "Thanks for helping me clean this up this morning by the way. Your nursing skills are excellent!"

John remembered this morning. Carl had told him a stray came into the backyard the night before, right up onto the patio, trying to steal some of his late-night snack, and bit him when he tried to shoo him away. The bite was in an awkward spot, so he hadn't been able to wrap it well. John had helped clean and re-bandage it after breakfast. He'd even felt sorry for the guy!

"Your fingerprints will be all over this gun by the time the police get here. I will tell them you shot Logan so she couldn't identify you, then you turned the gun on this little tyke here— probably just because he's annoying and now he can identify you. And speaking of annoying, you're also going to shoot that dog that's going ballistic in Logan's car."

Carl looked around him, vaguely confused.

"Where was I? Oh, yeah, I come home and save the day! I sneak up on you, wrestle the gun away from you—it goes off in the struggle, putting a stop to your madness, ending this whole bloody mess."

Looking quite pleased with himself, Carl said, "I should write for the movies!"

"Well, no sense waiting around," he added, pushing himself up off the chair.

"Scene one!"

***

Just then, Logan burst into the room, wild-haired, blood streaming down her right side, holding her gun straight out in front of her, keeping it trained on Carl, whose back was to her, even though her arms were shaking.

She had the drop on him, but didn't have a clear shot because Carl, who also had a gun and looked like he was about to use it, stood between her and Ian, who was stuck in the back of the bench seat near the window, John to his right.

Realizing he had company, Carl whirled around to face her, but almost lost his balance. He looked wobbly and kept blinking his eyes, as if trying to get Logan in focus.

Before anyone could decide what to do next, a snarling, snapping, blue and black blur shot past Logan and launched himself at Carl's throat.

A shot rang out, stopping Dixon mid leap. The dog's body jerked once, twisted in the air, then made a sickening thud when it landed.

Channeling his high-school football coach, John, who had been quietly making his way around to the front of the bench seat slid out. Lowering his left shoulder, he plowed into Carl with a loud grunt, putting all of his weight behind the tackle.

Carl's body hit the tile floor hard. Logan kicked his gun away, sending it skittering across the floor. Lying flat on his back, Carl was either knocked out or simply had the wind knocked out of him. Hard to tell. But he wasn't moving. Taking advantage of this, John ran over to the kitchen drawer, rummaged quickly, and pulled out some zip ties.

Putting her gun on the counter out of reach so Carl couldn't use it against her if he came to, Logan quickly knelt down beside him, intending to flip him over so John could secure his hands behind him with the ersatz handcuffs. But just as she tried to roll him over, Carl's eyes snapped open and locked onto her own, piercing her with a laser beam of pure hatred. With surprising speed and force, his left arm shot up and he grabbed her neck, squeezing it in his hand, pressing his thumb into her windpipe, cutting off all but a trickle of breath.

Panicked, Logan scratched and clawed at his fingers, trying to peel them away and free herself. As her vision began to blur, tiny stars danced at the edges of her sight, slowly engulfing her mind. Fighting panic before she lost consciousness, she jammed the heel of her hand upward with all her strength into her attacker's nose.

Blood spurted out and Carl let out a yell, instantly releasing his grip on her throat. Logan sank gratefully to the floor and drew several deep, long breaths as John took over.

Fashioning handcuffs out of the zip ties—he'd picked up a few tips and tricks from living with a mob boss all those years—he secured Carl's hands behind him, stuffing a towel between his almost definitely broken nose and the floor to stop the bleeding.

Surprisingly, Carl put up little resistance. His body had gone slack, and he seemed confused—almost drunk-like. The few words he got out around the blood-soaked towel were slurred and unintelligible.

Exhausted now, Logan tucked her gun inside her jacket pocket—putting on the safety first as Ben had taught her—and rushed over to take her frightened grandson in her arms.

Much crying, kissing, and hugging ensued.

As she was working at the edges of the duct tape to peel it off Ian's mouth gently, she remembered Dixon and was immediately flooded with guilt. Without any concern for his own safety, her dog had fearlessly launched himself into harm's way to protect her—twice in the last two days—and now he lay on the floor, not moving and losing a lot of blood.

While John kept an eye on Carl, Logan sat Ian down, took off her jacket and rolled Dixon carefully into it.

"Don't die, Dixon, please don't die!" she whispered in his ear.

Her first thought was to get him into her car and rush him to a vet, but she realized she had no idea where a vet was in this area. But she did know someone who could help if anyone could. Oletta. And she was just around the corner.

Keeping one hand on Dixon to comfort him and one arm around her grandson, Logan dialed with one hand. Oletta said she'd get her animal med kit and be right over. Next, Logan phoned Amy to let her know Ian was okay.

Then she dialed 911.

She knew Monson would ream her a new one for not calling 911 first, but she didn't care. She couldn't let her loyal dog die or Amy suffer one more second of worry because she was following the rules.

Logan was beyond grateful that Ian was safe, she just hoped Dixon was not beyond saving.

62

Logan woke to blinding light stabbing the backs of her eyeballs. She hadn't had a headache like this since she got wasted with Bonnie back in college. At least this one wasn't accompanied by repeated bouts of obeisance to the porcelain gods.

She gingerly touched the left side of her head. Bandage. Big one. But at least her hair hadn't been shaved off. At least not all of it. Raising her head carefully off the pillow, Logan waited to make sure this motion didn't bring on any waves of nausea. It didn't, so she slowly continued until she was sitting upright on the edge of the bed.

Squinting to block the bright sunlight streaming in her window, she assessed her situation. She was home in her own bedroom. Good so far. Someone had put her to bed in her PJs. Hopefully, Ben. Slipping her arms into a hoodie lying on the chair and her feet into a pair of warm Ugg slippers placed at the foot of the bed, she followed the wonderful smells of bacon and coffee into the kitchen.

She saw her broad-shouldered husband at the stove, easily tossing eggs in a heavy cast-iron pan.

Tears came unbidden to her eyes and threatened to spill over onto her cheeks. These small acts of thoughtful kindness just about undid her. How had she gotten so lucky to have found this wonderful man? Ben had had as little sleep as she'd had last night, but here he was, up early, taking care of her.

She came up behind him and wrapped her arms around his waist. He slid the eggs onto a plate and put down the pan. After returning her embrace, he firmly helped her to a chair at the kitchen table, poured her some coffee, and answered her two unasked questions.

"Kids are still asleep and no news, yet."

She hadn't expected to hear about Dixon yet, but she had hoped. At least the kids were getting some sleep.

It would take much more time for Logan to process the whole nightmare, but for now the caffeine helped her brain sort through at least last night's events.

***

Oletta had arrived with the vet practically on her heels. He had been in the area on another call, so came right over. He'd taken one look at Dixon's bleeding, prostrate form and shook his head. After a quick examination and getting the bleeding stopped, he'd said he could operate, but her dog was already pretty far gone. To be honest, he'd said, Dixon probably wouldn't make it. The decision was up to her whether to operate or not, but she had to decide now. Logan had quickly assented, and he'd whisked Dixon away.

When Logan had called Amy to tell her Ian was okay, Ben had just walked in the door. He must have run every red light and driven ninety miles an hour because his truck hadn't even come to a complete stop before Amy'd jumped out and raced into the house.

When the police and ambulance arrived ten minutes later, the EMTs, Narcan at the ready, made sure the tall, older man they found passed out on the floor hadn't ODed. He hadn't. John explained he'd slipped a roofie into Carl's wine earlier, which was probably why the bullet intended for Logan only grazed her head when Carl shot at her through her car window.

Ironically, the little bottle of Rohypnol in the kitchen drawer was Carl's. He'd said it was for when he had trouble sleeping. John suspected he'd used it for uncooperative female guests after Astrid died, but he'd never caught him at it. He had always kept as far away from Carl's personal life as possible.

Logan had the presence of mind to stay down on the passenger seat where she'd fallen, until Carl went back inside. She had left Dixon in the car but hadn't shut her door tight. Not about to be left behind, Dixon found his way out and followed her into the house.

Earlier, she'd tried to leave Dixon at home when she'd dropped off Amy, but he'd jumped in and refused to budge. Since there was no time to crowbar him out of there, he had come with.

Monson and Grant arrived last.

When Monson saw the EMTs working on Logan, he hadn't even acted surprised. His only comment was, "Oh, you again."

He had not been pleased with the trampled crime scene.

It took hours to straighten everything out and take everyone's statements, but sometime around two o'clock in the morning, Ben helped Amy place a sleeping Ian gently into his car seat and drove everyone home in Logan's car. They would pick up the truck another day. Logan had been in no shape to drive, and Amy wasn't leaving Ian's side for a second.

Logan had taken the passenger seat, which was soaked on one side with blood—hers. There wasn't even a beach towel to throw over the seat because she'd used it earlier for Amy. Maybe they'd have matching head wounds.

As the thought crossed her mind, Logan remembered barking out a sleepy laugh. Ben had given her a sideways look, but she had been too tired to explain.

***

Logan inhaled her bacon and eggs and had another cup of coffee.

When Ian bounced into the kitchen a few minutes later, he looked surprisingly none the worse for wear—in spite of yesterday's ordeal. He was, however, holding his mother's hand and rushed right over to give Logan a hug. Crawling up into her lap, he reached up and touched her bandage, asking if her 'owie' hurt.

"Nope," Logan said, giving him a kiss on the top of his head. "Just a scratch."

Keeping things light as long as Ian was in the room, Logan had him tell Ben all about their trip to the aquarium—the sea stars and anemones in the touch pool and about finding the octopus in her new digs.

"She was hiding, but I looked again and found her!" Ian said.

Watching her grandson chatter away, Logan wished she had the resilience of youth.

Amy had called Liam this morning already and filled him in. They'd moved up the timeline for their Hawaiian vacation. She and Ian were taking an Uber back to Portland this morning to join him, and they would catch the red-eye to Kailua-Kona out of PDX tonight.

After Ben got their bags in the Uber, the driver waited while Ian said his goodbyes to Max, who was almost as tall as he was. Max had no idea what was going on but was just thrilled to have an excuse to wriggle, bark, and distribute doggie kisses to his favorite little human.

63

After waving goodbye to Amy and Ian, both Logan and Ben went back to bed. Leaving her phone on full volume on the nightstand, she was asleep in two seconds and didn't wake up until almost four.

She grabbed her phone to make sure she hadn't missed any calls from the vet. She hadn't, so she decided to give him a call instead. No answer.

She hated waiting.

Maybe he was catching up on sleep, too. He had called early this morning after the surgery and left a message, saying he was able to remove the bullet successfully, but it had done quite a bit of damage as it passed through. They'd just have to wait and see how the patient did.

With nothing to do but wait, Logan gave Sam a call. She already knew about last night from her police scanner and law enforcement contacts, but just the basics. Logan filled her in on the details.

"Wow," Sam said when Logan wrapped it up. "You have the luck of the Irish, girl. You sure you're not a cat? What life are you working on now?"

Logan laughed, as was Sam's intent.

"Oh, and I forgot to tell you," Sam said. "Not that it matters anymore, but Ott's off the hook. His story checks out. One of the neighbors said Gloria was the volatile one in that marriage. Her ex has a steady job and no prior record of violence. His current girlfriend says he's never laid a hand on her."

"Thanks, Sam." Logan said. "You know, I feel bad we had him on the suspect list at all—or any of them."

"Yeah, but any one of those people could have killed Gloria. And most had good reason to."

"Not Keegan," Logan said. "He didn't even know Gloria."

"Oh yeah," Sam said. "That's something else I found out. Major Crimes Team did a lot of digging we didn't know about. They had Keegan on their radar because they found a chunk of money in his bank account, and it came from Carl."

"Wait, what?" said Logan.

"Well, not to kill Gloria, that just happened by accident, like it actually did when Davies went out there, but . . ."

"Wait, wait, start over!" Logan said.

"Okay," Sam said. "My bailiff friend says Carl, the actual owner of the place on Fordam Road, needed Oletta's property in order to build a racetrack he named after his dead wife. That lot was right in the middle. Without it, he couldn't build. And from his own bank records, my source said he needed to get it up and running fairly soon. It would take at least two or three years to build it out if he lived frugally, and Carl did not. He was over extended."

"Okay . . . ," Logan said.

"So we know Carl had been making offers on that land, not John, but Oletta and Lane kept turning the realtor down. They refused to sell."

"Yeah," Logan said, waiting impatiently for Sam to get to the point.

"So once he knew they had him dead to rights, Carl started talking. Bragging, more like it. Said he sent Fred Davies over there that night not to kill Gloria, but to set the arena on fire with the horses in it to force the Hartleys to sell. Gloria surprised Fred and his first reflex was to shoot her to stop her. Reflex—his lawyer is going to try to lessen the charges, but it turns out Davies has been dirty a long time, just never been caught. But this time it's murder, so no plea deal forthcoming."

"Does anyone know what Gloria was doing out there in the middle of the night in the first place?" Logan asked.

"Not specifically," Sam said. "But from past history, and because matches were found in her backpack, they think she was also there to burn down her rival's barn . . . and horses."

"Wow," said Logan.

"To avoid anyone discovering his true role in all this, Davies was focused on trying to put the blame on Keegan. Oletta says he knew about Keegan's troubled past and never let him forget it. In fact, he was the arresting officer when he got caught with drugs when he was a kid, before he turned his life around. With that knowledge, Davies must have thought Keegan made the perfect—and very convenient—scapegoat."

"What about Carl?" Logan said. "Is he going to wiggle out of this?"

"He may have been able to, but not now that the FBI's involved. The DA's office is very confident that with your and John's testimonies as well as a pile of physical evidence, they have enough to go to trial and win, several times over.

"Barbara Bianchi, the FBI agent assigned to the Major Crimes, is gleefully pursuing the leads John Carter provided. They're building multiple cases against Carl—or Carlo, his real name. He was a member of one of the crime families in New Jersey. Once they put him away, Carl's never going to see the outside of a prison again."

Logan digested this information, happy to see Carl get his just desserts, then said, "Speaking of Keegan, how much did Carl pay him and what did he pay him for?"

"To answer the first part of your question, he paid him $12,000," Sam said. "But my contact didn't know what for."

Logan put Sam on hold and called Oletta. She asked if she knew why Carl would pay Keegan $12,000 and if she knew of any work he had done for him."

"Don't know for sure," Oletta said, "but Keegan mentioned decommissioning a septic tank for a neighbor recently," she said. "Said it was a horrible, stinky job. The tank was in an awkward spot, tough to get to, and hadn't been installed properly to begin with. He had to get a buddy with the proper equipment to help, but Keegan took the work because he needed to pay for his daughter's new prosthesis. She got into that study and that was about the cost of the new leg."

Thanking Oletta again for helping with Dixon, Logan switched back to her call with Sam to share the update.

It wasn't until five o'clock that the vet finally called.

Dixon was alert and his vital signs had stabilized. He wouldn't be doing any leaping and jumping in the near future but with time and patience, other than a slight limp in his right hind leg, the vet expected him to recover completely. And yes, that included search and rescue training if she still wanted to do that. He said Oletta told him the dog had talent in that area.

To be on the safe side, he wanted to keep Dixon there another couple of days, but she and Ben were welcome to come see him in the morning. He gave her the address and said he'd be in by seven-thirty.

***

That night after a late dinner, instead of watching TV, Logan and Ben bundled up and went out and settled into their Adirondack chairs in the backyard. The large, comfortable chairs had drink holders that pulled out on the right side under the armrest. Ben brought out short glasses of a bourbon Clay had given them for Christmas, Elijah Craig. One large ice cube. Just what the doctor ordered.

They usually sat up on the back deck, which overlooked the forest, but tonight, Logan wanted to get as close to nature as possible. She needed to surround herself with the rustling of cedars and hemlocks, wrap herself in the embrace of their long, nodding branches. Reach out and touch their rough bark.

Taking a sip of her drink, she let the warmth burn down her throat, then burrowed into her chair. Breathing deeply, she took in the clean scent of cedars and the earthy scent of layers of untrodden leaves, sticks, and moss, and a thousand unnamed things she could not see that rose from the damp undergrowth.

Most of the birds were silent now, but there was a skitter or flutter here and there as prey escaped predator or simply found a more comfortable bed for the night.

As the moon rose slowly above the trees, she and Ben sat and sipped without saying a word.

Eyes closed, Logan smiled, remembering a parting comment Monson had tossed her way last night in Eddyville. He had just finished taking her statement and Grant was out loading Carl into the back of the waiting police vehicle. The venerable detective tucked his spiral notepad into his inside jacket pocket, then trained his blue eyes on her green ones.

"You're at my crime scenes so often anyway, Logan, you should consider making this your full-time job."

Logan reached over and took Ben's hand. She had no idea what tomorrow would bring, but right now life was very, very good.

EPILOGUE

John loaded a small suitcase into his car, then took one last walk around the house. He could have taken much more, but he didn't want any of it. He placed the house and mail keys into the small bowl on the entry table where the realtor instructed him to leave them, then closed the door behind him. The new owners were moving in this afternoon.

Last April, when he contacted her, Audra Branham had been thrilled to learn that all those listings she'd just made a killing on she was going to get to sell again! Forget two weeks in Hawaii! She was going to spend an entire month in a villa in the South of France. Her sister managed some luxury rentals there.

When Carl became confused and slurred his words, John thought it was the result of the roofie he had put in his red wine. It probably was, but they also discovered Carl had suffered a minor stroke that night. He later suffered a second, fatal stroke while awaiting trial.

It had taken over a year to sort out the will, go through probate, and track down the shell companies Carl had set up, but when it was finally done, Audra had lived up to her reputation and sold each lot quickly and for a good profit.

After paying the attorneys, John wasn't rich, but if he lived reasonably, he'd never have to work another day in his life.

This morning, he made his way to the large trees at the back of the property, near the stream that bordered the Hartleys. They were good people. He wished he could have them for neighbors, but he couldn't bring himself to live in what he still considered to be Astrid's home.

Astrid was the reason he made the trek down to the shaded patch of alders. A gentle, peaceful spot, it was where he often came to sit and think. A few months ago, he'd scattered her ashes here, knowing she would have liked this spot if she had lived. This morning he had gone to say goodbye.

It was time.

Out of habit, John patted his pockets as he got into his car, then smiled, remembering he quit smoking months ago. This time for good because he was doing it for himself.

Looking in the rearview mirror, John took one last look at the life he was leaving, then popped in his favorite CD and turned it up, singing along as he drove west to the coast. He no longer needed to plug in the address. He knew the way to Lauren's.

ACKNOWLEDGMENTS

As always, with a Logan book, which often takes me into new territory, I have many people to thank. First in line is Oletta Lewis, owner of Adventurous K9 where we often take our own dog, Finn, our six-year-old English Cream Golden Retriever, for fun and exercise. Oletta generously shared her knowledge and love of dogs, horses, and the world of national trail riding competitions. And they really do have a little yellow school bus that picks up the dogs in the Newport movie theater parking lot, seatbelts and all.

When I told her I thought her doggie daycare camp would make a great setting for a fictional murder, she loved the idea and invited me out for a tour around the property. You should see our Facebook messenger feed—it must be five miles long. Oletta was my source for animal questions from search and rescue, to tracking and horse training, to broken legs and hypothermia. I did my best to get it right, but any remaining errors are all mine.

Thank you also to Lane Lewis, Jean Paulette Goodyear, and Keegan Gray, who allowed me to borrow their first names for some of my characters. I didn't have the heart to make you the killer, Keegan, but I did manage to make you a suspect. Three of Oletta's trail riding competition friends, Donna, Denise, and Jan, make cameo appearances and cheer for Oletta when she takes on Gloria in the fight scene. The owner of J Fisher Training, Julie, an experienced horsewoman who holds national trail riding clinics out in Veneta, Oregon also allowed me to set the fight between Gloria and Oletta in the camping area at her place. I hope you all like your characters!

Thanks to my sister-in-law, Monique Fleming, and high school BFF, Cindy Havens, for sharing their equine expertise. Both were rodeo queens, but luckily, Gloria is an entirely fictional character and so none of Cindy or Monique's real horses were harmed in the making of this book.

Thanks also to our friends, John Bingham and Lauren Stenzel, who allowed me to use their first names and weave bits of their real lives into the story. I didn't have you do Carl in, John, but I hope you like how he got his just desserts.

I always try to include local businesses in the Logan series, so in this one I decided to have Logan sit in with popular entertainer and piano player, Michael Dane, one night at Gracie's Sea Hag, a local institution. Clary Grant, the owner along with her husband, Jerome, is as tough and generous as she is depicted, and manager Eli Ritter does make a mean Hangtown Fry.

And I was delighted to learn that Ulrike Bremer, the owner of Nye Beach Books in Newport, is also a positive reinforcement dog trainer. In that world, she goes by Pike Bremer, KPCT. No wonder her store dog, Meggie, is so well-behaved and loved. She manages to help Ben train the exuberant English Cream Golden Retriever, Max.

Newport PD Chief of Police (retired), Mark J. Miranda, patiently answered my many law enforcement questions, particularly how local police departments interact and are structured here on the coast. His knowledge and experience have proved invaluable for the last several books. Thank you, Mark!

Feedback from Beta Readers is always appreciated, but this year, extra thanks goes to attorney Kevin Chapman, author of the popular Mike Stoneman series, whose detailed feedback strengthened the story. Kimberly Peticolas came through again with another beautiful and powerful cover design. She gave me so many good options to choose from, I couldn't decide, so I had my newsletter subscribers weigh in. I love the lush, spooky octopus image they selected! And her editing always helps sharpen and polish the manuscript before publishing.

Interruptions are the bane of every author's existence, so when I'm working on a book, my husband, John, does more than his share of Finn walks and chores to make sure I have solid blocks of writing time. Beyond that, John has a law enforcement background and checks my weapons choices and cop dialogue for accuracy and believability.

And finally, a thank you to all the owls, eagles, coyotes, bears and other more familiar critters like stellar jays, hummingbirds, dark-eyed juncos, crows, chickadees, chipmunks, mice, and squirrels in the forest behind our house for just being you. In addition to Finn, you enrich our lives immensely.

Enjoyed the Book?

If you enjoyed *Lost and Found*, please consider leaving a review on Amazon, Goodreads, or BookBub. And be sure to check out the rest of the Logan McKenna series.

Novels

Shattered (Book 1)	*Lies That Bind* (Book 6)
Forest Park (Book 2)	*Whisper Creek* (Book 7)
Devil's Claw (Book 3)	*In Plain Sight* (Book 8)
Vanishing Day (Book 4)	*Lost and Found* (Book 9)
Safe Harbor (Book 5)	

Logan McKenna Prequel Novellas
Bella: An Appalachian Love Story
Jagged Dawn: Logan's Beginning

Want to know more about Valerie Davisson or her next book? Make sure to visit valeriedavisson.com and sign up for her newsletter.

ABOUT THE AUTHOR

A self-admitted book addict, Valerie Davisson was the kid with the flashlight under her pillow, reading long after lights out. After a life of travel, she now lives on the Oregon coast with her husband, John, and their English Cream Golden Retriever, Finn. When not working on her latest book, she's probably in the kitchen, cooking up a storm for family and friends.